by faerie light

Also from

BROKEN EYE BOOKS

The Hole Behind Midnight, by Clinton Boomer
Crooked, by Richard Pett

Coming Soon
Scourge of the Realm, by Erik Scott de Bie
Questions, by Stephen Norton & Clinton Boomer
Soapscum Unlimited, by Clinton Boomer

www.brokeneyebooks.com

Blowing minds, one book at a time, with cutting-edge fiction from today's rising stars. Broken Eye Books publishes innovative genre fiction. Fantasy, horror, science fiction, weird, we love it all! And the blurrier the boundaries, the better.

by faerie light

EDITED BY
SCOTT GABLE
CAROLINE DOMBROWSKI
DORA WANG

BROKEN
EYE
BOOKS

BY FAERIE LIGHT

Published by
Broken Eye Books
www.brokeneyebooks.com

ISBN: 978-1-940372-04-4

TABLE OF CONTENTS

VOLUME TWO

Introduction

Caroline Dombrowski & Scott Gable

When you catch movement out of the corner of your eye but can't find the source. When an uncanny child looks at you, unblinking, and you forget where you are. These are moments that the dark side of the fae seep into your mind, overwriting those glittering pastel images and clap-for-life stories. Living among us but not of us, the actions of the fae may or may not make sense. Their motivations are opaque to us, and though they are capable of great kindness, they are also capable of enormous terror.

Welcome to these tales of the fae and their influence over us. There are tricks and traps, loves and temptations, and in some small way, they may help you if you have the misfortune of entering their world one day . . .

Volume One

"Faeries, come take me out of this dull world,
For I would ride with you upon the wind . . ."
—W.B. Yeats, *The Land of Heart's Desire*

Shiro Hears the Cicadas

Dave Gross

At sunset on the southwest shore, the evening light paints the rock as the surf bathes the feet of basalt cliffs. Peasants and lords travel hundreds of miles to stand upon the precipice and listen to the song of the higurashi.

❊❊❊

Shiro paused, axe held above his head. The sea breeze bent the grass along the ridge, every stalk pointing toward him, his humble hut, and the forest surrounding them on three sides. As the wind subsided, Shiro heard the hush of the surf and the barking of the dog.

He let the axe fall and left it quivering in the stump. He collected the logs he had split into quarters and placed them on the woodpile. His back ached as he stretched. He would not have to feign infirmity, as once had been his custom when greeting visitors.

He fetched his straw hat and tied it snug under his chin. He fixed the buckets to the yoke and set it across his shoulders. Leaning into the wind, he walked out to the coast trail.

The yellow dog greeted him at the crest of the hill, dancing around him once before dashing back toward the intruder.

The visitor was a young man. Most of his visitors were young. Shiro believed that was because they had not yet become hardened against life's indignities. Yet not all of his visitors were young.

Shiro stood beside the trail. He raised his hand against the sun and estimated there was less than an hour before dark. It was not much time. He waited for his visitor.

As the young man approached, the yellow dog followed at his heel, looking up at him. Shiro bowed as low as his aching spine allowed.

"What are you doing here?" The young man spoke in a coastal dialect. Shiro noted the shape of the scars on the heels of his palms, the calluses on his fingers.

"I go to fetch water for my tea."

The young man looked astonished. "Who would live in such a place?"

"My name is Shiro." He bowed again.

"But what are you doing here?"

"Would you care for some tea? It tastes better when I can share it."

"Share it? But no one comes here except . . ."

Shiro bowed, this time to acknowledge that he understood. "Help me fetch the water, and I will brew tea for you before you throw yourself from the cliff."

"I did not say I had come to throw myself from the cliff."

"As you said, no one comes here except . . ."

The dubious expression of the young man's face gradually changed to one of pity as he looked down at Shiro. "Here, let me carry those buckets." He took the yoke and set it across his own shoulders. The weight of the empty buckets did not bow his strong back.

They walked to the crest of the hill. Shiro said, "Have you traveled far?"

"Two days along the coast road."

"You are from the village of the pearl divers."

The young man opened his mouth to speak, but he choked and nodded.

Shiro pointed to the fork in the path. To the right, the trail wound up to the farthest point on the cliffs, a spot overlooking the rocky shore, where most of Shiro's visitors wished to go. To the left, it clung to the side of the hill until it passed beneath a waterfall throwing itself into the sea.

"What is that sound?" asked the young man.

"My hearing is not so good."

"It comes from the forest. Is it cicadas?"

"I don't know how you can hear anything so close to the falls."

Shiro took one of the buckets and showed the young man how to fill it without stepping too close to the precipice. The fall would certainly kill but only after a dozen collisions with the rocky cliff face.

Shiro noticed the caution with which the young man filled the second bucket and replaced the yoke upon his shoulders. He followed carefully as Shiro led him back to the hut.

The young man set down the water buckets and rubbed his neck while the yellow dog settled beside the fire pit. Shiro fed the embers from the woodpile and stoked the fire to flame. Afterward, he fetched the dipper, filled a clay cup with water, and offered it to the young man. While his visitor drank, Shiro filled the iron kettle and hung it above the fire. Then he took a seat across from his visitor and waited for the water to boil.

"You live here all alone?"

Shiro nodded at the yellow dog. "Not entirely alone."

"What do you do here, so far from the nearest village?"

"I chop wood," said Shiro. "I carry water. Sometimes a visitor comes to help me."

The young man looked at the woodpile. "You will need much more before winter."

Shiro nodded.

The young man hopped up and plucked the axe from the stump. In his hands, it appeared no heavier than a switch. He split round logs in two blows, then halved and quartered them. After the first half-dozen logs, he slowed to a steady pace, the rhythm of his labor echoing through the trees.

As the young man worked, Shiro collected the split wood and added it to the pile. When the water boiled, he went into the hut and emerged with a pot and two covered cups on a carved tray. He poured a little water into the pot, swirled it, and poured it from the pot into each cup before splashing the water on the ground. He murmured a prayer and bowed to the forest, north and east.

The young man paused in his labors. "There it is again. What is that sound?"

Shiro tilted his head as if listening. He shrugged. "Come, have some tea."

He poured a measure of tea into the pot and filled it to the brim, spilling water over the sides as he set the lid in place.

The young man finished splitting a log and laid its quarters on the woodpile. He untied the kerchief from his neck and mopped the sweat from his face before returning to sit beside the fire. The yellow dog moved to sit near him, just within reach. The dog stared at the young man until he reached out to scratch the dog's jaw.

"I should go," said the young man. "It will be dusk soon."

"There is plenty of time before dark," said Shiro. He poured the yellow-brown tea into the cups, replacing the covers to capture the steam. The young man hesitated, watching as Shiro demonstrated how to hold the cup and move the lid just enough for a sip before covering the tea once more.

Mimicking Shiro, the young man sipped his tea. He frowned and nodded. "It has a strange flavor. But it is the best tea I have ever tasted."

Shiro smiled. He had felt the same way when he first discovered the tea growing wild at the foot of an ancient statue.

The young man sipped again. This time he smiled, and as he smiled, a yellow leaf that was not a leaf floated across the breeze to light upon his shoulder.

"What was her name?" asked Shiro.

The young man's smile vanished, replaced with an expression of feigned confusion. "Whose name?"

"The woman you lost."

"I did not say—" Another yellow leaf that was not a leaf skittered across the ground and clung to his shirt. There it swelled and breathed, as did the one on his shoulder. "Miyako."

"Tell me about her."

"I don't—" Two more not-leaves fell upon him, one in his hair, one on his neck. He did not notice. "We were to have married."

Shiro listened to the young man's tale.

The young man and Miyako had grown up together in the village of the pearl divers. The young man was not a diver but a fisherman. He did not fear the water, but he lacked the skill to hold his breath and force his body forty meters beneath the waves to gather oysters. Instead, he gathered fish all day and sang at night beside the fire with all the other villagers.

Miyako was the best diver in the village. She smoothed grease over her lithe, brown body and pinched greased cotton into her ears. She closed her nostrils with a tortoiseshell clip and leaped out of the boat with a heavy stone and a wide-mouthed basket in her arms.

Every time she dove, the young man watched her from his fishing boat, holding his breath for as long as he could. He watched until he grew dizzy, his face flushed, and finally gasped for air. Still Miyako did not appear, and panic fluttered in his heart. He would hold his breath again, hoping that by some sympathetic charm the air he did not breathe would find its way into her lungs, filling her with his love. He swore he would not take another breath until he saw her.

And then she would reappear, her basket full of oysters, and he would breathe again.

For every fifty times Miyako dove, one of the oysters she retrieved yielded a pearl fine enough to sell. For every pearl, the young man held his breath a hundred times. A hundred times, he did not die for loving Miyako.

Until the time she did not reappear. The other divers searched for her corpse, but they never found it. She was gone, whether swept out to sea or embraced by the weeds deeper than any of the other divers could go, no one knew.

Shiro refilled the young man's teacup.

"If only I could have held my breath longer," he said. "She would have made it back."

"So you came here to join her."

The young man nodded.

"What gift have you brought her?

"What do you mean?"

"If you go to Miyako now, what gift will you give her? You carry only sorrow."

"What else do I have?"

"You must go back home and fetch her better gifts."

"What kind of gifts?"

"What would you have given her if she had lived? What did you dream with her?"

The young man shuddered, unable to voice his thoughts. Still he did not notice the creatures clinging to his arms and shoulders, glowing in the light of dusk. With every sob from his chest, they grew larger. No longer resembling leaves, they now seemed like wedges of golden fruit with chubby little fingers clutching the young man's hair and clothing. A steady susurrus emanated from their bodies, a chorus of weird harmonies that sounded almost exactly like the song of the cicadas who sing at twilight in spring and autumn.

"Go back to your village," said Shiro.

"What will I do there without Miyako?"

"Do what you would have done with her. Live the life you promised her. Gather fish. Sing with your people. Choose another woman and make children. Raise them well. Teach them to gather fish and sing. Live that good life, and when it is over, you will take it with you to Miyako. That is the gift you should bring her."

One by one, the not-leaf, not-fruit creatures dropped from the young man. Their song ceased for an instant as they hit the ground, chortling as they righted themselves on chubby little fingers and skittered over to climb upon Shiro. They hung on him, resuming their song. Its music changed tenor as their glowing flesh changed from vibrant gold to green, then to blue, and finally to violet.

Shiro sighed as the weight of the yoke settled around his neck.

"You are right," said the young man. "I must—do you hear that?"

"What do you hear?"

"Nothing," said the young man. "Only the sea breeze."

"If you leave now, you can climb down from the hills before dark."

"Thank you," said the young man. "Thank you for the tea."

Shiro stood, faltering. The young man rose quickly to take him by the elbow. Shiro thanked him with a wan smile. The young man seemed to notice the weird little creatures for the first time as they fell from Shiro's body. The wind blew them back into the trees, where they clung to branches, now looking more like buds than leaves or fruits.

The young man stared at them, perplexed. At last, he said, "I forgot what I was saying."

"You wanted to go down the hill before dark," suggested Shiro. "If you hurry, you can reach home before the snow begins."

"Yes, that was it. Thank you for the tea." The young man hesitated. "But what will you do here all alone when winter comes?"

Shiro patted the young man's hard, strong arm. His arms had been like those of the young man when he first came to the coast to hear the song of the higurashi. They had leeched the sorrow from his heart, but without a place to put it, they sang it back to him the following morning. Every day Shiro mourned his wife, their two daughters, and their grandson, all lost to the typhoon. Every evening, he stood upon the precipice, preparing to throw himself into the sea, until once more he heard the song of the higurashi.

Since then, he had learned to bear the sorrow, if only long enough to send away the others who had come to commit suicide. One of them had left behind the yellow dog, whose company consoled Shiro on the worst days. On the others, Shiro had learned to bear the yoke of his sorrow.

"What will you do?" repeated the young man.

"I will carry water," said Shiro. "I will cut wood. And when visitors come, I will make tea."

MIDWIFE AND THE APOTHECARY

JULIA B. ELLINGBOE

From the journals of Margaret Birch, the midwife, and Aelfdene, the apothecary.

MARGARET

September 17

Summer flew by. I haven't documented more than the names of the babies I caught. It is a day of sevens. A good day to reflect and forecast.

Today marks seven months since my mother's passing, and I have caught the seventeenth child of the year to be born in our town, Jane Crabtree's seventh daughter. They named her Eleanor. A robust child weighing seven pounds, she even gave a lusty cry that filled the room. May the sevens around this birth bring her luck in her first year. It is the sevens that reminded me of Mother.

In a few days, Mr. Aelfdene, the apothecary, will return to his winter cottage just outside the walls of the town—and not a moment too soon! I will not have to trifle with Mr. Raven, the sloppy and dirty apothecary in Second Village. His tinctures are notoriously weak and smell of mold, and his dried herbs are dusty. When I last purchased dried lavender from him, I found mouse droppings throughout, and he refused to refund my money. I should have purchased all that I would need before Mr. Aelfdene left in the spring, but I was preoccupied with Mother's passing and my new position as First Village's only midwife.

September 24

Mr. Aelfdene arrived in First Village two days ago. I helped him move his crates and chests from the carriage as I have done since I was twelve. As is our custom, though I am a grown woman now, Mr. Aelfdene remarked that I must have grown seven inches since spring. I replied that I had only grown six inches but that the ground still rises to meet my feet. The smile that he returned warmed my cheeks.

He rewarded our labor with a shared pot of barley tea and something he called "friendship bread." The tea had a peculiar odor and hearty flavor unlike any barley tea I have tasted, but it restored my energy. The bread was sweet and rich with molasses and oats. Before I left for home, Mr. Aelfdene gave me two small, strange branches from an elder tree in full fruit (strange in that they look more like full trees than branches). When he handed them to me, he plucked the berries and promised to make an elixir for me. "A midwife must stay healthier than everyone in the town she serves," he said as he placed two ripe elderberries in my hand and waited for me to eat them. They tasted unremarkable, which disappointed me somewhat because I expected them to be sweeter. I put the branches in a jug of water and set them on the table.

Mother found Mr. Aelfdene's manners odd and at times disquieting, but she adored him. She called him the young man with an old man's heart. He knows this region's stories and superstitions better than the oldest among us. And he indulges them. He once told forgetful Mr. Hawthorne to place mistletoe in his cupboards to keep mischievous lobs—lubber fiends or brownies, as the older folks call them—from stealing his bread. All told, Mr. Hawthorne's memory of his food stocks did improve.

Mr. Aelfdene still looks to be my age, as he did when I first met him. I was five and mother was the apprentice midwife to Mrs. Copse. For years, Mrs. Copse would not go near Mr. Aelfdene's poultices and teas because she believed him to be from the Grove, but one year, nearly all the mothers in Mrs. Copse's care came down with childbed fever and half the children under two fell ill with roseola. Mrs. Copse's tried and true tinctures helped little. Mr. Aelfdene gently offered his own remedies, which proved to be more effective than what Mrs. Copse had been taught to use. All told, she didn't lose a single mother or baby that year. After that, she praised even the whiteness of his teeth. She didn't care if he came from the Grove.

The old people still talk about the Grove Folk and how they honored some ancient treaty to protect the seven unified villages from the Unseelie monsters that ravaged the villages, soured the milk, and stole the lives of our children. After the Unseelie were wiped from the area, the Grove Folk disappeared before anyone could properly thank them. Some of the old people still think Mr. Aelfdene is one of the Grove Folk. Mr. Aelfdene laughs about it and points out that the only known road to the Grove is overgrown with barberry and monkshood. It's not our custom to ask people from whence they come, so I leave it at that, as did my mother and Mrs. Copse. Mother said, "Trust the Aelfdene you see, not the one the townsfolk think they see."

AELFDENE

September 25

I have finally settled again into First Village, and my seasonal position as local apothecary. This is my favorite village, and as much as I enjoy tending to my family in the Grove in spring and summer, I look forward to returning to the Seven Villages more each year. Margaret Birch, the midwife, aided me in unpacking as she has for the past fifteen years.

As always, her smile and laugh are the two things I realize I have missed the most. She is a radiant beam of what is good in humanity, and she grows more radiant each year. Unlike her mother, she cannot see the fey, even though she has a vast colony of devoted lobs dwelling in and about her property, keeping her house warm and free of dust and pests. She does not notice. Even more have moved in since her mother's death. They were fond of Mrs. Birch and promised to keep her daughter's house safe and clean. She looks at me and just sees a travelling apothecary who settles in First Village in the colder months. When she looks at me, I have to catch my breath. I don't think she notices that any more than she notices the lobs in her walls.

I gave her my branch-antlers as a gift and promised to make her elderberry elixir. (I told her it would help to keep her healthy.) I suppose I am taking advantage of her blindness, though her inability to see what I am carries some immunity to my attempts to enchant her. If anything, possession of my antlers may cause me to linger in her thoughts, and my elixir may simply warm her heart to my advances the way any token of affection might. However, I don't know if I have the fortitude to make advances on her without my tricks.

My brother and sister in Third and Fifth Villages warned me that a small group of bendith y mamau are travelling north through the protected lands of the Seven Villages. They suffered a dreadful blight this summer and came south to the Grove in search of an alleged cure, a mushroom they call a "salamander's throne." They even sought the Green Lady of the Grove's help. No one could recall salamander's throne growing in these parts. I've only read about it. My mother gave them permission to pass through the Seven Villages to return north. For their sake, I hope that winter kills off the sickest of them and the blight simply runs its course.

The bendith y mamau are generally among the least troublesome or malicious of the Unseelie fey. Most of them are squat, ugly things with wiry black hair and knobby knees. They can transform themselves into various types of beasts and can hold a reasonably accurate but unattractive mortal form for several days. They are notorious baby thieves, especially when their numbers dwindle. Given their misfortune and devastation, any stealing and swapping of human babies for one of their crimbils (sometimes called "changelings" around here) as they pass through the Seven Villages is of little concern to the Green Lady of the Grove. Bendith y mamau ("The Mother's Blessing," as the Seelie fey have long called them in jest) are remarkably loving and loyal parents.

The Seven Villages have had a fruitful year. I've seen several beautiful and healthy babies, bountiful crops, and scores of young livestock. Many families no longer believe something unseen could snatch their children and swap them for a shriveling, ailing crimbil. Miss Margaret's disbelief is endearing, but I worry that her dismissal of what she calls superstitions and wives' tales may invite trouble with the bendith y mamau.

MARGARET

October 1

I caught the eighteenth child of the year to be born in First Village, Maeve Pennyroyal's fifth child (a boy—Maeve wanted a girl) with Calvin the blacksmith. The infant entered the world with a high-pitched cry. He was ten pounds and two ounces, sallow-skinned, hair as black as his father's iron. He was eager for Maeve's breast. His yellow hue will fade in the next few days, I hope. Maeve lost a great deal of blood. I gave her nettles and cramp bark for tea and told the parents to take the boy out in the sun as much as possible. Calvin, not known for his expressive nature or oratory prowess, smiled and cooed at the baby while Maeve's older daughter Clementine and I cleaned and cooked. More words burst forth from Calvin's mouth tonight than I have heard since he and I were children. He insisted that I give Maeve my lentil soup recipe. She is not known for her skills in the kitchen.

They do not have a name for the baby and did not care for my suggestion of Heath. Mrs. Copse believed that an unnamed newborn would be swapped for a crimbil. I am not concerned about crimbils or changelings, but I am worried that Maeve's disappointment in not having a girl will affect her ability to get to know this gentle little boy. Calvin will fill in while she comes to grips. I'm sure she will come to love the boy as much as Calvin does, as much as she loves her four other children.

Mr. Aelfdene's elder branches have started to grow roots and leaf buds! I told him about it this evening when he stopped by to return a ladle he had borrowed. He said to plant them, which I did. I will be surprised if they live through the winter, but while they stand, they remind me of him whenever I look out the window.

When I told him of the unnamed blacksmith's son, Mr. Aelfdene's eyes widened and darkened, and he pressed his warm, soft fingers over my mouth. "Best not to speak of this aloud," he whispered. "Tell the blacksmith's wife to leave a bowl of milk outside the door, and may they leave her child in his cradle." Aelfdene's hands smelled of elderberries and I breathed it in deeply. I wished he had pressed his lips on my mouth instead of his fingers. The thought of that made me blush.

Then he asked me a dozen questions about the blacksmith's house. How close was his forge to the home? Did they hammer any nails around the cradle? I told him to visit the Pennyroyals' himself. He furrowed his brow and looked away out the window, ignoring the fire. We did not speak for a long time. I was tongue-tied and flustered; he seemed lost in his thoughts. I tried not to look at him, tried not to fidget, so I picked up my knitting and watched his shadow flicker and dance on the wall behind him.

At some point I dozed off, and when I awoke, Mr. Aelfdene had left.

Aelfdene

October 2

The blacksmith's son has been stolen and replaced with a crimbil. In years past, a bendith y mamau wouldn't be so bold as to steal the blacksmith's son.

I wanted to see for myself, but I've never been able to stand too close to any blacksmith's dwelling because of all the iron. So I put a slumber spell on Miss Margaret by touching her mouth and leaning in close enough for her to breathe my breaths.

Miss Margaret sat in her chair, knitting to fill the awkward space between us. I just sat there, filling that space between us with more awkwardness, wishing I had stolen a kiss when I cast the spell, and relieved that I had overcome the impulse. I mapped the trail of windows while I waited for her to fall asleep. Then, as her eyelids grew heavy and she dozed, I crawled out of my body and into the glass. This is a modestly prosperous town, and nearly all the houses have glass windows now, so the leaps from house to house were easy and short.

The blacksmith's forge is far enough from the house that the iron did not affect me. That was, unfortunately, the best of the whole situation. The unnamed son of the blacksmith had already been swapped for a sickly, if not moribund, crimbil. Worse still, the Unseelie bendith y mamau slaughtered every hob and lob in the home. The house is filthy and stinks of death.

A hundred years ago in this region, a new mother wouldn't have dared let her baby see the first hour of his life without a name for fear that a fey of any stripe might have replaced the unnamed infant with a changeling. Mrs. Copse, the midwife who taught Margaret's mother midwifery, had little love for the Grove Folk. To her, all fey were the same: tricksters at best and perfidious murderers and thieves at the worst. But she sought my help when the Faerie Rades passed through the town, and I aided her as best I could. These days, no family leaves so much as a bowl of milk on their doorstep, not even that simplest prevention for infant swapping.

There is little I can do beyond recommend to Miss Margaret ways to rid the Pennyroyals of the crimbil. I'm forbidden to take arms against fey or mortal and can provide only magical protection. I may be able to negotiate a return of their baby, but without a name, it will be difficult to convince the bendith y mamau that the Pennyroyals deserve him. In their eyes, an unnamed baby is an unspoken offer to swap children.

October 5

I paid a visit (in the flesh) to Sage Pennyroyal, grandmother of the blacksmith's unnamed son. She recognized me as a Grove Folk. I had not noticed before, but it seems that my antlers are growing in earlier than usual, probably on account of my growing feelings for Margaret. Or, I hope, because she looks at my shed antlers and thinks fondly of me. I will have to start wearing a hat or grow my hair a bit longer. At any rate, Sage Pennyroyal is prepared to resort to drastic measures, which I hear Miss Margaret promptly disallowed, but grandmother Sage asked if I thought it might work. I told her firmly that she must not torture or hurt the changeling in any way. A baby is a baby.

I actually spoke to the crimbil's mother myself. The pitiful thing and her husband came to Miss Margaret's door disguised as beggars while Miss Margaret and I happened to be having supper together. When the couple saw me, they fled. Miss Margaret sent me after them with a portion of food.

The bendith y mamau parents are Acorn and Tom Wormfingers, and their baby's name is Phing. The son has the blight that claimed many of their kind this summer. Mrs. Wormfingers assures me that the blacksmith's son is safe and well, living in the blacksmith's brother's barn, wearing the skin of a newborn goat and being nursed and mothered by one of the dams. Phing the crimbil's condition is beyond the help of any known mortal or fey balm. He will likely die soon. Mrs. Wormfingers says her people plan to return to the north in two days, and if her baby could be restored to health, she would return the Pennyroyal's son and claim her own.

As the Green Lady of the Grove did not specifically prohibit the bendith y mamau from replacing their sick and dying children, I shall allow fey customs to guide my actions in this matter. As such, I will not return the Pennyroyal baby to his mortal parents. He will go with his foster family and grow up a stolen child. It could be worse. The Grove Folk have found themselves in need of restocking their numbers, as it were. Unseelie and Seelie fey alike can offer a mortal child a life of happiness among people who love him. Some of the best Grove Folk were once stolen children.

I told Acorn and Tom Wormfingers that they ought to stay long enough to plant heather on their son's grave. He will be the first infant to die in this town this year. The whole town will mourn him for the next year. The Wormfingers agreed to stay on and say goodbye to their child before they leave with their adopted baby. I asked what they would call the boy. Acorn said she liked the midwife's suggestion of Heath.

In the scant year Margaret has been the midwife for First Village, she's not lost a single child until now. One day I hope to tell her that the adoptive parents liked the name she chose. After I returned from meeting with the Wormfingers, Margaret and I finally dined together. I told her that they did not want to inconvenience us. Embarrassed, I said that I really meant "her." I meant "us."

As the stars as my witness, I'm in love with Margaret Birch. Eight hundred and seventy-eight years on the earth and I've never loved anyone as much as I love her. There, I've written it. I don't know what to do. She seems unaffected by my fumbling attempts to enchant her, and she is certainly not under my thrall. I suspect that she has feelings for me; whether they match my own, I don't know. My feelings for her are unenchanted. Human. I don't think I am able to enchant her, and without the veil of my tricks, I feel . . . naked. It's awful and terrifying and exhilarating. The uncertainty of whether she loves me as I do her worries me more than a roving band of sickly Unseelie, which is why I'm so concerned with the Wormfingers, I suppose. It's a simpler conundrum.

Margaret

October 5

The Pennyroyal child, still unnamed, is unwell. He is paler and more sallow than he was at birth, gaunt and bent like an old man. The strangest thing is that he is now covered with a light coat of downy hair.

I consulted Mother's notes and journals and found five similar instances where children practically wasted away and grew this strange hair. Two infants wasted away to nothing and died within six days of birth. In despair, one such mother threw herself into the river. One baby's family took the child to another midwife in Third Village, who recommended that they leave the child on a hilltop overnight. Apparently they followed her directions, and needless to say, the baby froze to death. Superstition should not supersede common sense!

One baby—Samara Winterfield, the oldest daughter of Violet and Basil—made a full recovery. Mother gave them the following instructions, which she learned from none other than Mr. Aelfdene: they procured a black hen with not a single white feather, wrung its neck, and roasted it unplucked. As they roasted the bird, they called the baby's name. As soon as all the feathers cooked off, Samara let out a robust wail, her "fur" fell away, and according to Mother, the color and fat returned to her body. Mother wrote that Samara was nearly a year old at the time, older than the others, and not as ill. Samara married a carpenter from South Harbor last summer.

Calvin Pennyroyal's mother believes the baby has been taken by the bendith y mamau ("The Mother's Blessing," as my mother called them) and swapped for a crimbil. She took Calvin and Maeve to task for not naming their baby, though she did not like my suggestion of Heath any more than Calvin and Maeve.

She advised that we hold the baby over the fire and threaten to cook him in order to provoke the real mother to claim her child. Calvin snatched the baby away and left. He had not returned by the time I left for home.

Mr. Aelfdene has visited the Pennyroyals, has seen the child, and agrees that the baby is not likely to live more than another day or two. Feeling bold, I invited him back for dinner. I made pumpkin stew and roasted the hare I caught in my pumpkin patch. Mr. Aelfdene brought his friendship bread, elderberry wine, birch beer, and candied violets. Where he acquired candied violets in October he would not say.

At dinner, I asked him about the advice he gave Mother in Samara's case.

"If I recall correctly," he said, "Samara's father was once a sailor. He had just returned home from his last trip when she fell ill. I think he brought something unseen and unseemly back with him." (At first I thought he said "Unseelie." I think I've had my fair share of faerie talk this week!)

Mr. Aelfdene went on to say that he indulges people's superstitions, if only to lift their spirits and give hope. He believed that Samara's greatest danger was that her parents were giving up. They needed to do something while she recovered from whatever ailed her, and recovery was up to her. She had taken all the herbs and tinctures anyone could give her.

Before he could continue, a strange couple wearing silken rags beneath fine wool coats came to my door. They said they were travelling north and seeking a hot meal. Naturally, I packed some bread, a bit of stew, and some hare, but when they saw Mr. Aelfdene sitting at my table, they fled. I asked Mr. Aelfdene to go after them to make sure they had a warm place to sleep (we're likely to have our first frost of fall tonight). When he returned, he said they took the food but did not want to inconvenience us—I mean, me. He said "us," then sheepishly corrected himself. (I liked the sound of "us" but he was so embarrassed I didn't tell him. Not yet.) He gave them enough silver to stay at the inn, though I later heard that Calvin's brother Malcolm Pennyroyal met them further down the road, and he let them stay in his barn (he's always kept it neater than his house). They gave him the silver and purchased three goats from him, a dam and her twins.

When Mr. Aelfdene and I returned to supper, he concluded the talk of superstitions saying that it would harm no one, least of all the blacksmith's son, if the family did some traditional or superstitious ceremonial act if it helped them to feel that they could help their baby: "Your mother didn't believe all the wives' tales, but if she thought that they might brighten the home or ignite the spirits, those acts became part of the course of medications as far as she was concerned. Your mother could not teach you the palliative side of midwifery. The first baby or mother who dies in your care, through no fault of your own, teaches you that."

Everything about his words brought comfort, from his lyric baritone, to the way he leaned into a whisper when he said, "ignite the spirits," to the way his mouth opened to a sad smile when he finished talking. I don't think he wanted to say "good night" any more than I wanted to hear it. He doesn't seem to know what to do with his love, so he wears it around his neck like a charm. One of the things I love about Mr. Aelfdene—yes, love—is that his plainness seems magical. His quirkiness is graceful. He brought violets in autumn.

But a baby that I caught is dying. My first infant death. I'm having trouble grasping Mr. Aelfdene's affection while my own grief and sense of powerlessness weigh on my heart.

October 7

Mother once warned me that midwives, shepherds of life and death, must learn to abandon disbelief in the face of the unbelievable.

I have loved Aelfdene since I was fourteen years old when his hand brushed mine as he handed me jars of sarsaparilla and rosehips to deliver to Mother. I've loved him ever since Jenny and Bernice Larkspur complained that he was handsome yet aloof, and I knew that he was to them, but he always offered his awkward openness to me. I have loved him all these seasons and was blind to my (and his) feelings. This evening, I told Aelfdene that I loved him. He was stunned and tongue-tied, and he stuttered and chuckled, looked away, shook his head, and then fell silent.

"I love you, too, Margaret Birch," he said, finally.

The day did not start as joyfully as it has ended. The Pennyroyals buried their infant son this morning. He finally nursed again on October 6. Maeve handed him to Calvin, and the boy died peacefully in his father's loving arms. They named the child Phinn. In addition to the Pennyroyal clan, Malcolm Pennyroyal's odd barn guests Acorn and Tom Wormfingers, Mr. Aelfdene, and I attended the funeral.

Coincidentally, the Wormfingers have recently lost an infant. They wept rivers of tears with Calvin and Maeve and planted on the grave heather and some other herb the name of which I did not catch but which resembled deadly nightshade.

Maeve and Calvin thanked me for my counsel and care. I have felt ineffective from the moment Phinn was born, but Maeve said Phinn was the easiest and most peaceful of all five of her labors and she attributed that to my "calm, straightforward presence." Calvin said he loved the lentil stew I cooked the night of Phinn's birth.

We roasted the (plucked) black hen Mr. Aelfdene and I had bought but not been able to use for ritual. Acorn Wormfingers seasoned it with a spicy but uplifting herb that they called goose tongue. It looked like white tansy to me, the herb that accidentally poisoned my mare Quince two years ago. Mr. Aelfdene said his stomach was being disagreeable, and he did not eat the chicken. The Wormfingers also made some sort of dessert that they called fuzz-ball pudding. It looked wholly unappetizing and smelled like very old and sour milk and dirty stockings. Everyone except Mr. Aelfdene declined a single helping. He and the Wormfingers gleefully gobbled the whole bowl. Mr. Aelfdene said his mother made a variation of it and added honeysuckle nectar to improve the odor. I did not ask for the recipe.

To my delight, Mr. Aelfdene walked me home. I remembered that we still had half a bottle of his elderberry wine and invited him to have a glass with me. The sweetness was of little comfort to my sadness, which rose to meet me when I considered my own part in this week's events. We buried the first child to die in my care. Mr. Aelfdene saw my tears and said, "Margaret, I'd like to tell you my secret." This is what he told me:

The Green Lady of the Grove and her concubine, the Elder Tree Lord, have seven hundred strong and healthy children. Most are firmly rooted around their father in a forest that the Grove Folk call the Elder Lord's Crèche. Seven of their children, however, resemble their mother and walk on feet, wear faces, and eat with mouths. They like mushrooms the best. These folk are called the Protectors, and they live in the Seven Villages and serve as apothecaries, doctors, itinerant farmers, and bards. They have sworn to protect the region (from what, he did not say), though they never carry weapons.

The Green Lady shows no preference for any of her children, but she does enjoy the company and conversation of the offspring who look more like her. And if she had a favorite, it would be her eldest son, Aelfdene, the apothecary of First Village, known to the Grove Folk as the Elderberry Prince.

Though he spends most of his time in the protected lands beyond the Grove disguised as a young-faced apothecary, Aelfdene does bear characteristics of most Grove Folk who are not trees. During the warmer months, his skin is light green, and two elder tree branches grow from the top of his head like the antlers on a buck. In the spring, his branch-antlers sprout green leaves and sprightly white flowers. In the summer, his antlers grow the sweet black elderberries. He makes syrups, elixirs, and wines from the berries from his branch-antlers, and just one sip will give the drinker long life and health, among other things. He spends his "green time" on his brother's farm in the Grove, just beyond the border of Seventh Village, tending herbs and mixing his tinctures.

When the weather turns cold, the leaves on Aelfdene's branch-antlers turn yellow and fall off. When they are entirely leafless, he sheds the branches, and his skin turns from light green to honey brown. Then he dons clothes and hats in the fashion of the townsmen of the Seven Villages who dwell beyond the Grove and takes residence in a tiny cottage just outside our town.

It pleases Aelfdene to help the mortals through their illnesses. He's always made a point to stay on good terms with the midwives of First Town, his favorite village in the Protected lands. The Grove Folk have long abandoned the act of falling ill, though some still pretend. Fainting and vomiting, a game where players feign mortal illness by actually fainting and vomiting, is popular among the common Grove Folk. To my relief, Aelfdene said that he does not care to play. He sees enough real illness.

Aelfdene told me this story with such sincerity that I would have believed him had it not been such a preposterous fable. It certainly cheered me up.

"Come spring, you will see that I'm telling you the truth." He said as he poured me another glass of elderberry wine. Then it was my turn to reveal my secret: boldness moved me to put my glass aside, to ignore the wine spilling on the table and the floor, and to draw Aelfdene into my arms and kiss him. In the initial shock of my action, he gasped and tried to say something, but I held on to him until we sunk into an embrace. His mouth tastes as I suspected: like elderberries and violets.

He purchased an acre of land around his home some years ago with the intention of settling there year round instead of staying with his brother. We'll marry the first of the year. Come spring, we'll move to his cottage outside of First Village.

I'm watching Aelfdene sleep. I'm sitting in my chair, wearing his fine blue silk shirt. He has a twig in his hair. If I were to pluck it out, I believe I might hurt him.

Aelfdene

October 8

Margaret Birch told me she loved me.

I told her that I was a Grove Folk. At first she did not believe me but assumed I was telling her a fanciful tale to cheer her up. Margaret then told me her secret, which cheered me up.

She said, "I've loved you since I was fourteen years old."

I told her that I loved her, as well. I was relieved to say it and relieved to hear it reciprocated. She said, "Aelfdene the apothecary or Aelfdene the Elderberry Prince are all well and good. Aelfdene, Margaret the midwife's husband is even better."

So be it.

A Nightmare for Anna

Jennifer Brozek

The forest was dark, and Anna was scared. She tried to stay as close to Mother as she could while they walked deeper. Even though it was morning, the tall trees shut out the light, making it seem like dusk. Strange birds cried overhead as Anna, who had not yet seen nine summers, tried to huddle closer. She stopped before Mother's skirt dragged against her, though. Touching Mother was forbidden. Especially as she sang to her baby boy, Aiden.

"We're almost there," her mother cooed to the sleeping baby. "Almost to the best place to find the best mushrooms."

"I don't see any, Momma."

"Not yet. You will." Her mother stopped and looked around. "Here we are." She turned to Anna and smiled. "Are you ready?"

Looking around the dark forest with its giant trees, flickering shadows, and strange noises, Anna nodded, giving her bravest smile. Mother was happy and that was rare. Ever since Aiden was born, Mother had been short-tempered with Anna—even though she tried to be the best big sister she could.

"Do you know what to look for?"

Anna nodded. "The big white mushrooms with the caps, not the bowls."

"Very good."

"We're gonna make Daddy the best mushroom and turnip soup we can." Anna paused, seeing her mother's smile crack and disappear. "When he gets home from the castle, that is." She did her best to make her voice as smooth and happy as possible.

"Mother is tired, Anna." She spoke to the sleeping baby rather than to her daughter. "We're going to rest here. I want you to fill the basket halfway with the mushrooms before you come back."

Anna bowed her head, still not sure what she did wrong. "Yes, Mother." She picked up the small, grass-woven basket and turned to the dark trees. She took several uncertain steps before looking back, but Mother, without looking up from Aiden, waved her on. Anna nodded, straightened her back, and faced the scary forest. She would find Daddy's favorite mushrooms, and all would be well once more.

Anna circled the small grove again. She hadn't been gone that long. Not long at all. Mother had to be here. But she wasn't, and after the third time Anna circled the two trees she'd marked with crossed sticks, she knew either she was lost or Mother had left her here alone in the Old Forest. Both possibilities amounted to the same thing: death. No children came out of the Old Forest once they went in. Not any child alone, that is.

She sat against the tree she was sure Mother sat against, and she muttered, "Think, child. Think." She even used the same amused tone Daddy used when the answer was right there in front of her and she couldn't see it. Just the thought of him made Anna's throat close up. She missed him so much. She hated that he had to take such long trips away to the castle.

Sitting up, Anna knew that she needed to face the fact that Mother left her behind, and it was up to her to get herself out of this mess. Her heart sobbed at the abandonment while her mind set upon the task of finding her way home. She was her father's daughter, after all.

Anna stood and turned in the direction she was certain would take her home. All she needed to do was follow their own tracks back the way they'd come. Simple. She looked at the ground and saw the trampled grass. She could find her way home. When she did, Mother would be so sorry that she had left her that she'd welcome Anna home with open arms.

By the time Anna found the ruins of the manor house, she knew she was well and truly lost. Having lost the trail of footsteps—if there had been any to follow and not just wishful thinking—she had no way to know how to make it out of the forest alive. The discovery of the stone ruins with its partial roof raised her low spirits. It was something new and interesting, something more than just endless trees and loamy earth. Even the scent of stone cleared her senses. Best of all, a small opening in the treetops allowed the sun in.

Running to the shaft of sunlight, Anna could have cried with relief. In the warmth of the sun, feeling it against her chilled skin, it seemed like the forest creatures following her could not touch her. In her mind's eye, they were afraid of the light. As she turned back to the forest, she even saw some of them slink away. For the moment, she was safe.

Of course, Anna was too young to wonder what might frighten a predator away from an easy meal.

❀❀❀

As night fell and the sky morphed from shades of blue into black, Anna huddled in the corner of the broken room. She wondered if the night creatures would come or if it would rain. Her tummy rumbled its hunger, but the mushrooms she had found were long gone.

The sound of something close by in the forest brought Anna to her feet. The following growl had her looking for a weapon. Scrabbling against the broken wall, her hand found a loose stone. She pulled it free and raised it up, ready to throw at whatever was coming. More stones fell to her side as she watched the large shape prowl the edge of the forest.

It was watching her. That much was certain.

Anna took two steps forward and threw the stone at the monster. "Go away! I'll hit you! Go away!" She snatched three more stones from around her and threw them, too. None of them hit even halfway to the forest line, but the monster came no closer.

Moonlight glinted green and yellow off its eyes. Anna picked up the largest stone near her feet and threw it as far and as hard as she could. The glowing eyes disappeared, and Anna felt a surge of pride.

She backed up into the corner again and sat. Still watching where she last saw the monster, she searched out another stone. Just one to keep with her as guard.

Her hand found something that felt like stone but was warm. Startled, Anna looked down to see what it was.

Her hand was on a long, black stick that was as wide as her wrist and disappeared into the wall. The wall was actually two walls with a space in-between. Whatever the black stick was, the rest of it was still hidden. She would figure out what it was in the morning.

Finding a different rock to hold and comfort her, she settled in to sleep.

❀❀❀

Anna knew she was dreaming, and that was a strange thing. Not the dreaming but the realizing that what she was seeing wasn't real. Something had just been happening. She frowned. Something awful. Something she couldn't quite remember. She reached for it . . .

"Do not do that, little one. I took it away because it would frighten you." The voice was as dark as the shadow it came from. "Do not look for it."

Anna tilted her head, looking up at the shadowed figure. It was so tall, as tall as one of the trees in the forest. Things moved all around it, but curiously, she was not afraid. "Was it a nightmare?"

"Yes, little one."

"My name's Anna." When it did not reply, she asked, "Who are you?"

"Sigis. You may call me Sigis." The shadow moved closer and shrank in size. "Why are you here?"

There was a long pause. "I am old and alone. You are lost and afraid."

Somehow, that answered the question without answering it. Anna looked down at her hands, remembering her mother's abandonment and that she was lost in the Old Forest.

"Will you help me?"

She looked up again. The shadow was closer now and not much taller than her father. "What do you look like? Why are you hiding in the dark?" Anna knew she should be afraid, but she wasn't and didn't know why. But more than anything, she wanted to see who she was talking to. It was important.

The shadow shook its head. "I do not wish to frighten you."

"I want to see. Show me your face." Anna didn't know why it was important, but it was. "Please?"

Sigis nodded. He didn't move out of the darkness so much as the shadows withdrew from him.

Anna saw what she needed to see.

❀❀❀

Waking with the first light of day, Anna knew there was something she needed to do. To remember. She sat blinking into the twilight, unafraid at her unusual surroundings. The glade and its broken rocks, rambling vines, and sprouting grasses all glistened with dew. The entire ruin looked like it was covered in little jewels.

Anna stood and stretched, realizing she was not cold. At all. Her little corner had remained warm throughout the chill forest night. She discovered it was only her little corner that was warm when she had to do her necessary. This little bit of magic made her smile. It had to be magic. There was no other explanation.

As she hurried back to her shelter, Anna saw what she needed to remember. There, in the left side of her shelter, part of the fallen wall revealed that the pieces of black stick were actually dirty pieces of a statue. Brushing at the stone, she saw that it was not just black. It had a red hue that reminded her of bloodstone. She could not make out the form, but from her dream, she knew exactly who she was looking at: Sigis . . . and he was stuck in the wall. She had promised to help him.

Without hesitation, Anna moved to the wall and pulled at the crumbling rock. Each stone that came loose showed more of the reddish-black statue beneath. Once the easy rocks were done, the wall seemed unbreakable. No matter what she did, she couldn't shift or move anything more. Only half of Sigis was uncovered.

Anna touched one of the spider-like legs, feeling its warmth, and sighed. "What do I do? The wall won't move." While a ripple of reddish light moved down the leg and over her hand before receding, there was no answer. She took that as encouragement to try harder. Sigis was trapped, and only she could free him.

After a moment's thought, Anna picked up a large rock and started beating the base of the wall with it. At first, it looked like nothing was happening, but then, the chips and cracks started. Harder and harder she worked until she thought her heart would burst and her hands were bloody with the effort. At last, the wall started to crumble.

From that point, it was just a matter of time and diligence. If nothing else, Anna was a diligent child.

Anna was forced to flee when her efforts succeeded in the sudden breaking and tumbling and crumbling of the wall all around her. She barely got out of the way of the ceiling that had been her shelter as it crashed to the ruined floor. The noise of the falling rock startled all of the nearby forest into silence.

When the dust cleared, she picked herself up and faced the form she had met in her dream. He was taller than her father and made of reddish-black stone that was smooth to the touch. His fingers and toes were clawed, his head horned, his eyes solid black. The eight spider legs that sprouted from his back, four curling around each of his sides, were the most disturbing thing about him. Even though his face was twisted into a long-tongued leer, it was easier to look at than those legs.

"Sigis?" Anna moved forward and stopped at the sight of something glinting in the rubble around her. With a bloody, sweaty hand, she picked it up. It was a light-blue gem as fair as the summer sky. She looked up, and the statue began to move.

"Sigis?" she asked again, this time with a hint of fear in her voice.

The statue shifted down to one knee before her. "Never fear me, little one. By blood and bone, by sweat and toil, we have a pact, you and I. I am yours to command." Sigis bowed his head to her.

Startled, she lifted the jewel up to him. "Is this yours?"

He nodded. "It is. Given in good faith to the wizard I had a pact with."

"What pact?"

"I . . . protected him and his. Those who came to his home with malice in their hearts suffered the guilt of nightmares. Those who were true had no worries for their sleep."

"Oh." Anna thought about this. "Do you want it back?" She offered the jewel to him, her palm up.

Sigis looked at her. "I do. Do you give it to me of your own free will?"

"Yes."

"Then I accept my freedom." His large clawed hand engulfed hers. When she looked up again, instead of solid black eyes, Sigis now had eyes the color of the summer sky. He stood and smiled at her. "But I do owe you, child. What do you want?"

"My name is Anna." She smiled at him. "I want to travel with you for a while." Her smile disappeared. "I want to know why Mother left me here in the Old Forest."

Sigis looked around. "Is that what they call it?"

She nodded. "How old are you?"

"I was old when this forest was young and the manor house was but a dream." He looked down at her. "I can take you with me. I have tasted your blood. You have tasted my dreams. We will walk the Dreamtime." He offered his hand to her, and she accepted it.

"You'll take me away from here?" Never had she wanted to leave a place so much.

"Wherever you wish to go, Anna. Even in freedom, I am yours to command."

"Why?"

"Because there are rules that were old when I was young. You freed me. Also, I, too, am alone."

Anna nodded, understanding the fear of being alone in a strange place.

✵✵✵

"Are you certain you wish to know? To find out why your mother abandoned you?"

There was concern in his voice, and Anna heard it as she stopped to play with a creature that looked like a cross between a caterpillar and a puppy. "I think I'm going to name you Pupapiller," she said, not answering him. She had her own fears as well. "Isn't he cute?"

"Careful." The concern in Sigis's voice morphed into affection. "Here in the Dreamtime, names have power. What was once a passing dream for someone is now a very real creature. What will you do with him now?"

She stood and looked between them—Sigis as still as the statue he once was and Pupapiller cavorting about her feet. "I'll keep him. You want to stay with me, don't you?"

Pupapiller leapt to her arms and licked her face, wagging his whole body. She laughed. "See? Pupapiller wants to stay."

What Anna did not see while holding her new pet was the nightmarish monster that appeared out of the ever-shifting landscape and Sigis waving a hand at it, forcing it away. Anna had no idea that she, as a human child, called to all of the creatures in the Dreamtime.

"We need to go. You are certain you wish to see your mother?"

Anna nodded, putting Pupapiller on the ground. "Yes."

Sigis offered his hand once more. "Think of your mother. Think of home."

Trying to keep her heart hidden, Anna smiled bravely. "I will." She closed her eyes and thought of home with her mother and father and baby brother, Aiden. She missed all of them so much her heart ached with just the thought of them.

"We have arrived."

Opening her eyes, Anna smiled wide. It *was* her home, the small but snug farmhouse on the edge of the wood. There was a fire in the fireplace, and her mother was standing over Aiden's crib, humming the same song she had been singing the last time Anna saw her.

For a moment, Anna did not know what to do. She looked up at Sigis, who nodded and stepped away. Anna nodded back and stepped forward. "Hello, Mother."

Her mother whirled in surprise and fear. "You shouldn't be here. You can't be here. I've already sent the letter to Niall that you've run away. He's coming home!" She put her hand to her breast, looking like she had said too much. "You shouldn't be here."

Anna's nervousness changed to sudden fury at the accusation of her running away from the home she'd loved all her life. "Why, Mother? Why'd you abandon me? I was lost and alone and scared! I'm a good girl! Why?"

"Stop calling me that! I'm not your mother."

Anna's fury faded, and she took another step forward in confusion. "But . . . you are."

"No. I'm not. Your father brought you with him to me. I wet-nursed you. He and I fell in love. I never thought I'd have my own child again. I wanted to die, but Niall needed a wet nurse. One child died. One mother died. I needed a baby. You were it." She glanced at the crib. "It never felt right. You weren't my child. But until Aiden, my lovely baby boy, I never knew what a real mother's love for her child was like."

The woman looked at her with something akin to disgust. "You were nothing but a leech to me. One I thought I had to love because of the man I married. I thought I loved you. I tried to love you. Thought maybe something was wrong with me . . . but there wasn't. It was you. Not my baby. Not worth the love of a mother. Not like my Aiden." She turned back to the crib. "Not like my Arthur before him. You were a poor substitute."

Tears spilled down Anna's face, her heart breaking all over again. She didn't understand. She didn't want to understand. Anna didn't want to know why she felt "wrong" to the only mother she'd ever known. She reached out a hand but could not make herself touch the woman who had already rejected her and let it fall to her side again. Then, a warm, clawed hand rested on her shoulder. Anna turned to Sigis, throwing herself into his arms. He picked her up and held her close with both arms and four of his spider limbs as she sobbed on his shoulder.

After an eternity of pain, Anna became aware of her mother's rising voice, panic clear. She turned to see what was happening but held onto Sigis's neck.

"Aiden, honey. Aiden, my love, where are you?" Her mother—for she would always be Mother in Anna's heart—dug through the crib, pulling far too many baby blankets from it. "Where are you?" She turned from the crib and looked through everything in the room that could possibly hold a baby. "Aiden!"

Anna was alarmed. "What's happened to Aiden?"

Sigis stroked her hair with a spider leg. "Nothing. Aiden is safe and sound. I will show you." He turned around, and there was Aiden in a floor crib with bright butterflies and flowers floating around him.

Anna wiggled to get down. Sigis allowed it. She hurried to him, kneeling to give him a kiss. Aiden giggled and grabbed for her hair. She smiled. "He's a good baby."

"He is. It is my experience that those who abandon the innocent do not deserve them. It is your mother's guilt that gave her the nightmare of losing her baby."

She looked up at him. "I've decided what I want."

"What is my command?"

"I want to become like you."

Sigis paused. "You wish to become a nightmare?"

"I want to become like you. I want to stay with you."

"You would have to leave all you love behind."

Anna looked at her mother sitting in the middle of the farmhouse, sobbing for her lost baby. "She doesn't love me. She doesn't want me." The words brought fresh tears to her eyes.

Sigis offered his hand. Anna accepted it, and he scooped her up into his arms again. "I know someone who does."

❋❋❋

Thirteen steps through the Dreamtime, passing through many strange and wonderful and frightening dreams, Sigis brought Anna to a familiar place, though she'd never been there. It was a castle with a drawbridge—one described to her in many of her father's tales about his journeys to the castle. This was his dream. Sitting on the edge of the drawbridge overlooking the moat was her father. "Daddy!"

Sigis let Anna down and watched as the little girl ran down the bridge to her father, who grabbed her in a huge bear hug.

"Anna, my girl. What are you doing in the city?" He ruffled her hair. "I won't be home for another moon."

"I missed you, Daddy. So much." She hugged him and kissed his cheek.

"I know it's hard. But when the king calls . . ." He pulled back from his hug. "What are you doing here? How did you get here? The road to the castle is long and dangerous."

She wriggled out of his arms and then sat next to him on the drawbridge. "My friend Sigis brought me." Anna looked between Sigis and her father. "Daddy, why does Mommy say she's not my mother?"

Her father looked like she had slapped him. "Oh, honey. Oh, darling. We were going to wait until you were older . . ." He looked sad.

"She's not my mother?"

He shook his head, pain clear on his face.

"Who is she?"

"Your mother died. It wasn't your fault. Birthing's hard on a woman. You saw that with Aiden. But I love you. We both love you so much. You'll always be our daughter."

She smiled through the pain and nodded. "I know, Daddy. I know." She stood again. "I've got to go. And I don't think I'll be back. Not for a while. Maybe not ever."

He stood as well. "Where are you going?"

"Far away, Daddy. But I do love you. I'm going to miss you. I think this is the best thing for you and . . . and Mommy . . . and Aiden." Anna stepped back from him. "I'm going to travel to new places and new dreams. I'll see you sometimes. I'll watch over you and Aiden. I promise." While she spoke, he grew farther and farther away from her.

"No, Anna. Wait! Don't go!" He reached for her and would keep reaching for her forever. Except for those rare times when she would visit him in dream.

As he disappeared from sight and sound, Anna turned to Sigis. "I couldn't tell him. I couldn't make him upset. Maybe now he'll think I didn't run away but tried to come to the castle and got lost."

Sigis nodded. "You are certain you wish to be like me?"

The two of them did not walk the Dreamtime so much as watch it pass them by. Pupapiller showed up again and stayed by their side. The sound and color and sights were a kaleidoscope of dreams, nightmares, and the passing denizens of the realm.

"Yes. Do you promise to stay with me? To never let me go?"

He was silent for a moment. "Never is a long time. When you become like me, we will have all the time in the universe. I can promise that by blood and bone, by sweat and toil, I will be your nightmare father for as long as you will have me."

She smiled up at him. "Then, yes, I'm certain."

Sigis leaned down and kissed her on the forehead. Anna felt warmth like a hot bath spread over her, down from her head to her shoulders to her waist, arms, and feet. She watched as her pale, soft skin became hard and smooth and the color of bloodstone. Whole worlds opened up in her mind as her humanity died a quiet death, and she was reborn a nightmare.

Blinking eyes the color of the perfect summer sky, she asked, "What do we do now?"

"Anything you wish, my child." Sigis smiled at her and meant every word.

As the two of them walked deeper into the Dreamtime, Anna's small human form lay curled up in the corner of a broken room in the ruins of a manor house deep within the Old Forest. In her hand was a small gem the blue of a summer sky—a most precious gift of death and life.

GOBLIN FRUIT

LILLIAN COHEN-MOORE

I'd been told that if I wanted stories about the spirits that infest forests, bless houses, and strike down livestock, I'd best wander the country. That the people who believed, truly believed in those stories, were the ones outside the places most people considered civilization. Standing on the porch of what looked to be a farm, if the outline of the land was not a lie beneath the late summer deluge, I wasn't sure I particularly cared anymore. I gave no thought to the notebooks likely dissolving in my rucksack as I waited, having tugged the bell-pull more heartbeats ago than I cared to count. I was wet, numb, and miserable. Academia could hang itself. I just wanted to remember what feeling my toes was like.

The woman who opened the door was not an otherworldly beauty. Button nose, freckles, pointed chin and dark eyes—she was not the stuff of tremble-inducing glories. But her smile. The edges of her eyes crinkled in sheer perverse amusement before she half-turned in the hallway, hollering, "If no one brings me a mop, I'm using their bed linens!" She looked me up and down neatly, smile widening as I somehow managed to flush. "You might as well come in. I doubt you're some forest sprite come to do us harm, and if you are, I would still like to have my lunch first." She gathered up the excess material of her skirt in one hand, holding the door open as she stepped to the side. "Enter, be ye man or sprite." Her delivery was dry, the words accompanied by a flourishing half-bow. She looked up, laughing.

As she stood back upright, the hall into the farmhouse proper filled with multiple sets of footsteps. The now-crowded threshold soon also held a man and woman who appeared to be quite clearly related, both rangy and black haired, and a bear of a man who towered over all of us. He was the first to start laughing and haul me over the lintel. "By the Graces, get in already!"

❀❀❀

My mocking greeter's name was Moira Gates. The dark-haired relations were first cousins, Amelia and David Collis. The bear of a man was Ivan Fiske. Amelia was married to Ivan, David had a long-time association with one of his models—

Alma waved a hand airily, nearly flinging her toast. "They don't much care out here in the country. Our money spends as well as anyone else's."

My interrogation was brief and conducted entirely by Ivan. I was from Lenore. I was in the countryside collecting stories, particularly about local spirits. My notebooks, carefully wrapped, had been largely undamaged but were still set to dry near the stove. Moira watched the conversation but rarely spoke over lunch, content with popping raspberries into her mouth, observing as conversation devolved into an argument about the demands of the art forms of each resident of the house. She watched me as I, bewildered by the turn of the day, attempted to take in the conversation. "David, you have some spare clothes in the studio, don't you? I'm sure our new guest could use not catching his death of cold."

Alerted by the sound of his name, David jerked his head up, blinking. "Mmm? Oh, yes. Just pull something out of the wardrobe."

She glanced at me as she slid off her stool, gesturing for me to follow as she popped one last raspberry into her mouth.

"So, you're an artist colony?"

"After a fashion, I suppose. The land is taken care of by an actual farmer. We have some chickens, a horse to get to the village proper, an outbuilding that Ivan uses for sculpture—" She stopped speaking as she opened the door. "You're really a story collector?"

I shuffled, self-conscious and still wet, into David's studio. "Do I strike you as one to fib, ma'am?"

"You collect stories. It's in your nature to fib." She pointed to a screen, discreetly tucked against one corner. "You can undress. I'll see if I can find you something suitable." She made a shooing motion as I hesitated, opening the wardrobe only after I had scooted behind the screen. "So you decided to spend your summer collecting stories?"

I could hear her rifling through the clothes as I fought with sodden shoes. "I find it better described as keeping oral traditions alive."

Moira snorted. "I say collect, you say keep alive." She giggled as I dropped one boot, then the other, to the floor. "If you just strip down, we can add the clothes to the washing. Should be able to get it done tomorrow." As I debated stripping down, albeit behind a screen, she sighed. "I'm an artist. I have seen and heard far more interesting things than a man changing." As I began to divest myself of clothes, each garment hitting the wood floor with a slap of water-heavy fabric, she sighed contently. "I remember Amelia whipping these together. This should be your size."

The garments tossed over the screen, while of a more eccentric cut than my own, were at the very least warmer. I could hear her pace as I dressed. "Are you kept from some pressing task, ma'am?"

"Am I to call you *sir*?"

"I beg your pardon?"

"If you're going to insist you call me *ma'am*, I shall have to call you *sir*. Unless you'd rather like it if I call you *Colin*?"

I finished dressing before exiting from behind the screen, executing a more sincere half-bow than her earlier one. "As the lady—Moira—wishes."

She laughed, pressing her fingertips to her lips for a moment. "I do believe I like that. The lady." Moira chuckled, stepping behind the screen to retrieve my wet clothes. "Flattery will get you everywhere, you know."

"Then I suppose you would be willing to answer a question, as I've so flattered you."

She stuck her head out from behind the curtain, a stray curl hanging near her right eye. "Yes?"

"Why did the last village say to come here for the stories I'm looking for?"

Moira laughed. "They said that? Such wagging tongues. They sent you here because of the goblins."

❀❀❀

The rain didn't clear till the following morning. David sketched a map of some of the nearby homes; Amelia armed me with a basket of country remedies to dole out to sick neighbors. Her curatives opened a number of doors that may have otherwise stayed closed to me. Over ashen cookies, tea of varying strengths, and a morning spent walking through strangely heavy fog, the shape of the land—both physical and supernatural—began to take form. Every household had stories, and the first day gave way to several spent by me walking the wide-flung community, meeting the inhabitants, and observing the phantasmagoric landscape once the fog lifted. This corner of the countryside was given to peculiar weather, tall hedgerows, and copses of trees no light could penetrate, their branches were so deeply intertwined.

After the first week, I was unsure if the countryside bred the stories in fertile imaginations or if I should instead be less cavalier about taking my rambles at odd hours. I didn't particularly believe a land could hold actual, willful malice. Moira quickly took to teasing me, going so far as walking me to the end of the artist's lane, smirking as she'd wish me goodbye for the day.

Nine days on, we'd linger by the gate, becoming alarmingly familiar in our language. I was loath to contemplate that I should likely leave within the month, a thought that would leave my head the moment Moira appeared.

I had been at the farmhouse for two weeks when their girl, Nell, quit. *Girl* is a disingenuous descriptor; Nell occupied the twilight state somewhere past 40 years of age but before "truly ancient." I came home from a night of teeth-achingly sweet tea and a lecture on the local undead creatures—none of whom had appeared to me. Nell, often cheerful, was leaving the gate, tight-lipped and walking past as if she had seen the creatures of the night , if not worse.

After a fortnight of daily tales and dire warnings to not ignore that which is out of place, I made for the farmhouse with haste that equaled Nell's efforts to leave it in the dust. David and Ivan were hauling the laundry baskets up in the blue twilight. Moira and Amelia were standing in front of the door. Moira leaned heavily against the older woman, head resting on her shoulder.

I held my hands up to placate a suddenly tense Amelia as I broke a branch underfoot, crossing into the remaining twilight illumination. "Just Colin. No forest sprites."

Moira's laugh was a sudden, bleak bark, the sound edged and dangerous.

I raised my eyebrows.

Moira pulled away from Amelia, turning on her heel and entering the farmhouse.

Amelia's smile was tight. "Moira will need some time to calm her nerves. Nothing to worry about." She watched as David and Ivan finished carrying the laundry baskets—something Moira and Nell usually handled together—back into the house.

In a moment, we had exchanged nods, and I was left to stand in front of the door, now alone, in front of the farmhouse. The usually brightly lit and loud household was now walking on eggshells. I shut the door behind me and excused myself to the room I had been allowed to use during my stay: a warm and plain room tucked neatly beneath the narrow stairs that led into the upper reaches of the house.

After the household had been quiet for some time, the stairs creaked with someone's attempt at stealth. Moira slipped into my room, wrapped neck to toes in a heavy dressing gown. I turned in my chair, motioning to the bed. Decorum would die of apoplexy about an unmarried man and woman in the same room, alone, at night. It didn't mean I couldn't let her take the more comfortable seat. She took it, pressed her hands against her knees, and tried to speak.

It took a long, uncomfortable time for her false starts to become words, even after I restrained myself to a look of concerned encouragement.

"I saw them. Nell and I both saw them."

"Saw who, Moira?"

She kept her head up, her gaze on my face. "The goblins. Just like in the stories."

I held my hands out to buy time, squeezing her hands as she placed them in mine. I rubbed my hands around her cold ones. The stories went the same way every time: someone encountered the goblins while away from their home, came home crazed and babbling, fell ill, died. Moira was shaken and still sporting scratches but seemed far from ill. I squeezed her hands, eliciting a brief, fragile smile.

"I went down with Nell to help along the wash. She has a niece, Ginny, who comes by when she can to help her with it. Poor mite is sick." She licked her lips, smile nervous. "They sang. I don't even remember it all. Just 'come buy, come buy.'" She shuddered, closing her eyes for a minute. "Nell told me to run." Moira opened her eyes again, their surface gleaming. "They had fruit. Such amazing fruit, smells I'd never smelled before. I'd never craved a sweet like that."

I held her hands, painfully aware that if I interrupted, my questions could do harm. I waited.

"I didn't take one. I wanted to. So much." Her smile was confused and bleak. "I don't believe in stories, Colin. I don't—" she took a breath, deep and pained.

I moved beside her, held her when she sought my arms, and petted her hair. Stories said that sprites could steal pieces of the very heart of man, so I did what I could. My own lifelong fascination—and scoffing—at sprites was silenced by that gleam of unshed tears. She had been wounded by something, not even touched but wounded all the same.

I held her for what must have been hours, as if I could somehow help her incubate a sense of safety, a warmth like sunrise. When we began to doze, I shook off sleep to touch her shoulder.

"You should seek out your own bed, lest your household upbraid me for unbecoming behavior on such a night."

Her smile still pulled a twinge within my chest, and that sweet twinge became an ache when she kissed me. A brief, warm press of lips and a hand to my face before she drew backward.

"Goodnight, Colin."

❀❀❀

Nell did not quit for good, but once Ginny was once again able to stand without a spinning head, she was sent in Nell's place to help around the farm. Moira seemed distractible and nervous, but that ebbed enough that, a week later, she notified everyone over breakfast that she would be painting in a nearby field for a number of hours. Over dinner, her compatriots expressed a desire to go past the village and down to the next "proper outpost of civilization" to drop off a painting for one of David's clients and pick up new materials for Amelia's next artistic endeavor at the loom.

"We'd be gone for a week." Amelia's tone was cheerful as she speared greenery with her fork.

Moira and I shared a glance, the briefest moment, as if attempting to ascertain how the other felt. Might feel.

"I hope you won't, Amelia, but the light's too lovely this week. I can't go with that sort of color out there waiting for me to paint it." Moira shrugged, as if regretful.

Ivan lifted his glass, pausing for a moment as he looked at me. "I'm sure if Colin is still attending to his tale collecting, he should stay behind as well."

It was settled so casually I felt almost numb. I didn't know what either of us would do with the time without three far-too-clever companions.

The next day dawned, the cart was loaded, and we . . . *bolted* is the most honest word. Moira had painting to do and things to fetch, and I had a few miles' walk to go learn many important stories about tiny spirits that slept in . . . shoes. Possibly shoes. I still can't remember that first part of the day clearly. In the early evening hours, I walked back anxious and happy and briefly unintimidated by the countryside, tales of goblins notwithstanding.

She wasn't there. I checked every room when my calls went unanswered, just to know, to satisfy curiosity that she was not merely painting in a corner, or perhaps napping by the fire in obscenely warm weather.

Moira was gone. And as dusk crept closer, I left a note, lit a lantern, and went looking. I found her out in the fields she'd been painting, breathing slow and labored, kneeling half-limp in the grass.

"Moira?"

She looked up the third time I said her name, and I nearly dropped the lantern. She was pale-faced, cheeks bright with fever, lips smudged with some faint and luminescent substance. She blinked, wide-eyed, only half-present. "They smelled like peaches and strawberry and pomegranate. But better."

❀❀❀

I left the broken, spattered canvas behind but managed to marshal the wit and fortitude to guide Moira back to the farmhouse, toting paint box, easel, and lantern. She followed like a sleepwalker, skin hot to touch when I laid the back of my hand against her brow. I had younger sisters and did my best to think not about what eating goblin fruit could do to a mortal, man or woman, and instead to follow the steps to aid her. I washed her face, helped her strip down to her shift, and put her to bed. When she wept, I patted her hair. I slept with her head resting on my chest, the rest of her carefully tucked into the blankets of her bed.

Ginny, who arrived at noon, was informed that Miss Moira had taken ill and that I would need help during the days until her friends returned to nurse her. One day turned into two. I could hear, as if at the edges of the world, some strange musical vibration. But Moira heard nothing.

Every night I would try to lure her out of her strange fog of bewilderment and intermittent weeping with the most everyday stories I could think of. My childhood. What my family was like, had been like. People I had met, and stories

I knew about them. I did not speak of sprites or goblins. But she grew paler by the day and spoke only of their cries. *Come buy, come buy.* She could not remember why they had given her the fruit, only that when she took it, it was all she wanted. I kissed her brow and held her and listened. I, the story collector, could only listen.

On that third night, when she drifted off to sleep, she murmured, "Come back." I hesitated but slid my way out from her fevered, unconscious embrace. And I left in search of the goblins. My chest felt weighed down with fear for Moira and feelings for her too closely knitted, like the copses, to peel away from one another. I wanted nothing but answers, some cure.

As I thought about that fear, my imperiled, unnamed hopes, I could hear the nigh-musical cries. Down, in the darkness of the copses of trees, by the river. Down where she first saw them.

"Come buy, come buy!"

The smell hit me before I even saw them. It was the purest, sweetest smell, one so strong as to be unimaginable until that moment. The heart of summer, ripe, made flesh in fruit. It dizzied me, the smell, and their cries, and before long, I was surrounded by the goblins. Like untold numbers before me . Had they all been would-be lovers, afraid for the one who held their heart? Parents seeking their children?

"I have no coin."

They chuckled. Leered. They wore crowns of twig and vine in the dark, moved and rustled, and I salivated at the very smell. And their dark laughter became dark muttering, wary and undercut with violence. When I reached for one of the fruits in the hand of the goblin nearest to me, I spoke.

"I want her back."

It screeched. "Buy! BUY!"

They shrieked and chortled, shook, and gnashed their teeth. My senses said they were ugly, underneath the shifting smell of goblin fruit, a smell that seemed sweeter than her kiss and softer than her skin. I was bewitched, and as a collector of stories, I did the only thing I could think of. I thrust my fist into that goblin's face, pain searing, knuckles bruising, a cut forming where my skin skid across one of its teeth. With that blow, all pretense of flowery seduction was gone. When the blood of the goblin hit my eye, I screamed.

I understood.

I fought my way out like a cornered animal, biting, tearing, snapping, screaming. Everywhere, the howling rage of cheated goblins and crushed fruit. One eye tried to seduce me still, while the other saw their ugly rage, their hideous forms. Their fruit smelled as dangerous since it smelled of desire. I was no longer interested in stealing or purchasing fruit for her in some hope it could be curative. I was concerned only with meting out all the violence I could. Not only to escape and return, but to make them suffer. Suffer as we had suffered already, and only the Graces could know how many before us. I know not if I managed to kill any of them, but even with stinging bruises from their cudgels, I made them hurt twice as much. I stumbled, dizzied, away from them as they retreated, finding me too motivated a match.

It was so warm as to be obscene that night. My eye stung, countless places along me ached and burned, I smelled of goblin blood and goblin fruit. But I walked, one foot in front of the other. I had to see her. I had likely failed. I had no answers and no cure. The burning in my eye had drifted deeper, a cold fire of flickering understanding. A sense that, perhaps, if I could get back . . .

Perhaps this could end more happily than other goblin tales.

❀❀❀

I lingered outside in the summer heat, still unabated hours after sunset. In the end, I chose to enter, afraid of what I might find.

My boots left slick trails of broken fruit flesh on the floor as I walked over the threshold. The only sound in the house was the wood creaking under my feet. When I pushed at the half-open door to her room at the top of the narrow stairs, I still felt all too aware of the bruises left behind by the goblins. I was awash in the marks of their cudgels, still in pain and drenched in the violent color of the goblin fruit. Rind, flesh, pulp, seeds. I was covered from neck to toes, had risked myself body and soul because I could not bear to sit idly by her and watch her die.

I shut the door behind me with a sore and trembling hand, breathing in the miasma of the fruit's many odors. Noxious, sweet, intoxicating. I knelt by her on the bed, gently cupping my hands around her face. "Moira."

I had hoped she'd look at me and answer, but she merely breathed, rasping and hollow. She hadn't returned to her senses. Moira had not improved with the simple passage of hours. Desperate, willing to try anything, I used my fingers to scrape pulp from my shirt.

She breathed in pained rasps, cheeks bright with fever.

I hesitated, then pressed the wine-colored smear of goblin fruit to her lips. She shuddered, some flicker of color inside her visible to my still-stinging eye. One of her hands rose to grasp mine, sucking the pulp from my fingers, nipping at them with her teeth. She drew me closer, teeth and tongue scraping at the remnants of fruit on my clothes, sucking the juice from my coat. Moira was warm, too warm and pressing against me. She held me tight, her weakened grip becoming increasingly strong. Moira knotted her fingers in my shirt, whimpering ecstatically as she sucked the fruit from my neck. My short, heavy breaths were the only other sounds in the bedroom. I murmured, in my tongue or some sprite-blood fused language, I couldn't say. I couldn't hear them calling from the river anymore. I could barely think of anything but Moira's whispers in my ear, happy, breathy, "You came back to me."

My senses were muddled, heart pounding as she slipped her hands beneath my shirt, nails scraping into skin. When she pressed her mouth against mine, tongue teasing my lips open, I tasted the traces of goblin fruit in her mouth.

In that moment, I was hers. We wrapped our arms around each other, shuddering and devouring. Moira's bites came with force, leaving new bruises, the sensation of her nails scraping down my body only dimly felt. The bedding was shoved aside as we burrowed into the bed, clinging with the force of shared desire. We had never once kissed like this, and as her hands pulled the clothes from my body, all wonderment and thought ceased as my mouth made its way down her neck, chasing her freckles as intently as her cries.

❀❀❀

We woke awkwardly but without regret.

Amelia and the others knew something had changed when they returned the following afternoon. They have been gracious about continuing to host an "itinerant storyteller" under their roof, making the agreement simple: stay on as an extra set of hands through winter, and I was welcome. I don't know what this winter will hold for us, but as days turn into weeks, Moira returns to health. Every day I've watched the lingering grip of their fruit recede from her, the sickly incandescence fading. But when I hold my hands up, a strange dark hue lingers in my eyes. She and I go down to the river together, now, to do the wash—a chore Amelia was delighted to cede to the season's house guest.

Moira cannot hear them anymore, nor can she see them. But with my right eye, which tasted their blood, I see things I never had before. And where her mouth was pressed to mine, still stained with Goblin fruit? There still buzzes a faint, insistent thirst that never fades. Whether for the fruit or for their flesh, I do not know. But in the corner of the fields where one goes to burn brush, in which I buried my clothes from that strange night, there is an odor in the air, faint and familiar.

I fear the fruit of spring.

Endless Castle

Torah Cottrill

Gozen ran through the forest. The howling storm blinded her, and low branches snatched at her hair. Her robes tangled around her legs, and she fell, bloody hands vivid against the snow. Faintly, she could hear her pursuers through the wind. She scrambled to her feet and ran on.

A low building shown through gaps in the sheets of snow. It might have been a forgotten tomb, its turtleback roof sunk into the hill, or a woodcutter's home. Gozen stumbled to it and scratched at the door with broken fingernails.

"Let me in!" she called. "Please, let me in!"

There was no answer.

She sagged to the ground, leaning against the door. It was a tomb after all. Gozen closed her eyes and waited to be caught. Or to die.

The door opened silently, and orange light stained the snow. Strong arms lifted the unconscious woman and carried her inside. Outside, the wind soon erased all traces of her passage.

When Gozen opened her eyes, she lay on a sleeping mat in a warm, wood-paneled room. A man dressed in layers of white silk stood by a fire. Although his hair was white, he had a young man's face, angular and beardless. His eyes were the color of the winter sky.

The pale man handed her a cup of broth. Gozen grimaced at the taste, but its warmth brought a flush to her face. She pulled the blankets closer and looked quickly around the room. There was no sign of her blood-soaked dress. Gozen took another sip to disguise her curiosity.

"I'm Gozen," she said, looking up at the man through dark lashes. "Who are you? Where are we?"

"My name is Tsuchigumo. This is my home."

"Thank you," the young woman murmured indistinctly, sinking fast into exhaustion. "Thank you for letting me in."

Gozen woke to morning light. Wrapping a blanket around her shoulders, she explored the bedroom. Sunlight glowed through papered windows that wouldn't open. She found a bathing room behind a folding door. A white robe and a beautifully woven red sash were laid out next to a basin of hot water and soap that smelled like unfamiliar flowers. When she felt clean, she slid the robe on. It was light and soft and very warm.

Gozen tied the wide belt and investigated the tall wooden chest in the main room. It had dozens of drawers of all sizes. Most were empty, but in one, she found an ivory comb, which she used to smooth her hair. She fastened it with two jade pins from another drawer.

Gozen tried the door. It was locked.

She frowned and sat by the fire to wait. Eventually, she heard a quick knock, and the door opened. An old woman entered with a lacquered tray.

"Ah, my dear, I thought you might be awake! And hungry too, I imagine. Here, take a look at what I've brought you."

The old woman put the tray on the table and opened the lids of various small ceramic pots. "Here's some rice porridge, and an egg, and some smoked eel, and an orange . . ."

"An orange?" interrupted Gozen. "How did you find an orange in the middle of winter?"

The servant chuckled indulgently. "My lord can get anything he wishes," she said. The old woman paused. "You're very lucky the master opened a door for you. He doesn't often let people in here."

"Tsuchigumo is the master of the house?" Gozen asked eagerly.

"Bless you, child," the old woman cackled. "This is Mugen-jo, the Endless Castle. Tsuchigumo-denka is our prince and the master of the doors."

"A prince," Gozen breathed. She stared at the array of delicacies before her, then ate as quickly as good manners allowed. The old servant looked on, smiling indulgently at Gozen's appetite. When the young woman was finished, the servant gathered the empty dishes.

"Where is your master?" Gozen asked. "I'd like to thank him for his help and beg his continued hospitality."

"No doubt," the old woman replied, opening the door. "My lord is away now. You wait here until he returns. I'll see to anything you need."

Alone in the room, Gozen paced its length many times. She inspected the bathing room and the many drawers of the chest again but discovered nothing new. She poked at the fire until its heat made her sleepy.

Gozen awoke from a doze to see Tsuchigumo's silhouette as he stirred the fire. She leaped to her feet, but he gestured. "Jorogumo has made you dinner. Eat."

Obediently, Gozen knelt at the table and opened the clay pots. When she offered to serve the pale man, though, he declined with a wave of his hand. She poured him tea and then ate slowly and decorously.

While she ate, Tsuchigumo sipped his tea. "Do you like your room?" he asked. "It can be changed."

"The room is comfortable, my lord, but I'd like to be able to leave it. The day is very long without occupation."

"The door is locked to keep you safe. The Endless Castle is a dangerous place for you. But you're not a prisoner. If you want to leave, I'll take you back to the door into the forest."

"No, no!" Gozen protested quickly. "Please, my lord, I didn't mean to complain. Don't make me leave! Nothing here could be as dangerous to me as the things in the forest."

Tsuchigumo nodded. "Very well, you may stay. I suppose you don't need to remain in this room all the time. Perhaps you'd like to visit Jorogumo in the kitchen? You can always find it from this room by turning left at each hallway. I'll tell her to expect you."

"Tsuchigumo-denka," Gozen reached out to touch his hand where it rested on the table. "You saved my life." The tips of her fingers rested lightly against the bones of his wrist. His eyes followed the curve of her arm. Her skin was the color of honey. Gozen's fingers tightened, pulling him to sit beside her.

Tsuchigumo studied the delicate bones of the woman's hands, then looked up into her dark eyes. The heavy curtain of her hair fell across her face, and he reached to brush it back. Suddenly, they were very close. "What a strange creature you are," he murmured, "but very lovely. I suppose I'll have to find a place for you here."

Gozen stroked Tsuchigumo's cheek, leaned forward, and kissed him. "Thank you," she whispered and drew him toward the bed with a smile.

Later, Tsuchigumo left the sleeping woman's bed and crept out of the room. He spoke into the darkness, "I know you're there."

From the shadows came the sound of striking flint, and a candle flared. The old woman stepped toward him with a reproving hiss. "Put her back, my lord. No good comes from interfering with these things."

"I was sorry for her," he replied. "And as I recall, you once had a weakness for dark hair and a flushed cheek."

The old woman grinned. "As you say. But you can't afford this distraction."

"True. My mother is restless to claim new territory, and she wants me to find it for her. Take care of this one for me. If we're going to keep her, I want her to be safe."

The old woman bowed low. Tsuchigumo vanished into the maze of dark corridors.

"Strays wander," the old woman muttered as she walked away. "If she gets lost and doesn't come back, you'd be better off."

The next morning, Gozen stood before the door. She took a deep breath and tried the handle. The door opened to her touch. With a small smile, she peered out. Identical whitewashed hallways stretched away before her and to either side. Dark wooden doors broke the monotony of the corridors at uneven intervals.

Gozen stepped into the hall, her slippers noiseless on the polished bamboo floors. She walked down the long hallway before her, anxious to see more of the castle. When she glanced back at her room, the door was indistinguishable from every other door.

Gozen rushed back, eyes firmly fixed on her own door. She checked that it was really hers, then unknotted the red sash at her waist and tied it to the door handle. From halfway down the hall, she looked back. The sash glowed brightly against the dark wood.

Many of the doors on either side of the long hall were locked. Gozen peeked inside those that would open. One room was full of colored glass globes, each glowing as if it contained a captive star. She found a room containing only a suit of chain armor with an iron cuirass. As she came closer to peer into the empty helmet and admire the gold-washed steel, she left a trail of footprints in the thick dust. Gozen quickly shut the door of a room that exhaled a steady, cold wind from no apparent source and realized that she had come a long way—she could no longer see her own door. She continued down the corridor.

Ahead of her, at the end of the long corridor, a spot of color appeared. Gozen's steps quickened. As she drew closer, Gozen could see another hallway crossing the one in which she walked. Tied to the door was a red sash.

Gozen opened the door with shaking hands and saw the familiar contents of her room. The color drained from her face and her knees buckled. She sat in the doorway, staring into the long, straight corridor she had followed.

It was a long time before Gozen felt steady enough to leave the room again. Finally, she returned to the hallway. Carefully, following Tsuchigumo's directions, she turned left and left again, many times, until she reached a broad flight of stone steps leading down into a kitchen warm with steam and full of the colors and scents of cooking.

Jorogumo looked up from a large loom, where she sat weaving in the light from a paper-covered window. "Welcome, child, to my domain within Mugen-jo. Can you weave? Spin?"

Gozen shook her head, mute at the extravagant detail in the kitchen after the endless stark hallways. Copper pans gleamed on racks, bunches of onions hung from the rafters, sacks of rice and vials of spices lined the walls, and everywhere skeins of thread were piled. Most were white or the palest shades of blue or green, but a few were brilliantly colored. Gozen carefully untangled a mass of indigo thread from a wooden chair and sat.

"What thread is this? Flax? Lotus stem?"

"That one is made from nettles, dyed with persimmons. Most of these are a kind of silk, though. Here, girl. If you can't weave, at least you can wind the thread neatly."

Gozen obeyed, untangling skein after unruly skein of gossamer thread and carefully winding each around a bamboo frame. As she did, she darted curious glances at Jorogumo.

"How long have you served the prince?"

"Oh, a long time! I've cared for him since he was a child, and I'll care for his children, too."

"What domain is your lord the prince of? I suppose he has many palaces more lavish than this!" Gozen's face was sharp and eager.

The old woman cast a shrewd look at the young one. "You're flushed, child. Sit, and I'll make you some bark tea and flower cakes."

While Jorogumo drew hot water from the pot over the fire, Gozen hid a pair of scissors in the folds of her sash and a length of tangled thread in her sleeve.

By the time the old woman returned with a tray, Gozen was once again placidly winding skeins.

After that first glimpse of the castle's treasures, Gozen eagerly explored more of its endless maze of rooms and stairs and corridors. Each morning, she tied a sash to the door of her room. As she explored, she marked her way with bits of thread tied to the handles of doors. Each afternoon, she followed her knots back, undoing each as she passed.

The many whitewashed corridors led to other corridors, sometimes at right angles, sometimes not. Staircases of wood or stone brought Gozen to new levels of the castle, although some led to locked door or blank walls. Hallways and rooms were illuminated by the diffuse light from papered windows that could not be opened.

Most of the doors were locked. Some opened to reveal only empty rooms. But sometimes, behind the door, there were scenes of wonder. Gozen found a room barely large enough to contain the giant stone horse inside. She walked around it, running her hands along its chilly flanks and carved mane, her eyes round with awe.

Another day's wanderings brought her to a room with shining gilt walls and a deep drift of overlapping carpets worked in the colors of jewels. "One day," she murmured, stroking the silky carpets, "I'll be the mistress of all this." Gozen smiled and pressed a hand to the hint of roundness beneath her sash.

As the days became weeks, Gozen slipped down innumerable white corridors and through the dark doors that would open to her. A room bristling with masks of a thousand different faces, made out of wood or ivory or leather or feathers or bronze, startled her to a shrill cry. Gozen clapped a hand over her mouth and hurriedly checked that the corridors remained empty. After gulping a few steadying breaths, she inspected the masks closest to the door. A few moved, eyes and mouths and snouts and tendrils shifting slowly. As Gozen stared, she could hear voices, a multitude of overlapping conversations, some in languages she couldn't name. With a shudder, Gozen fled.

The weeks blurred together, and the young woman lost count of the time spent in the shifting castle. One morning, she found a spiral stairway leading to an iron-bound door. Through this door, Gozen found a room with an impossibly high ceiling, carpeted in lush grass, pillared by living trees taller than any in the forest where she'd lived. She followed the sound of water to a stream that flowed out of a blank white wall. It led to a pond dense with lotus blooms. Beneath the gently rippling water, the shadows of fish glided. Gozen lay on the grass and feathered a hand through the cool water, humming a cradle song.

Most afternoons, when she had finished the day's explorations, Gozen made the familiar leftward turnings from her room to the kitchen to sit with Jorogumo by the fire. The old woman gave no indication that she was aware of Gozen's clandestine wanderings through the castle.

One afternoon, Gozen arrived to find the kitchen empty. She began opening cabinets, quickly inspecting the contents of each. In the back of a low cabinet behind Jorogumo's loom, Gozen found a bundle of dirty cloth. She reached for it. It was her old dress, stiff with dried blood. Gozen's hands trembled and she squeezed her eyes shut, fighting off the memories.

A sudden noise startled Gozen from her daze. Hastily, she shoved the dress back into the cabinet and stood.

Jorogumo was watching her from the door. "Why, child," the old woman chuckled, though her sharp eyes did not echo the mirth, "the fire has brought a flush to your cheeks. Look at you! You came to us like a ghost and now here you are in my kitchen, lovely as a song."

Gozen flinched. "Someone else told me that once. The daimyo, as he rode through woods."

"A daimyo, eh?" said Jorogumo. "Lucky girl to have attracted the notice of such a powerful man."

"Oh, no, it was nothing," Gozen said, bowing so that her hair hid her face. "And a provincial daimyo is not so important, compared to a prince. Please, tell me when our lord will honor us with his presence."

The old woman laughed and patted Gozen's hand with hard, dry fingers.

"Ah, you hope for another visit from the prince, do you? He's not often here. Right now, I imagine he's in court."

"Have you been to court? Tell me about it."

Gozen listened to Jorogumo's stories and wound thread or hung bundles of unfamiliar herbs to dry. Some days she simply sat and stared into the kitchen fire. She moved more slowly now, afflicted with a strange lassitude. One morning, as she reached for a packet of spices from a high shelf, the old woman laid her bony hand on the swell of Gozen's belly.

"As I thought! Soon I'll have another child to care for." Gozen dropped the packet, and a puff of ground ginger rose around her. Jorogumo helped her to her seat by the fire and brought her a cup of mushroom broth.

"More princelings for the castle! This is good fortune, indeed."

Gozen hid a smile behind a sip of broth.

When she woke the next morning, Tsuchigumo was standing by the fire.

"Are you well?" he asked.

"Yes, my lord, very well. The morning illness no longer comes."

Tsuchigumo turned away. "Do you require anything?"

"More clothes, please," Gozen replied. "This robe never shows wear, but it would be nice to have more than one." The man nodded and left without another word. Gozen stared at the door for a moment, then shrugged and prepared for the morning's exploration.

Although she tried to find the path back to the forest room many times, the way had changed. Gozen found rooms with groves of tinkling jeweled trees and rooms with murals so cleverly painted that it seemed she could walk right into them, but no door led her to the cool forest with the gently rippling pond.

Gradually, Gozen became heavier and slower. As the baby crowded her breathing and dragged her steps, she spent more mornings resting than exploring. The old woman brought her lotions to ease her skin, and teas to ease her aches. And new things appeared inside the drawers of the tansu chest.

At first, Gozen found an ivory silk robe shot with threads of gold and a pale lavender sash. Another morning, the drawers revealed a linen envelope containing a pair of silver bracelets etched with a pattern of cherry blossoms. As her belly swelled taut, Gozen found a gossamer wrap the color of the palest sky, damasked with gray cranes in flight. Although the castle was neither warmer nor colder than ever, Gozen often sat in the evenings with the wrap around her shoulders, staring into her fire.

Some drawers were now full of scrolls, containing ink drawings or poetry or folktales. At first, Gozen set these aside impatiently. But as she stopped exploring the castle, Gozen began to read. Tales of the planes and their broken worlds, sketches of the islands of the Forever Sea, and strange transcripts from Aralu absorbed her days and filled her dreams.

Jorogumo brought dainty morsels to tempt Gozen's failing appetite. Each meal began with mushroom broth. She no longer winced at the taste.

"Have some while it's hot. There's a good girl," the old woman urged Gozen. "It'll keep up your strength, and it's very good for babies!"

"Where's your master?" Gozen fretted, querulous in late pregnancy. "I should have attendants and doctors! And I'll want things for the baby."

"There, there, child," Jorogumo soothed the young woman, patting her hand. "Don't you worry. Here in Mugen-jo, we have everything you need."

One night, Gozen woke with an aching back and a restless urge to walk. She drew the crane wrapper around her shoulders and made her way slowly to the kitchen.

"Old woman!" she called, her voice pinched shrill by pain. "Where are you? Summon the doctor!"

Jorogumo appeared suddenly at Gozen's elbow, startling her into a backward step that almost unbalanced her. "Don't be silly, child. You'd think this was your first baby! Come back to your room."

Many difficult hours later, Gozen delivered a boy into the old woman's waiting hands. He had Gozen's smoke-dark eyes and black hair, but his skin was as pale as moonlight.

The old woman helped her into bed and brought her tea and rice. "Eat now. Babies drain your energy." She picked up the baby and, crooning a low song, carried him to the door.

"Wait!" Gozen cried.

"Hush, girl. Don't worry. I've raised many princelings! I'll keep this one safe and sound and bring him back to you in the morning. You need to rest now."

Soon, Gozen was asleep. She dreamed of a room with walls made of shelves, each lined with the bleached skulls of animals. Some were as small as her thumb, the bones of mice or voles. Others had strange horns or stiff frills of bone. One was as large as a loom, with cruelly curved fangs. Its empty gaze seemed to follow her, and from its mouth, a hollow voice called her name. Gozen woke with a cry.

In the days that followed, Gozen didn't regain her strength. Eaten by fever and tormented by dreams of blood and snow, she woke when urged by the old woman to swallow sips of mushroom broth, then fell back into sweat and chills.

A cool hand on her forehead brought Gozen awake from dreams of wandering lost. Tsuchigumo was kneeling by her bed, speaking to Jorogumo.

"Spinner, what have you done?"

"I? Nothing, my lord. You knew the risks, bringing her here."

"Perhaps you were right, and I should have left her to her fate. Can she be saved?"

"Her kind rarely survives the birth of princes."

Gozen lifted a weak arm toward the pale man's face. He caught her hand in his and allowed her to clutch it.

"My lord!" she rasped through dry lips. "You have a son."

"Yes," he said, absently stroking the damp hair from her forehead. "You have given me an heir. You'll be rewarded, I promise, when you're better."

Gozen sighed deeply and closed her eyes again. Her grip on his hand slackened, and her arm fell back to the bed.

Tsuchigumo knelt, studying the sleeping woman. After some thought, he lit sticks of harsh incense. When the room was full of acrid smoke, he pried Gozen's mouth open and thrust a sliver of resin under her tongue. She thrashed in her sleep, and he placed a pale hand over her mouth to keep her from spitting the resin out. Finally, she was still, and he left her to sleep.

When Gozen woke, she was clear-headed at last. She brushed her hair until it gleamed, wrapped herself in a dawn pink robe with a yellow sash, and made her way with quick steps to the kitchen. She found Jorogumo weaving, rocking a cradle with one foot.

When Gozen approached, the old woman grinned.

"There you are, well and whole! You owe the master double thanks now, my pet," Jorogumo said and patted Gozen's cheek.

"My debt is paid and more," replied Gozen cheerfully. "There he lies!" She leaned into the cradle and lifted the baby. He opened his eyes and waved his arms vigorously, snagging a fistful of Gozen's loose hair and yanking with enthusiasm. Gozen smiled broadly. "An heir for the prince," she whispered into the baby's soft starburst of hair. "You're a treasure indeed!" She turned to the old woman. "Where is my lord? I'd like to show him his son."

"The master is gone," replied Jorogumo as she assembled a tray of sweet bean cakes for Gozen's breakfast. "But he's seen the child and given him a name. He's called Yosei Obake."

"Yosei-chan," Gozen laughed, bouncing the baby on her lap. "Where's your father?"

The old woman placed the tray in front of the Gozen and took the child. "Eat now, and build your strength. My lord disapproves, but I say you should feed the child if you can. Princelings grow faster if they take strength from their mothers." She crooned to the baby in her arms, "Isn't that right, small one?"

The next morning, Jorogumo brought the child when she came with Gozen's breakfast. "Here, now," she urged. "Feed him, there's a good girl. I'll come back for him later."

Gozen offered Yosei her breast as she ate honeyed apricots. Soon, though, Gozen was leaning heavily against the table, the child clasped loosely in her arms. She slumped to the floor, eyes blank and face the color of ashes. His meal interrupted, the baby yowled vigorously. Gozen's eyelids fluttered at his cries, and she roused herself to comfort the child. She tightened her robe, brought Yosei into her bed, and fell asleep immediately. Gozen didn't awaken when Jorogumo took the baby from her.

"Heh," she chuckled, stroking Yosei's rosy cheek. "That was just what you wanted, wasn't it? At last, that woman is good for something." She placed a covered bowl of mushroom broth on Gozen's table and left.

In the days that followed, Gozen fed Yosei in the morning. She was careful to stop before the lightheaded feeling overwhelmed her, against the baby's protests. He was growing quickly, becoming stronger every day. Gozen's glossy hair lost its sheen, and her face drew tight against its bones, but as the days passed, she gained a restless energy. "Where is your master?" she demanded each time she saw Jorogumo. "Tell him that I need to talk to him!"

One morning, as Gozen paced her room with Yosei in her arms, Tsuchigumo came.

"Welcome, my lord," Gozen said, offering him the child.

"Yosei Obake." He smiled. "Jorogumo tells me that you're growing strong. Soon you can come with me to meet your kin."

"Tsuchigumo-denka," Gozen said, taking the baby, "now that I'm your urakata, I should accompany you to court. It's time I give my respect to your royal parents and take my place with you there." Gozen paced the room with growing energy. "I'll need better clothes, and jewels, and a nurse to take care of Yosei-chan, and a girl to do my hair and take care of the rooms, and . . ."

Tsuchigumo held up a hand, cutting off the flow of words.

"Urukata? You can't be my consort, Gozen."

"What do you mean?" Gozen demanded, her face twisting. "I gave you a son. You promised to reward me!"

Tsuchigumo shook his head. "Ask for something else, Gozen. Your kind isn't welcome at court, and my mother would eat you alive if I took you there. You have care and shelter here, and a child. Be content."

"Content!" she shrieked, spots of color flaring on her cheeks. "Content to live my life humble and forgotten? No!"

Gozen ran from the room, the baby in her arms. Tsuchigumo followed her.

"Stop! The castle isn't safe for you."

Gozen fled before him down the featureless halls. Around an abrupt corner, she found a tight spiral of stairs. At the top was a landing and a heavy door banded in iron. Clutching the rail in one hand and Yosei in the other, Gozen climbed.

Tsuchigumo called up the stairs, "Gozen! Don't open that door. Come back!"

"Did you think that I'd stay hidden away here with a baby and an old woman?" Gozen reached the top of the stairs and whirled, her hair flying loose around her shoulders. "You're just like the daimyo. You think you can have what you want from me and then cast me aside. But I will be a great lady!

"Since this child is all you wanted, give me what I want." Gozen dangled the baby over the railing. "Make me your royal consort, or I'll drop him, and you'll have nothing."

The baby's shuddering wails echoed in the emptiness.

"Gozen, what you ask is impossible." Tsuchigumo reached the top of the stairs.

Gozen leaned farther over the rail. "Then you have only yourself to blame," she hissed, anger bright in her eyes.

"Yosei Obake," the pale man called. "Come to me!"

The baby in Gozen's grasp fragmented into a multitude of white spiders, each no larger than the tip of a finger. They swarmed over Gozen's body and across the landing to Tsuchigumo. Gozen shrieked. Tsuchigumo approached slowly, his hands held out to her. His clothes and hair rippled with the motion of his children.

"Gozen, come away from the door."

"Stay away from me!" Gozen screamed and leapt at him, the silver scissors bright in her fist. Gozen stabbed the pale man once, and again. He staggered back, clear fluid seeping from his wounds.

Tsuchigumo's form blurred like a summer cloud. In place of the pale man was a white spider, as tall as Gozen's waist. A swarm of tiny spiders clung to its bone-white carapace. From its gray-dappled abdomen angled many long, jointed legs.

The front two, larger and longer than the other six, were raised in the air to either side. The spider's many pale blue eyes regarded Gozen.

Gozen groped behind her for the handle of the door. It turned with a rusty moan.

"Gozen, no!" Tsuchigumo's voice came from the spider's mandibles.

Panting with fear, Gozen dragged the door open and flung herself through.

She stood in the winter woods in the midst of a blinding snowstorm. She turned to claw at the door, but found only the blank face of a turtleback tomb.

Gozen heard a voice behind her. "Wife, you have returned." She whirled. A man stood before her, his face gray and his clothes bloody. In his arms, he clutched the limp form of a small girl.

Wide eyed, Gozen pressed herself back against the unyielding stone.

"You aren't my husband. Unkei is dead."

"Yes, and our daughter, too. Why, Gozen?"

"If I didn't have a husband and a child, the daimyo would have made me his concubine."

The man shook his head. "You murdered us in our sleep for this foolish hope?"

Gozen's voice spiraled high above the shriek of the wind. "It was not foolish! I could have lived in the palace instead of this forest. I would have been someone important! But your apprentices discovered me, and nothing turned out as I planned." Gozen's features lost their animation. "Nothing," she repeated.

The ghost leaned to whisper in her ear. "A year and a day I've waited for you in these woods, to take you with us." Unkei placed a gray hand over her face, and Gozen crumpled to the snow at his feet. He waited, patient as stone.

Finally, the wavering outline of a young woman rose from the lifeless body. "No! No, no no no!!!" Gozen wailed.

Her husband pressed the dead child into her arms and dragged her into the endless storm.

THE FOREST ALSO REMEMBERS

ANDREW PENN ROMINE

They cut her husband down at first light, sawing through the thick web of ropes where he dangles like a spider's supper from the water tower at the center of the Village-in-the-Forest. Braeg's beard glistens with the sparkling jewels of morning dew. Numb and tearless, Gilly stares as the townsfolk lower him gently to the damp black earth. He's dead, but his anguish is not. It still bruises his sightless eyes.

Such is the power of the forest to make sorrow from joy.

His brother, Alwun, rises above the crowd of villagers, tall and sturdy like a knotted pine—and twice Gilly's age. As they cover Braeg with a traditional shroud sewn from broadmaple leaves, Alwun lifts his palm in greeting. His face is a mask of grief and fawning pity for her and the babe, Rufen, carried in her arms. Gilly pulls Rufen closer and studies Braeg's cocooned body instead. Alwun's wife died three years ago. She knows how lonely he has been. As elder of the Village-in-the-Forest, he has his pick of mates—there are widows and widowers alike who would share his company. Alwun has picked Gilly, had picked her even before Braeg began his long decline into sadness and death.

Gilly wonders if Braeg's melancholy was genuine or some conjuration of Alwun's. As elder, he traffics with the powers of the forest to keep the village traditions secure. With Braeg gone, there is nothing to stop Alwun. As if to confirm her fears, his gaze rarely wavers from her even as he sprinkles Braeg's body with sacred, black loam.

The bogles around the village washing pond pause in their scrubbing, lifting their tiny, horrid faces, like melted lumps of lye, in mute witness to Braeg's last rites. Underneath one of the mulberry bushes that line the pond, another bogle with a hide like spoiled milk waits—this one is Braeg's creature. Hers now, she supposes. She hates it, though, shuddering as it pleads with eyes like glistening orbs of tallow and glass. The bogle has served Braeg and Alwun's family ever since there has been a Village-in-the-Forest. Every family has its bogle. The villagers' debt to the forest for allowing them to settle in the wild will never be fully repaid.

In Brandlevok, the Town-Upon-the-River where Gilly is from, no woman or man profits by the labors of bogles of the earth or spriggans of the air or even nixies of the currents, but only by their own hard work.

In happier days, when Braeg first brought her to the village, he had begged Gilly follow tradition and employ the diminutive creature for household chores as the other families did. Still in love with her mysterious boy of the forest, she relented for a time, letting it wash and mend the clothes and sweep the floors, but when it tried to scrub her clean with its rubbery mushroom fingers, she had sent it away immediately.

Braeg's night-promises in that sultry summer of his visit to Brandlevok had not unveiled all the truths of eloping with him to the forest. His sadness might have begun upon realizing his maid of the river would never truly take on his ways.

Rufen squirms, sucking air with thin, leechy lips. The bogle winces at the sound and withdraws deeper into the bushes. The babe frightens it for reasons Gilly can't explain, even though Rufen's barely six weeks old and already sallow and deflated. Like his father, she fears. She feeds him, and he grows stronger, but there are bags under his eyes, and his mouth is stubbornly inclined to a frown. This forest air, reeking of pine and moss and rotting things, is bad for him. She vows that soon he will breathe the clean, pure air of the riverside.

At Alwun's approach, the wretched bogle disappears into the foliage. It knows better than to approach her now. Alwun does not. The elder places a warm, callused hand on her shoulder and puffs the ghost vapors of the chilly morning.

"Now you must come live with me, Gilly."

"I must do nothing of the sort. Braeg's body is not even cool," she chides.

Alwun shrugs. "Your steading languishes. Another season and the forest will reclaim it." He makes a show at whispering, but the other villagers can hear. Do they blame her for Braeg's sadness? For his death?

Gilly ignores their busybody glances.

"Mourn then. It is proper. But at least take your bogle back into service," Alwun nods toward where the creature has vanished. "You will need the extra hands in this difficult time."

Gilly wonders how Alwun can ask for her companionship yet know her so little.

"No. If someone must take the creature, it should be you."

Alwun sighs, and some of Braeg's sadness droops the planks of his face. "I am village elder, Gilly. I will make you a good husband."

"That is kind, but I mean to return to Brandlevok, the Town-Upon-the-River, where I belong. My mother's house will welcome me."

Shock whitens Alwun's face.

She tries to mollify him. "I will quit all claim to Braeg's lands. They shall remain with his family."

Alwun's posture shifts, his stoop-shouldered sympathy sloughing away as he rises to his full height.

"So should Rufen, Gilly. The forest is already calling to him. It is his home." Alwun says.

Impossible. She and Rufen belong together, no matter his fragile skin or rattling cough. She would not raise him here where the dense forest air chokes the joy from life. The green weight of the woods would make him into another sour, serious villager like Alwun, like Braeg.

"I am his mother. I am his home."

Alwun narrows his eyes and scratches his beard. Too many wrinkles furrow his brow and crease his eyes. Loneliness has depleted him, aged him.

"Please don't abandon us now."

Gilly pities him, but exhaustion creeps into every length of her. She raises a hand in farewell. "I am so very tired, Alwun. And there is still Braeg to plant."

"I will find good cause for you to stay," Alwun calls to her as she walks toward the other villagers, waiting with her husband's shrouded body. Rufen's tiny hands beat at her breast as if in solidarity with his uncle.

"We shall see," Gilly replies.

❋❋❋

In the afternoon, with Braeg planted on his feet in the yew grove in the custom of his ancestors, Gilly takes her clothes to the creek to wash them. The silver water tumbles free of the emerald verge of the forest seven dozen paces behind her cottage. The water is shivery with the snowmelt of early spring. She refuses to do the washing in the still, scummy tank at the village center with the bogles. She had refused even before the water tower above it became the site of Braeg's death. She's sure Braeg's bogle will loiter at the pond, melt-eyed and pitiful. But her creek splashes bright and clear through the boulders that ring it like a castle wall. Somewhere to the south, it pours itself, laughing, into the river.

She sighs, restless, but this is the last time she'll wash clothes here. In the morning, she'll bundle Rufen and a few possessions and strike out for her mother's house in Brandlevok. She's still young enough to learn her mother's ferry pilot trade or start her own public house on the bluff where the kiteships moor.

On the grass beside her, Rufen fusses, so she wraps him in a blanket the color of the river in summer and places him atop a flat, sun-kissed rock. He squints his stormy eyes in the dappled light. The amber glow lights his cheeks, and he grins. Gilly's heart catches at the joy of him. In such moments, she's certain that her son will not share his father's fate.

She scrubs the pine-and-leaf stink from the clothes until the creek runs cloudy with soap and the mud-bugs scuttling along the bottom are lost from view. It is a disservice to the gleaming water, but she imagines the suds being carried all the way to the river itself, and it already feels like she is going home. She loses herself in the happy blur of the daydream until she realizes the forest has become still.

Terror dives from above—a swoop of golden feathers and grasping talons. With a cry, Gilly upends her washboard into the creek as she clutches for Rufen. Before she can reach him, a large eagle snatches him from the rocks. Like an azure banner, the tattered blanket trails from the eagle's claws as it spreads its golden wings and glides across the shallow creek.

Gilly hurls a smooth, gray stone, but it misses, falling into the creek with an icy splash. Three more follow, but they clatter uselessly into the gloom of the forest. Gilly snarls, splashing across the creek. She refuses to let her child become dinner for a wicked bird. Rufen does not cry, and a panic in her bones whispers that he is already dead. On the opposite bank, she clutches a stone, her knuckles the color of the frothy soap.

The eagle lands atop of a tall, spiky ironthorn. It does not eat but dares her with its golden eyes. *Throw the stone and you will lose him*, it seems to mock with a shrill cry. Moaning, Gilly falls to her knees. The barbed roots of the ironthorn tear her flesh. She rocks forward, and fat, salty tears splash to the forest floor. Her only hope is to climb, she thinks, and she digs already bloodied fingers into the serrated bark.

"Don't," comes a low, tremulous voice.

Gilly wheels, expecting to see Alwun but, instead, finds her bogle clambering up the creek bed. No, *Braeg's bogle*, she reminds herself. It stares at her with its rotten-egg eyes, clutching a red felt hat between its doughy, fused fingers. Worse than the eyes is its smile—an expression she has never seen on a bogle. The teeth crowd its mouth like smashed pebbles. Wriggling like a slug, its tongue leaves thick trails of slime across its bruised lips. Gilly's heart flutters in her throat. For a moment, she fears it will attack her.

It raises a placating mitten-hand. "No. I am here to help, lady."

"I-I don't want your kind of help," she sobs.

Still perching in the tree, the eagle preens and regards Rufen with a diamond-bright gleam in its amber eyes.

"That eagle looks hungry," the bogle says, "but as you wish. I have maddercaps to pick."

The eagle pokes its beak into the tangled waves of Rufen's blanket, probing for the soft flesh inside. Rufen remains strangely quiet. Gilly will not let herself think of what that dread silence might mean.

"Wait!" she calls over her shoulder.

The bogle has not gone far, standing on its root-like legs near a rainbow spray of wildflowers.

"Why help me?" she asks. Her throat tries to clamp off the words, but they come anyway. "All I've ever done is send you away."

"There was a time when more riverfolk lived under the trees. The forest remembers their music. It aches for their company."

"I won't stay, bogle."

"There is one who desperately desires that you do. One who may call the beasts and the birds to his bidding," the bogle replies, thrusting a stubby finger up toward the bower where the eagle is pacing.

"Alwun." The thought whispers like smoke from Gilly's trembling lips. The elder had said that she should not take Rufen from the Village. Is this how he meant to stop her? Now, where fear had gripped her with icy claws, rage howls like a fire through an overgrown forest. She burns inside, and anger threatens to sear away her skin, exposing the coal-bright embers of her bones.

"Are you not loyal to your own family?" she asks the bogle.

"My service belongs to your husband and to you, lady of Brandlevok. And to young Rufen, of course."

The bogle points again to the treetop where the eagle preens.

"Name your price, bogle."

"To serve you again, lady. To serve Braeg's son. The forest has chosen him. If you take him away, he will need me more than ever."

"There are no bogles in Brandlevok," she tells it.

"Not now," it answers, "but once there were. Even the river was once part of the forest before your people cast us out and cut down our trees. From fungus, sap, and root, my kind were fashioned to serve you. To bargain with the wild places on your behalf."

"At what price? We make our own bargains with the river."

The bogle glances at the top of the ironthorn and then back at Gilly, his eyebrow raised in estimation of her negotiation skills.

"Very well. But you shall have to remain hidden." She relents, unable to suppress a shudder. "And you shall never touch me. Or Rufen."

The bogle emits a low, scraping cough that Gilly takes for a chuckle.

"Of course. Until the child comes of age, your word is my law, Gilly of Brandlevok, wife of Braeg."

Gilly peers at the bogle for some glimpse of treachery, but whatever drives it to make its bargain remains opaque beneath its sagging, mottled face. The mere thought of the lumpy creature underfoot in all the uncounted days ahead fills her with a dull misery.

"It's agreed, then," she says, with a glance at the ironthorn and the feathered death that glares back atop it. "Come to the cottage in the morning."

The bogle places its battered cap on its melted brow.

"Then I am, as always, at your service, lady."

She has a sudden vision of being on the road to Brandlevok before the sun fires the panes of her house. When the bogle arrives at the empty home, it will be Alwun's problem then.

The bogle reaches into its filthy woolen coat and pulls out a pair of black stones. They are flattened black ovals, not unlike river stones, but polished to such a luster that Gilly thinks they must be of extravagant pedigree, perhaps jewels in some ancient bogle crown.

"Fashioned from the heart of a lightning-struck ironthorn, lady," the bogle explains. "They have considerable heft and are balanced for throwing. They will not miss."

It is Gilly's turn to smile.

"Just give me the stones, creature."

The bogle obliges with something like a twinkle in its eye. It retreats a few paces to give her room.

Gilly wipes away the remaining tears and looses the first black stone with the image of Rufen's face burning in her mind. Her aim is true, and the bogle's stone catches the eagle square between the eyes. The bird squawks in pain, rising from its perch, flapping in the air. In the chaos, Rufen falls from the branch, but his blanket catches on a thorn, and he hangs as if it were a cradle. The eagle cries after its fallen prize. Before it can pounce, Gilly throws again. The second stone also finds its mark. The eagle, screeching profanities in the language of the sky, vanishes into the forest.

The climb up the ironthorn wounds her body, but not her spirit, and she is soon on the ground again with Rufen. He squalls, but his howls sound like cries of contentment to Gilly. He is safe.

She turns to thank the bogle, but it too has vanished. *No matter*, she thinks. *If I do not have to see it again, so much the better.*

✹✹✹

Alwun is waiting for Gilly when she returns to her cottage. He sits upon a knobbly stump by the door, the gnarled brown trunk of his frame rising from it like a leafless tree. The crinkles around his eyes draw in, pinching his gaze as he spies Gilly and Rufen coming up the path from the forest. Upon his face spreads a dark bruise, and Gilly wonders if it was more than just a hungry eagle doing Alwun's bidding at the creek.

"Gilly," he says, his voice creaking like the wind in the trees.

"Alwun. What happened to your face, brother?" she asks. Her heart thumps feverishly, like a rabbit's in a snare. Despite her fear, she can feel her anger building again. She clasps Rufen closer, and his tiny presence calms her. Fortunately, he continues to doze, content for once.

"I ran into a branch coming up the path," Alwun chuckles, fingering his bruise. Concern etches his brow, but Alwun's eyes glitter with flecks of amber and gold, like a raptor's. "But I am fine. How is your child, poor Gilly?"

"A strange question to ask, brother," she says, playing along. "He fares well."

Alwun stands, unfolding himself in a manner that recalls to Gilly the lean thrift of the wood mantis. He frowns, a black crevice like the hollow of a tree.

"As the elder, I often hear whispers from the forest. Today, I heard Rufen's cries among them."

"He sleeps now, but you know how troubled he can be. As I washed my things he broke into quite a fit. Perhaps he knows his father is gone."

At mention of Braeg, Alwun grows wistful. "I miss him, too, Gilly."

Gilly wonders why Alwun is playing at worry. In the downturned creases of his face, she sees his complicity in Rufen's peril. Surely, he knows that she knows, and it sets her on edge, like an old bull sniffing a challenger upwind.

"I saw your bogle upon the village road. Have you taken it in yet?"

It occurs to Gilly that the bogle's help may not have been motivated purely by circumstance. The bogle, after all, had served Braeg's family when he and Alwun had lived under the same roof.

"Indeed. It begins work on the morrow." She is careful not to sound angry. She senses a chance to turn things to her advantage.

This time, Alwun's jaw hangs open in surprise.

"Then you are staying?" The note of joy in Alwun's reply is almost too much for Gilly to bear.

"As you said, Rufen's home is here," she lies, "but I long to see my mother again, in Brandlevok."

"And visit her you shall, Gilly! I have business there in a fortnight. We could all go together?" His eagerness smothers her, and she imagines a lifetime of Alwun's earnest pandering.

Gilly takes a deep breath and pretends to study Rufen's face. Asleep, he is placid and at ease. She sees less of Braeg's heavy brow and more of her own delicate, upturned nose and wide riverfolk features. A boy needs the blue, open air of the river and not the stultifying verdancy of the forest.

"Come tomorrow, Alwun. Perhaps we can talk again of such things. But I have no more spirit for weighty matters tonight."

Alwun steps closer, presses the stems of his fingers into Gilly's shoulder. His honey-yellow eyes are shining with sentiment. For all of his power as elder, she thinks him a fool. He is blinded by his love for his village, for his station. For her.

He is not unlike the bogle, Gilly realizes. Trapped in an inflexible tradition of how things must be, he cannot see that the village is rooted like the great ironthorns that surround it. But a river must always flow onward and, sometimes, so must a person.

"I might stay for supper," Alwun suggests.

Gilly shakes her head and places a hand on his shaggy cheek. His skin is warm and rough, like firewood long in the sun.

"Tomorrow," she laughs, remembering she told the same thing to the bogle.

✦✦✦

Night falls quickly, as if the forest cups its hands and traps the leafy miasma close about her cottage. The incessant chirping of the cicadas wheedle her with promises of happiness in the bosom of the trees, but Gilly has embarked upon a frenzy of packing. There is little to take, and most of it is for Rufen: a heavy blanket against the night's chill, a pacifier of hardened resin, a salve to combat his frequent rashes. For herself, there is only a tunic and breeches, a pair of oilcloth waders that had once belonged to her father. If she follows the creek bed south, like her soap suds, she will arrive at Brandlevok by midday at the latest. There will be no trail for Alwun—or the bogle, for that matter—to follow. Though both will no doubt guess her destination, they will have no power over her there.

Rufen's mood sours, but it seems idle discomfort and no consequence of his ordeal with the eagle. Gilly sings to him that soon he will return to the flowing currents of his forefathers. In faint moonlight that shines through the window, his knitted brow smooths.

She waits as long as she dares, until the moon has wheeled across the narrow slice of sky afforded her by the greedy trees. The creek, limned with the silver fire of westering moonlight, gurgles with joy in a greeting to her. Its waters harbor a deep chill, but here it is barely calf deep, and her father's waders keep the worst of the cold from her bones. Indeed, the biting waters fire her soul and spur her homeward. The birrup of frogs, invisible in the dark, cheers her spirits.

Rufen she carries in a sling across her breast. He dozes, as if he knows they are finally leaving the forest. The rucksack across her back helps to balance his awkward weight. She fears no misstep or slime-slick stone—her feet prod the water with an instinct for firm ground.

Perhaps an hour has passed when she becomes aware of a rustling along the bank, an occasional discordant splash behind her. She has traveled too quickly to let a fear of the forest infect her spirit, but the sounds dog her heels, too close for coincidence or transient nocturnal creatures.

"To Brandlevok, laaa-dy?" The wail swirls down the creek bed like a torrent in spring. The chill rises from her legs and up her backbone.

"To Brandlevok without your faithful servant?" The last breaks off into an anguished cry like rabbits screaming. Gilly wades faster, her surefootedness giving way in her haste. The creek deepens to her knees.

Ahead, the timber of the babbling water becomes a rushing chorus. It pulls at her, eager to surge over the small cascade that awaits around the bend. Even in her urgency, she does not fear the tumble to the lower creek bed. But the rocks along the edge of the fall are large, and one of them shifts, gray and craggy in the waning moon.

"Gilly!"

Alwun's deep voice booms above the rushing water. He stands at the edge of the cascade, the tree trunks of his legs steadying him against the current. Even in the gloom, his anger and disappointment shine like a lantern. Rufen begins to cry, a piteous howl that upsets her more than that of the bogle.

"You lied!"

Gilly wonders if the bogle and Alwun have been working together all along or whether they followed her into the forest on their own. All that matters now is that she frees herself from their plans for her. That she frees Rufen from the grasping tangle of the forest.

For an instant, she considers charging up the bank and into the trees, but she knows that Alwun and the bogle have more power amid the ironthorns. The forest will trap her. Only the water can take her home. Clutching Rufen closer to her chest, she strides right at Alwun. The elder, prepared to give chase, falters at her sudden bravado. A dozen paces away, Gilly wraps her arms around Rufen and throws herself into the turbulent water, kicking hard in the direction of the elder.

The icy current loops around her, through her. Her momentum is multiplied by the strength of the water, and she hurtles into Alwun's legs. The elder is no river man, and his footing is that of the loamy forest, of the rooted tree. Even a great ironthorn cannot grow in a river. Alwun grunts, and together, they sail over the edge to the water below. Gilly bobs in the arms of the stream, and Rufen screeches happily in the swirling current. A true child of the river.

Alwun tumbles in the shallows near the bank, clawing for purchase. He spits water and sucks air in great, whooping gulps. The elder forgets Gilly and his nephew for the moment.

The bogle does not.

It perches at the edge of the cataract, a misshapen lump of flesh and fury.

"Now who steals a baby, lady?" it shrieks. "Now who steals a child of the forest?"

Gilly laughs, for the creek is spiriting her away from the impotent rage of the forest bogle. She lifts Rufen to transfer him to her back. She can swim all the way home if she must. Then she sees the bogle raise a tiny fist. In it is a smooth, oval stone, black as coal.

They will not miss.

The bogle hurls the ironthorn heart, and Gilly spins to shield herself and Rufen. There is a dull thump, and for a moment, she fears she has been hit but is too cold to feel it. Then there is another thud.

Rufen falls abruptly silent. Gilly refuses to give in to the raw panic.

"The forest will not forget you, lady! And you will not forget the forest!"

Gilly cannot determine if Rufen still breathes, but she kicks off downstream to gain distance from the bogle. She greets the pull of the water, allowing it to speed her away. The bogle and Alwun vanish from her sight as the creek bends and becomes a stream and bends again to become a river. She swims, her arms and legs numb. As the cool gray mist of dawn rises from the river, Gilly and Rufen leave the forest at last.

✵✵✵

Later, on the riverbank, Rufen wakes, and his cries make Gilly's heart surge with joy. The river recalls its own, and it has brought them to safety. But when the child opens his eyes, they are glassy and black like the lightning-struck heart of an ironthorn, and Gilly knows that the bogle was right. The forest also remembers.

THE NIGHT MAIDEN

ERIK SCOTT DE BIE

Sweat plastered his clothes to his skin as he crouched low in the brush, hand over Elta's mouth to keep her from giving away their hiding place. "Peace," Dorn said. "They'll hear us."

His niece went rigid with fear, even as heavy breathing alerted them to the monsters not a dozen paces distant.

Of course she was terrified. Not an hour before, Elta had watched the creatures beat her mother's head in with their sodden war clubs. Dorn had watched too, unable to do anything but pull Elta away at a run. The creatures were everywhere, and the screams of the dying wrestled with pleas for mercy in the smoky night.

Dorn held Elta tighter, cursing his misfortune. A fool stumbling in the dark, he'd led them right into the grasping vine, trapping them for their pursuers to find. The more they fought, the tighter its needles hooked them like drowning fish. Their only hope was to stay still.

One of the creatures stepped into the cold moonlight outside their hiding place, breath rank with blood and rotting flesh. It sniffed the ground, more a beast than man, rippling with muscle and covered in coarse hair, rough skins and a macabre necklace strung with bones and withered ears. As Dorn watched, a second joined the first, this one wearing a helmet adorned with feathers and bones. In one massive hand, it held aloft a thick war club soaked in blood. Dorn realized, of a sudden, that this was the one who had killed his sister Anett. He recognized a clump of her straw-yellow hair stuck to the brutal weapon.

Trembling, Dorn grasped the heavy knife that was all he'd been able to take from the house. The blade was old and stained from long use, but the woodsman kept it sharp enough. He would defend Elta with his last breath.

The creature was close now, pushing through the nettles easily. He could feel its rotting breath on his face, making his skin slimy with sweat. He waited, breath quickening with every heartbeat, until it was almost on top of them. Then he wrenched free of the vine, heedless of his tearing skin and clothes, and thrust the knife at the creature's neck with a roar.

The beast flinched in surprise, and the knife skipped across its rough skin. Then Dorn was falling as the creature shoved him back and staggered off balance. It fell and the grasping vine entangled the creature with renewed fervor, as though jealous of how easily the intruder had ignored it before.

The creature's yelp of dismay broke Dorn's stunned hesitation, and he stabbed at the thing again. This time, it raised a hand to ward off his attack, and the knife sank in halfway. The point tented the thick leather on the back of the monster's glove. Dorn's heart thudded. *He was winning. He—*

Then the creature shot out its other hand and grasped him around the throat.

Dorn hiccupped just before the air cut off, then immediately started thrashing. He couldn't breathe. He couldn't think. Elta was screaming somewhere behind Dorn, and terror ripped through his body. She was going to die. They were both going to die.

The bigger of the two—the one in the helmet, the one that had killed Dorn's sister—stepped forward, hefting its club. It looked both mischievous and vicious. It held the club over Dorn's head as he stood, strangling, and dripped blood into his eyes. The club swung back.

Something moved in the dark, something big, fast, and very, very strong. A blur swept through the bestial creatures, and the leader's elaborate helmet went flying through the air. Dorn realized what had happened only when the garish thing struck a tree, and its owner's disembodied head slid out of it and rolled across the ground. The one holding Dorn released him and bolted upright, yowling in fear and challenge. Then the night spun again, and blood showered Dorn. The headless body collapsed atop him, smearing gore across his body. He cowered, as much to keep the stuff out of his face as to take cover. He felt something sharp prod his head, like a spear, and he recoiled instantly.

"Uncle?" Elta asked.

"Stay!" He started loud but finished the command in a whisper. "Don't move. Don't—"

Air blasted over him in an explosion of breath and an oddly derisive snort. He dared to open his eyes and saw the snout of a massive black horse poised a handsbreadth from his face. A knight's steed? Had the Golden Crown sent aid after all?

He looked up into the animal's eyes, which glowed in its dark face like twin moons. It had some sort of silvery helm on its head that protected the length of its snout and extended as a long spike between its eyebrow ridges. Dorn started to stand, and the horse's head rose to match him, it's gaze averted almost haughtily. He had ceased to matter in its eyes. The beast stared past him at Elta, whose expression was amazed. He opened his mouth to speak to her when he saw the horse's rider, and his breath caught.

Astride the midnight stallion towered a rider in gleaming armor rendered luminous against the night. As he looked closer, he realized the light radiated from beneath the plates of steel, rather than from the moon. It seemed more like cloth than armor, or perhaps webbing woven of silver. Dark blood dripped from the rider's curved sword and sizzled into the ground. The sound brought him to his senses.

"Elta, mind yourself." Dorn looked to the rider. "Sir—"

Without explanation, the rider turned as if to go.

"Wait!" Dorn said. "Thank—thank you for saving us."

"You—" The rider hesitated over the words, as though surprised to be addressed—or to find herself answering. "You are welcome, man of the woods."

He was not prepared for the sheer beauty of the rider's voice. He knew women sometimes became knights of the Golden Crown, but to hear her speak gave the rider both substance and voice as such. It was not a human voice, either. He thought he had never heard his tongue given such eloquence, not in all the poems and songs he had heard.

The rider stared, waiting, and terror threatened to crash back in.

He had to hear her voice because he thought, if he did not, he would weep. "What—what are these beasts?"

"In the tongue of my people, they are *orakh*, imperfect reflections of men," said the rider. "They dwell in lands far north of yours but have come south in search of game and sport."

She cut off her words abruptly and stared at him as though this was sufficient explanation for why his scattered people were dying. There was a hint of empathy in her gaze but not pity. Her black steed shared the cold expression, and Dorn wondered if it shared its mistress's mind as well.

"Your people," Dorn said, finally understanding the significance of her words. "You are not a knight in service to the Golden Crown, then? You—"

It was then he saw the horn.

A long, spiraled horn extended like a spear from the stallion's forehead, graceful and very, very sharp at the end. At first, he had taken it for armor, but now he realized the silver crest was part of its skin, the horn an extension of its ivory bones. The stallion wore no bridle, harness, or even saddle. The black horse was not a horse at all but something Dorn had dreamed of since he was a boy and knew could not truly exist: a unicorn.

An old memory stirred, of dreams or fantasies he had never been able to let go.

As though she could hear his thoughts, the rider reached up to her helm of curling branches and lifted it from her face. Beneath, her face was a vision to match her majestic stance: cheekbones chiseled from living tree bark, eyes like the first rain, skin the rich russet of autumnal leaves, and hair like spun midnight. Her expression was one of inestimable sadness, and all Dorn wanted to do was soothe her. He thought perhaps the world would be saved if she would only smile.

"You—" he said.

What could he say to her? She was a half-remembered dream, one his mind fought desperately to recover. She gazed upon him the same way, as though she recognized him as he did her, as though their spirits spoke to one another across time and legend, but neither knew the other's name. The rest of the world fell away into the distant past, and only they two existed. He loved her and knew she loved him.

Her mouth opened, but the words caught in her throat too. She saw in him something she had never expected, and it set her at ease. For a heartbeat, her perfect exterior wavered, the corners of her lips rose, and he saw something like happiness in her eyes.

The black unicorn gave an uncertain snuffle and looked to him, its eyes dangerous, and Dorn's ease shivered. The creature offered him a threat without words.

Then a scream echoed in the forest, and the world they had occupied fell apart. Dorn remembered the horror of the night and was stunned that he could have forgotten. At just that moment, the clouds opened and rain flooded down.

Dorn heard a guttural howl and saw a group of the orakh heading their way, war clubs raised. The rider's expression turned from one of blissful contentment to something serious and deadly. She looked that way, and the unicorn turned in concert with her will.

"Stay!" Dorn held up a hand. "You must stay and help us, else we will die."

"I must do nothing," she said. "But you speak true. You will die unless I aid you."

"Please," he said. "My people. My—my niece. She'll die."

The Rider hesitated a long moment, then nodded. "Very well. Wait."

"Wait?" he asked. "What do you—?"

Without another word, she reined around and charged straight into a great pine that grew near them. Dorn drew in air for a shout, but unicorn and rider vanished into the tree as though into a bank of fog. Near the pack of orakh charging toward them, the rider appeared anew, astride the unicorn, and tore into their midst. She slashed the head from the lead orakh, and her unicorn speared a second and hurled it into the air. The remaining orakh stumbled, taken by surprise, and ran screaming into the night. The rider barely paused and charged on, shifting through yet another tree to spring upon their party as they fled. She rode the orakh down and slew them all within seconds, then sprang into another tree.

Elsewhere, Dorn heard screams of more orakh.

Dorn flinched as Elta suddenly took his hand in hers. "Uncle?" she said. "Is that her? The Night Maiden?"

Now Dorn remembered the night when, as a boy, he had heard his sister repeat a fantastical tale she had learned from their mother and from their grandmother before her. Anett had spoken the ancient story with reverence. On certain nights, when the moon was full and the need great, the most beauteous of maidens rode astride a great unicorn through the darkest heart of the woods. Father had interrupted the tale and chastised Anett for telling such refuse, but the imagery stuck in Dorn's imagination.

How could he have forgotten that story when he had dreamed of it for so many nights?

The fantasy faded, and the real world intruded once more.

Vegetation crackled, and he drew Elta behind him as he turned toward the new threat. A hulking form passed among the trees and into the moonlight, but it was not one of the creatures. Instead, a haggard man with muddy hair hanging in his face swaggered into the clearing, eyes fixed dully on Dorn and Elta. It was Mudir, the husband of Dorn's sister—former husband, now that she was dead.

"Papa!" Elta started toward her father, and though Dorn hesitated to let her go, he ultimately gave way. The girl threw herself into Mudir's arms, almost knocking him over.

"Enough, girl," he said, his words slurred by drink.

"Gods, even now?" Dorn asked. "Our world is ending, and you are deep in your cups? Do you even know your wife is dead?"

"So?" Mudir shrugged.

To Dorn, indifference was a greater insult than ignorance. Mudir and Anett had grown apart ever since Elta was born, but to dishonor the memory of Dorn's sister was too much to bear. He stepped forward, thrust Elta aside, and slammed a fist into Mudir's ear. The two ended up in the mud, wrestling and gouging. Mudir flailed with drunken strength, but Dorn could think clearly. He punched Mudir over the kidney, and the man shivered as his limbs failed him. He landed a knuckle-splitting blow on Mudir's jaw, knocking him into the mud. Mudir lay there, eyes rolling and blood leaking out his nose.

Dorn drew back his aching hand for another strike, but tiny hands encircled his wrist and held him back. Elta stared at him, her eyes wet with tears, and shook her head.

In that moment, Dorn realized that his sister's husband might be a worthless wretch, but he was Elta's family. He withdrew his hand and let Mudir up. Elta helped him rise as best she could, then clung to his leg. She was the man's daughter, even if Mudir did not deserve to be a father.

Mudir focused, as much as a drunken sot could. "Broke my burned jaw . . ."

Dorn knew that was untrue, or else Mudir could not speak. His fury would not let him pursue the thought further. "How could you?" he asked. "How could you leave them alone?"

"Was—" Mudir wheezed, though not out of injury. "Was just a night . . . like any other. Wasn't home . . . Anett didn't want me."

That was true enough. Dorn remembered his sister tearfully extracting a promise from him never to let Mudir cross their threshold drunk, and he'd complied. Perhaps if he'd not listened, Mudir might have been in the house. Perhaps he might have died, and not Anett. Or—

Dorn shook his head, as doubts like that would drive him mad. "Come," he said. "It's not safe here. We have to go."

"Go where?" Mudir waved around weakly. "Monsters in the woods. We can't—"

"The man has no heart," said a voice from the trees. "He fears every shadow in this place."

Heart pounding in his throat, Dorn turned and raised his knife smeared with orakh blood. Mudir tried to take a fighting stance as well, a fallen war club in his shaking hands. Only Elta showed no fear, eyes wide at the newcomers.

Three lithe figures moved in the darkness toward the men and the girl. They looked like the rider—slight women in armor of glowing cloth—and carried spears from which hung bright feathers and bleached finger bones on leathern thongs. They stood taller than the men, like willow trees gracefully swaying in the wind.

"Nightsisters." Dorn made a warding sign. These creatures he also knew from legends—the lesser but vicious sisters of the Night Maiden—but he had never thought they would scare him so. The myths said they were hideously ugly, twisted monstrosities. Clearly, those stories lied, but their spears looked menacing enough.

Mudir seemed not to have heard those tales, or else they did not frighten him. He had served in the King's militia years past, before Elta's birth and his descent into drink, and he was no stranger to being menaced by folk with weapons. "Come, you woodland wenches," he bellowed in his warrior's voice. "I'll never have a woman speak so to me."

"Perhaps this one has strength after all." The lead sister—the one who had spoken—stepped forward in response to Mudir's challenge. She drew off her helm and gazed at them through eyes like pits of darkness in a nut-brown face. "I see you and am for you, man of the wood. I will water this ground with your blood."

"Murre!" cried the other woman, this one smaller but no less wondrous. She doffed her helm as well, and her skin was the color of new spring foliage. She entwined herself around the leader, like a lover or an ivy vine. "He has drunk too much of the fruit, sister, and it has clouded his mind."

"Then this world will not mourn his passing, Serre." Murre shrugged the smaller maiden off and raised her spear.

The third Nightsister had neither moved nor spoken. She merely stared at Dorn and his family, watching as her leader came toward them, spear at the ready.

Elta trembled, and even Mudir looked concerned. A club was nothing to a spear in the hands of a trained killer. It fell to Dorn to do something, or they would die as they stood.

"Hold, in the name of the Night Maiden!" Dorn cried. "She has saved me this night and would not see me harmed."

That gave the women pause, and they exchanged incredulous looks. The one called Serre looked convinced, while Murre turned her scowl on Dorn. "For what purpose? You are a man and not an impressive one. You have no purpose to offer and no need to fulfill other than to cleanse my spear of orakh blood."

"Sister," Serre said, but the more aggressive maiden stepped directly toward them, spear raised and ready.

The night parted, and the black unicorn was among them between the menfolk and the Nightsisters. It heaved and threw the corpse of an orakh off its horn to sail into the night. The rider towered over the gathering, bloody sword naked in her fist.

"Mistress!" Immediately, Serre fell to one knee, while Murre knelt more slowly, though with no less reverence. The third Nightsister bowed readily but kept an eye on Dorn.

"Who's this now—?" Mudir asked before Dorn could silence him with a look.

"Show respect, men," said Murre. "She is Lythe the Night Maiden, Princess of the Ykai. You will shed your blood for her and spend your life at her whim."

"Doubtful," Mudir murmured, but Dorn elbowed him.

"This place is overrun," Lythe said, her words falling like rain. "We must flee."

To Dorn, such a confession seemed impossible. He had witnessed the ease with which Lythe slaughtered the orakh, and he couldn't imagine them presenting a challenge to her. But the Nightsisters took her at her word. They stepped back toward the shadows of the forest and raised their voices into keening wails. The unicorn reacted to the song as though to a challenge. He rose up on his hind legs and radiance leaked from his horn. He waved his head back and forth, slashing the air with his elegant horn until the cool night crackled with a lightning-rush of power. Then the very air bent and ultimately broke at the pitch of the keening, and Dorn realized he was now gazing into another world: one filled with mist and deeper darkness than this place. Towers rose from among the trees and motes of silvery light floating like snowflakes threaded the pathways. A gorgeous woodland city rose beyond the veil of the worlds, and he knew it was the realm of the Nightsisters.

Behind, back in his world, the war cries of orakh chased them from deeper in the forest, and Dorn saw torches working their way toward them. Only death waited here.

Murre stepped toward the rift, but she paused when no one followed her. "Mistress?"

Dorn realized that Lythe was gazing down at him intently—him and Elta as well.

"They come with us," she said.

The Nightsisters seemed taken aback. Serre looked startled, while Murre's face darkened with fury. The third stayed silent.

"What do you mean, mistress?" asked Murre. "They are men and of no use to us. Leave them here."

"Listen to Lythe," Serre said. "We can't simply leave them to die!"

"What meaning do their lives have? They are diseased rodents, born for little but dying," Murre said. "Mistress, if you bring them, they will infect our world with their stench, and we will never be rid of it. They—"

"Enough," said Lythe, silencing the headstrong Nightsister. "I will not command you to do what you do not agree to do. What say you, Corre?"

The third Nightsister gazed at the men and girl. Particularly, she watched Mudir, as though she could see something about him no one else could. He stared back levelly as long as he could stand it before he cursed and looked down at the ground. Finally, she nodded.

"Go quickly, then," Murre said. "Fall behind, and no one will carry you."

As if in defiance of her bold words, Serre dropped back and put her arm around Mudir to help him along. The man grumbled an objection, but ultimately, he could barely walk a straight path, so he leaned on her shoulder. Murre watched them carefully as they passed through the rift, then followed. Corre gave him a nod, and he thought her expression deeply sad. Then the silent Nightsister too stepped through the portal.

"Hear me, man," Lythe said. "We must not tarry long. What you call time exists differently in my world. Go quickly, or you may never find your fellows again."

As they stood before the darkness of the other world, Elta tugged on Dorn's coat. "I'm scared, Uncle," she said. "I don't want to go."

"We have to, love." Dorn looked back into the forest and saw the torches growing closer still. "We have no choice."

Elta shut her eyes tight and shook her head.

"Here." Lythe swung down from her steed, as graceful as falling rain, and knelt before Elta. The child looked up into her face with wide eyes. Lythe took Elta's hand and put it on the unicorn's flank. "In the tongue of my people, he is called Nkai, which means 'night dream.' Will you ride him?"

All of Elta's fear drained away, and her face brightened. Lythe lifted her onto the unicorn's back, where Elta clung to the beast's neck with all her might. Dorn made to help, but the unicorn gave him a fearsome glare and warded him off with his horn.

"He does not tolerate the touch of men, upon his riders or upon his person," said Lythe. "It is only out of loyalty to me that he does not kill you."

Dorn backed away. "You are very kind," he said softly.

"She will not panic," Lythe said. "No place is safer than upon Nkai's back."

"I mean, for helping us." Dorn reached out as though to take her hand. "Thank you."

Lythe looked at his hand uncertainly, then nodded to him—the curt nod of a soldier. She swung up onto Nkai behind Elta and winced terribly. In the moonlight, Dorn saw the hint of bright blood dribbled upon her skirts. She must have been injured. When she saw him looking, she glared. "Come," Lythe said. "Fall behind and no one will help you."

She spurred Nkai and Elta through the portal, leaving Dorn alone. He could see the flames of his village, deeper in the wood, and hear the triumphant roars of the orakh.

He was about to step through the portal when something hot and sharp ripped past his head. Reeling, he thought he must have run into a tree branch, but finally he realized the thing quivering in a nearby tree was an orakh spear. More spears flew toward him, and he scrambled toward the rift. It was shrinking, closing the doorway between his world and the other. A moment later, he staggered through—

And sank to his waist in a deep snowdrift.

The forest had been muggy, soaking him with sweat, which became ice almost instantly. His breath steamed up in front of his face, and he coughed on the cold air. Wind danced across the snow drifts, and he took shelter as best he could behind his cloak. The others were nowhere in sight, and this was not the effervescent world he had glimpsed through the rift.

"Hail!" he shouted, but the wind ripped his voice away. Opening his mouth made his throat ache instantly, and he coughed and sputtered for breath. He thought he would freeze to death in moments.

Darkness loomed, and Dorn felt hot breath on his neck. Nkai perched like a mountain above him, his horn hanging like a stalactite over Dorn's upturned face. The unicorn's dark eyes gleamed dangerously, and fear, rather than cold, made Dorn's body cease to obey his commands. He put out his hands in surrender and tried to determine a way out.

"Easy." Dorn reached out, as he had done thousands of times to calm standoffish horses. The unicorn thrust his horn at the man's face. Dorn threw himself backward into the snow, and Nkai reared up, hooves flailing. So this was how Dorn would die—trapped in a snowbank in a foreign world, crushed under the tread of a creature he knew only in legends.

Sibilant words he did not understand shot across the wintry field, and the unicorn fell back, away from him. Nkai made a derisive snuffling sound and trotted back several paces, where he watched Dorn warily.

"Man." Near him—standing across from Nkai rather than sitting on the unicorn—a white-wrapped figure shook loose a flurry of snow. Lythe gazed at him from deep within the cowl of the cloak. "You tarried too long in your world, so you have allowed grief to enter our land."

"What?" Dorn asked. "What do you mean? What has happened?"

For a moment, Lythe gazed at him as though he was a foreign, strange thing to him, and they had not just been together a moment before. Finally, she extended a hand. "Come."

It was the first time Dorn had touched Lythe, and he found she radiated an inner cold that made his heart beat only sluggishly. She looked pale, her ageless face almost seeming old. He realized she was different than when he had last seen her: worn with unfulfilled longing.

She led him to Nkai, who strayed away from them on their approach. Even when Lythe reached out to touch the unicorn, he menaced her with his horn.

What had come over the beast? She spoke words to Nkai in her own language, and the unicorn relaxed and let her climb atop his back. Nkai still looked at Dorn warily.

"Come," Lythe said. "You must see for yourself."

He climbed uneasily astride the unicorn, and they were off. They ran so fast Dorn had to take cover behind Lythe's shoulder against the cutting wind. He hadn't seen Nkai really run, and the sheer speed with which they flew across the snow made Dorn's eyes water and his lungs heave. Clinging to Lythe, who seemed unaffected by the rush, it was all Dorn could do to keep his seat.

"What's the matter?" Dorn shouted over the wind. "Is it Elta? Mudir? What—?"

But the Night Maiden said nothing, only spurred the unicorn on to greater speed.

They crested a rise, and Nkai mercifully halted. "There," Lythe said.

Dorn shook loose a hazy beard of frost and slapped ice off his hood so he could see where she pointed. Before them rose hulking towers of black stone in the misty snowfield. At first he thought it a mountain, but then it took shape in his eyes as a castle. An ancient, crumbling wreck of a place, it nonetheless evoked the grandeur of another time. Tattered banners hung limply over the entry gate, and Lythe held them aside with her black spear. They crossed the threshold, and Dorn shivered as he looked up at the twisted, rusted gate that hung precariously over their heads. They rode Nkai into the ancient palace, the walls thick with dust and the withered remnants of paper doors flapping in the cold breeze. The castle felt empty and dead.

"What is this place?" he asked Lythe.

The Night Maiden spoke without looking at him. "This holdfast has as many names as it has had masters. Shujan, Koritokos, Voritir, and most recently, mine. It is the throne of the Ykai, and soon it will fall nameless once more, as we in turn pass away."

"What do you mean?"

Lythe did not respond, but her lip trembled. Seeing fear on her face made his heart ache.

Nkai bore them into a vast, nearly empty hall choked with dust. At its very center, four female figures in robes spun of white silk knelt around a raised bier of black stone, upon which lay a man's body. His skin was shrunken, his hair white, and he wore a beard that spread out across his chest, woven with withered leaves and tarnished silver bangles. And somehow, Dorn knew him.

"That—that's Mudir." Dorn could not believe it. "What happened to him?"

Lythe glanced at him for the first time since the snow fields. "He died."

As they approached, one of the women looked up, her hand on a spear seemingly made of glass—or ice. Dorn recognized Murre instantly, and he fairly leaped off Nkai to confront her.

"You!" he cried. "You hated him! You did this!"

He tried to strike her, but she swept his hand aside, knocked him off his feet, and put the point of the spear to his throat. "I have done this? You were the one who destroyed us!"

"Hold!"

Lythe's voice gave Murre pause, just as it had before. All eyes fell upon her now. Two of the other women were rising, while the one at the head of the bier had not moved.

Lythe swung down from Nkai, strode to Murre, and knocked the spear aside with her sword. "You will not slay him. He does not understand."

"He is a fool, then," Murre said. "I told you this would come to pass, but you did not listen. You obey your heart and not your mind. You are as foolish as he!"

Lythe slapped Murre, who flew back. The ice spear shattered against the floor. There Murre lay, glaring up at Lythe as though at the worst of traitors.

"Uncle?" A woman he barely recognized rose from where she knelt beside the old man's body. "Uncle! It has been so long!"

"Elta?"

The vision before him was his niece, as a woman grown, nearing her thirtieth winter if he guessed correctly. Her strong arms encircled him, and she pressed her head into his neck, as she had as a girl.

"What is this?" he asked. "What has happened?"

"I told you long ago," Lythe said. "What you call time in your world means little here. You might be gone a moment in your world while an eternity passes in ours, or the reverse. In this case, fifty of your years have passed since the night of our meeting. You can see the changes wrought in your long absence—and the costs we have paid."

Lythe gestured across at the fourth attendant at Mudir's side. It was Serre, but unlike the other Ykai, she had grown old and shriveled. Dorn realized he could see right through her as though she were not there at all.

"The one called Mudir was a good husband to her," Lythe said. "They dwelt together for years and loved each other so deeply. He never struck her or spoke crossly or drank of the grape or barley. There was no violence in this land, but now, his curse lies upon us."

"Curse? What curse?"

Lythe shook her head, but it was Murre who answered. "Serre fell in love with him, of course. And he was but a man, so would die long before her. And now her heart is broken, and she will fade and vanish, and we will all go with her. For we cannot exist apart from her."

"Because she dared to love a mortal man?" Dorn asked. "That is madness."

"That is the world," Murre said. "And now you must leave this place before you too bring disaster upon us."

"No!" Elta cried. "Uncle, you must stay. Don't leave me again!"

Elta hugged him tight, threatening to crush him. No longer a little girl, she felt terribly strange in his arms. It was as though she had grown into a woman—an adult—while he remained a boy. And perhaps exactly that had come to pass.

"How is this possible?" he asked. "Fifty years . . . you should be an old woman."

"I am, Uncle," Elta said. "The land of Ykai, it . . ."

"It brings life to those who have little," said the last of the four—Corre, whose words echoed through the empty palace like the pronouncement of a king. "But the sons and daughters of men cannot live forever. Death must come for them, and now, death has entered our realm. Now, we will all of us fade."

Tears in his eyes, Dorn looked over Elta's shoulder and saw Lythe watching them, her eyes soft. Slowly, she smiled at him.

Then, as Dorn stood embracing his niece, Nkai let out a wild cry and charged. The unicorn barreled toward Dorn in a seemingly unstoppable rush, horn down to gore him through the middle. Instinctively, he thrust Elta behind himself and presented his chest like a shield. He might die, but he would suffer no harm to befall his niece.

Something interposed between them and came staggering back as Nkai struck. The horn burst out her back, toward Dorn and Elta, but fell short. Lythe reeled and fell to one knee, grasping at her chest. Around and through her fingers, dark blood stained her moonlight armor.

"No!" Murre cried.

The fierce, sudden attack drew Serre out of her misery for a moment, and she stared at Lythe with wide, uncomprehending eyes. Then she vanished, as though she had never been there.

"It is done," Corre said.

The unicorn stood panting, its sides heaving, and sweat turned to ice strung along its dark flanks. It stared at Lythe without pity or so much as concern.

"Gods!" Dorn ran to Lythe's side and pressed his hands to her wound. His heart beat in time with hers. "Help me! We need to stop the bleeding!"

Elta looked shocked. Corre looked impassive. Murre looked angry.

"You betrayed us!" Murre spat at Lythe. "You, who were our queen!"

Corre stopped her before she could move toward Lythe. "All things must end," she said. "All stories must weave their final words, and all hearts must beat their last."

Murre glared at Lythe, then turned and strode away. She was gone before she had taken seven steps. Corre vanished in a similar fashion, leaving the mortals alone with Lythe.

"Our world is ending." Lythe tried to sit up but failed, and Dorn cradled her tightly. "And all because I took pity on you. Because I loved you." She coughed flecks of blood. "I have loved you so long—longer than you loved me."

Uncomprehending sorrow choked off Dorn's words. "I don't understand," Dorn said.

"We must dwell apart from the world of men, inviolate and enduring," Lythe said. "We are Ykai—'in dream'—and my own name means 'to forget.' We are a fantasy, nothing more, and when we are broken, we are lost." She gazed in the direction Serre had gone, and her eyes seemed infinitely sad. "She will wither and fade now, lost and alone and without purpose. You have done this—she should never have known the touch of man. Nor I."

"But why?" Dorn asked. "I have done nothing to deserve your love."

"Have you not?" Lythe's voice was small now, but its strength remained. "You alone among your kind was brave in the face of the orakh. Even Mudir, who won glory and renown in this world, could not match your heart. How—" She coughed. "How could I not love you?"

"But we have known each other so little," Dorn said.

"You have worshipped me since you were a child," she said. "And though to you, we met less than an hour past, I have loved you for so many years. But you were gone, and my sorrow drained the life from this world. It was not Mudir and Serre who have caused the most harm, but I. I have betrayed my people."

"I am so sorry," Dorn said.

"It does not matter." Lythe sighed. "You have done what my sisters said you would. You have brought darkness upon us, and now that our circle is broken, we will cease to be, save for those who live in the hearts of those who remember us."

"Remember you? I don't—"

She took his chin between her fingers and kissed him. In that moment, he touched a world deeper than any he had known. He caressed a passion pure as the driven snow and more powerful than a storm at sea. The second her lips touched his, he saw the truth, and it was all he could do not to weep.

"You're leaving," he said.

Lythe nodded. "Help me stand."

Hardly able to breathe, Dorn did as she asked. He expected her to collapse at any second, but once on her feet, she remained there. Even near death, Lythe had a strength a mortal man could not fathom. She stood and looked off into the gathering night outside the palace, where the snows whirled and deepened.

"You and Elta are the last ones holding me," she said. "She has dwelt among us long enough that she is one of us now, so it does not matter. She will go forth and do great and terrible things. But you—" She turned toward him and took his face in her hands. "Do me this kindness. Forget me. Release me. Let me fade away."

The sheer tragedy of it all filled him with sorrow and regret. She was in such pain, her entire world falling apart around her. It was too much—too much in such a short time. They had not had the chance to do more than fall in love, to be together and face the trials the worlds had to offer. The unfairness of it all crashed in around him. Had he dodged that spear and come through the rift with her, would things have been different? If he had not dodged it at all and perished in that lonely grove in his own world, would she have loved him still, or would she have forgot him, and let her world live?

"No," Dorn said. "No, I cannot. I will not."

Lythe looked at him with profound sadness. Then she narrowed her eyes and tightened her hands on either side of his head. He started to speak—to ask what she was doing—but he understood as soon as his head started to ache. His arms thrashed of their own accord, striking at her in vain. He knew he could not stop her. Instead, he put his arms around Lythe and embraced her as best he could. If he was to die, he would die loving her.

His world crumbled at the edges, fraying like burning paper, and he could feel his heart thundering in his head. Breath scratched in and out of his throat, and he wanted to vomit. Her eyes burned into his, the focal point of his shrinking vision. He would not look away.

Then, finally, her eyes softened, and she drew away with a cry. He collapsed to his knees, panting and grasping his exploding head. She watched him—he who loved her, and could not forget her. She who loved him and could not destroy him. She nodded.

"Wait—" he said. "Don't . . . don't go . . ."

After she gave him one last look, the night swallowed Lythe, and she was gone.

Dorn staggered after her, casting about blindly, but it was no use. She could not stay, he could not go with her, and she could not fade away. He knew he would never see her again.

A form appeared in the night, approaching him, and his heart leaped in hope. But it was Elta, running toward her beleaguered uncle. He opened his arms, and she pressed her face into his chest.

"Uncle," she said, "Why are you crying?"

He looked down at her—at her earnest eyes glowing up at him with a courage and fire he would never have expected. She did not remember Lythe. She had forgotten her just as she had asked. He smiled with all his strength. "Happy tears, my love," he said. "We are together once more. These are happy tears."

Elta's smile faded, and she released him. She looked away into the snowy night.

"What is it?" he asked. "You'll not leave me too."

"I must. I am the Night Maiden, and I must protect this world."

She raised her arms and sang a keening melody, like the one Dorn had seen strike asunder the worlds before. Her voice seemed deeper than that of Nightsisters, but she sang with as much force as they had. Nkai acted now as he had then, slashing at the air viciously with his horn, cutting the fabric of reality until it shattered and unwove at the seams. When the snow flurries cleared, Dorn found himself looking into a barren world of burned tree trunks. In the distance, smoke rose from a cookfire, and he thought he could see shadows moving against the flames. This was his world—or one like it.

"Come with me," he said. "Elta, I—"

She shook her head. "Nkai must have a rider, Uncle, and the Ykai must have a champion."

She climbed onto the unicorn's back, and the great stallion let out a sigh of mingled relief and anticipation. Dorn looked into its face and saw finally a measure of peace. At long last, Nkai's purpose could once again be fulfilled.

Elta looked down to Dorn. "You brought me to this world to save me—now let me save you. A man cannot exist in this place without destroying it. Return home. Remember me. And perhaps we shall meet again when the time comes for you to walk the lonely path."

And with that, Nkai gave a cry, reared, and vanished into the snow.

Dorn stood, stricken with grief and loneliness. In the span of an hour, he had lost everything that ever mattered to him: dream, sister, niece, even marriage-brother. He looked back into his own world—perhaps his home, intact, or perhaps a nightmare he could not face. But if he remained, he would freeze to death within moments.

He made the only decision he could.

Dorn stepped through the portal to an uncertain destiny.

FAE BLADES FOR THE DREAD DUKE

ED GREENWOOD

"There will be . . . much blood," Father warned me, his hands warm and reassuring on my shoulders.

Humans were always so warm.

"We need you to watch it all, so you can tell us what befalls."

Only the most powerful wizards and fae could see from afar. And the Free People couldn't possibly afford—or trust—wizards.

And I was the only fae the Free People could trust.

It had not always been this way, but here in Darrove, where the Dread Duke killed fae on sight, there was only one left. Me.

Oh, there were fae aplenty in other lands, but they hated and feared the likes of Duke Landur Meldrune and came here only unwillingly.

In order to bring two fae Blades here for this latest attempt, we'd had to pay more than the worth of the duke's newest castle, the tall and forbidding keep down at Riversar. We hadn't been able to afford three.

"If the Fates are with us," Father said softly, "two will be enough." Then his voice had gone grim and inward. "And if the Fates turn from us, not even the largest army of Blades will prevail."

I was far from being a Blade and always would be. Small and dark and quiet, I. The infamous Blades were skilled sword wielders, as graceful as dancers. Not just feared for their fighting skills, they could disappear like smoke when cornered.

Some folk believed the most powerful fae could read thoughts. I was becoming one of those folk, for at that moment, one of the Blades turned and lifted her head from the long, slender sword in her hand to regard me.

And smiled.

It had been a long time since I'd seen a fae smile, even counting myself in a mirror. Then she added a wink. In the next instant, she turned her face back to a mysterious mask as she and her fellow Blade looked around at us all. They raised their blades in silent salute. Dull, unadorned steel. Cold iron. The tales lie, you see. Cold iron slices fae just as anything sharp does. It's silver that kills us, poison creeping through us, turning us blue . . .

They looked magnificent with their great dark eyes, sad mouths, and long unbound hair, all silver and green and pearly sheen. And they looked dangerous. And as mysterious as the deep secrets the Fates guarded.

They would not give names, but we could call them Left and Right, distinguishing them by which of their forearms bore the bracers to scabbard their rows of throwing-knives.

"Now, dearest," Father murmured. "Scry him well, so that our . . . guests can see all they need to see."

Ceremoniously, I held up the waterstone in both hands, so what I saw would be shared with the Blades in the air above it, and I bent my will to seek out the man who'd ravaged me and so unwittingly spun a link between us.

Deep, rich hues whirled for a moment in my head, then spun up in a winking whorl in the waterstone, then in the air above it, coalescing suddenly into a scene.

I felt the cool, minty breath of the two Blades as they bent over me, leaning over Father's shoulders to peer at what I saw . . .

✖✖✖

The duke was alone in his bedchamber this night, no doxies to bring him to sweating and grunting and snarling out curses.

Instead, his companionship seemed to reside at the bottom of a goblet larger than many a man's head.

He'd just signed three dozen death warrants. Such grim work sobered even the likes of the Dread Duke, it seemed.

Perhaps he had come to know what we fae are born knowing: that every life he extinguished left fewer people he knew, a dwindling fellowship that brought death closer and closer to the one at its heart.

He happened to be the man most hated and feared in the Five Kingdoms and the Three Old Realms. The beast of the Long Siege, the traitor who'd used a poisoned blade even under the sacred truce of the High Parley. The last of the Seven Rich Men who'd formed a pact to bring down corrupt thrones—and to replace them with their own infinitely more grasping, venal rule. The man who'd arranged "accidents" that befell the other six wealthy magnates, accidents he had not had a literal hand in, yet somehow knew about beforehand.

Landur Meldrune, Duke of Darrove, Baron of Lhavaray, Lord of Riversar. Better known as the Dread Duke, in all the lands from one sea to the other. The man none dared slay because everyone knew the wizard Havalass of Thontaeray had death-bound a fangjaws to appear and fly to bite off the faces of anyone within sight of the duke when he died, and everyone knew that the wizard Ulmulaer of Khessk had worked a death-binding to make whatever building the duke died in collapse with a roar within moments of his passing. And everyone knew that the wizard Zorsczlaran of Iltarroy had woven a death-binding that would bring down a curse on anyone the duke had named as a foe within a tenday of his passing.

Not to mention all the death-bindings that everyone didn't know about. There were sure to be many.

"The Dread Duke and his death bindings are why you called us," Left remarked calmly, checking her knives in their sheaths, "You have engaged Blades to do this deed that so sorely needs doing. Dangerous—and wise."

"Yes," Father admitted, steadily meeting her eyes and then those of Right.

They both smiled fleetingly. The danger was that Blades were so few. If risked in frivolous causes, they might be gone entirely when truly needed. One of the reasons the Duke of Darrove had gone unchecked this long.

"I wish you well," Father whispered then, bowing his head to them as if they were kings.

They nodded back, as gravely as if he'd favored them with great honor.

Then the air blinked, and they were gone, leaving behind a scattering of soft sparks that were not sparks and a sound like distant jangled harp strings.

And then I pulled my scrying back until it showed them there, in the receiving room outside the duke's bedchamber, where all the guards sat at dice and cards or snored on couches or stood facing the door on duty, swords in hand.

Almost floating forward, like a calm and unhurried wave, Left and Right bounded high as the duty guards shouted and raised their blades and slashed open two throats before the other guards could do more than turn and slap down cards in exasperation.

Right's man staggered a few agonized steps before falling and was in her way. She danced sharply sideways to get around him and ended up behind Left, whose man had crumpled obligingly to one side and left her path clear to the table. Like an infuriated reaper hacking down stalks without regard for the harm, Left hewed about, heads lolling and seated men reeling as startled curses swelled. The men doing that cursing snatched for their swords as they sprang upright, chairs toppling.

"Sing, dearest one," Father said softly, his hands warm on my shoulders. "Sing to anchor them. The Lament."

Unable to look away from the distant vision, I swallowed. We'd discussed this, yes. But . . . but the Lament was so short. Just twelve lines, albeit intended to be sung slowly. Twelve lines.

Father's warm grip tightened. Well, I would just have to sing it over and over, until this was done.

I opened my mouth and sang.

Weep for the fallen,

Their heads went up, those two fae blades, like proud horses hearing their names.

Those now in shadow,

They hadn't paused in the slightest, but I knew they could hear me. I made my voice as deep and rich as I knew how, trying to sing as the elders did.

Now beyond all mercy,

Left was around one end of the table like a storm wind, her blade flicking now, slashing at faces and throats and hands without pause, disabling rather than slaying, moving, always moving.

Mere faces in shadow.

Right turned the other way for a moment, along the line of seated men Left had already slain, then bent between two of them and was suddenly not there. Two guards stared at where she'd been as if someone had robbed them.

O weep for the fallen,

They were still staring when the table, driven by Right's shoulder beneath it, went up and over in a whirling chaos of cards and dice and beer and flagons, into their faces—and then crashed down on their toes with a heavy booming.

Who in the shadows shall bear witness,

So they were busy shrieking and hopping in pain as Right reached them, chopping at their necks and throats like a butcher calmly getting on with jointing carcasses.

Who from the shadows hear all,

As they reeled and started to fall, she was already past them, circling back to the part of the room behind where she and Left had appeared, the couches of snoring men—some of them snorting fitfully now, some of them stirring—and the door they were supposed to be guarding.

As they await every one of us

Right raced along the couches like a ruthless whirlwind, stabbing and slicing as men spasmed and stiffened and then sank back to drip, drip, drip over the edges of their couches onto the uncaring floor.

Who are fated to join the shadows

Left danced backward now, extricating herself from a tangle of slumped men in chairs beside a table that now, on its side, was a confining rampart manned by furious guards lunging and hacking at her over their dying comrades.

No deliverance from shadow

She spun watchfully, all around, and espied a man crawling stealthily from his bed toward the pull cord of an alarm gong. She plucked up a chair and hurled it, dashing him against the wall.

Oh, no deliverance from shadow

In its wake, she charged him, her sword opening his face in a spray of blood and teeth and squealing agony.

No deliverance at all.

The Lament was done—and so were the Duke's guards. In the time it had taken me to sing twelve lines.

Right was at the outer door now, and in a whirling instant, had checked that the bars across it were in place and secure, then put her back to it to stare warily around the room.

Left was the only other entity still on her feet. The two Blades exchanged glances, their faces two sad masks sick with disgust, then started around the room. Ignoring the dead but gathering up the dying, heedless of blood and gasps of agony, to kiss them fiercely.

And where lips met, brief fire flickered.

It did not take long. Then, in silent unison, besmirched now with the blood of those they'd slain, they drew a knife each and strode together to the inner door.

Right tossed hers underhand, gently, to thunk into the door right in the midst of its ornate carvings. It caught blue fire, first blade and then door, magics wrestling in a silent snarling that left the knife a cascade of dust and the door no longer warded against intruders.

Left tossed her knife harder, waving a hand to cover her eyes in a showy gesture that I knew—knew—was meant for me.

Even so, I was almost too slow and saw the rest of it through a red haze, after knife and door vanished together in a red flash that awakened screams heard miles from the Ducal Tower.

"Sing the Lament again," Father murmured, his breath against my ear. "They need it now."

I swallowed as I watched them stride forward, swords raised to strike aside the whirling blades that came winking and spinning at them. On into the palatial gloom where the man with the goblet sat waiting for them, scorn on his face but fear in his eyes.

"Sing," Father said, his voice sudden steel. "*Now.*"

So I sang.

Weep for the fallen,

The Blades turned sideways in mid-step, striding apart—and the stone block that would have crashed down on their heads instead shattered into golden tiles as the duke cursed. He did something to his goblet and then flung it, but fae grace swayed aside, and it crashed harmlessly against the wall to spit its sudden lightning across shields and crossed swords and empty suits of trophy armor the duke had never worn.

Those now in shadow,

Right had dodged the goblet, so Left struck first, tossing another knife—and then her last, following the first so swiftly they were like two arrows, streaking at the same target.

A flash in the air claimed the first knife, but the second passed through where that flash had arisen, whole and undeterred, to—vanish. A brighter conflagration flared, closer to the now-smiling-again Duke's face.

Now beyond all mercy,

Right threw a knife, and it became a bright and snarling nothing right in front of the long and pointed Meldrune nose above a suddenly unsmiling mouth.

Mere faces in shadow.

Right threw her last knife, and a spark as fat as a giant's eyeball snapped from that nose, just before the blade would have sliced into it, and made of it a bright spray of dust.

O weep for the fallen,

"Keep singing," Father murmured in my ear. "Whatever befalls, keep on, steadily. Just keep singing."

Who in the shadows shall bear witness,

The duke sneered again, but both Blades danced and whirled closer with their blades out, hacking and parrying and thrusting with a speed that made Father gasp.

They were bleeding, leaking blue-white glowing droplets as the duke gloated.

Who from the shadows hear all,

Suddenly they were both beside him, blue-white blood raining in torrents, wholly focused on the duke.

As they await every one of us

The duke's sneer changed.

I will never forget the surprise that blossomed on his face.

Sick surprise at how smoothly a blade could slide in. And come out again on the far side of his body. Two blades, right through him in different directions.

Who are fated to join the shadows

The blades, all wet with dark red blood, plunged in again, through his ears this time, his head lolling wildly . Then the blades came out again, red-black gore spraying.

No deliverance from shadow

Left and Right turned to face me, tears streaming down their faces, mouths twisted in disgust. They raised their bloodied blades to their lips in upright salute—and then became smoke, two pillars that soared up and were gone as two swords clattered to the floor.

Oh, no deliverance from shadow

"This is how they manage it," Father said hoarsely, sounding on the edge of tears. "So swift . . . so when reinforcements come, they're just in time to catch the death-bindings in their faces."

No deliverance at all.

I held that last note long and quaveringly, not wanting them to be gone, not wanting it to be over.

"End it now, dearest. Don't doom them by holding them where magics can reach them. Give us silence—but keep watching," Father commanded.

So I did, and the duke's guards thundered into the chamber with their swords drawn, shouting.

And the empty air sighed and gave them a fangjaws, long and sinuous as it beat its leathery wings once. It glided, jaws agape impossibly wide, ignoring the desperately swung swords, too hungry to feel the pain. The fangjaws bit, taking heads and helms and all in its hunger.

It was still feasting when ceiling, walls, floor, and all shivered, tremors that became shudders, as if the tower was revolted by what had happened within it—and then, with a roar, the great canopied bed and dying guards and gliding fangjaws were all swept away in a dark, tumbling tumult that left me blinking at the distant sky, emptiness where there had been a mighty fortress a moment before. The dust of its collapse billowed.

❀❀❀

I blinked through sudden tears and looked around my home.

Father squeezed my shoulders, then strode briskly away as Free People laughed and cheered around us, only to turn and come stalking back, like a restless warrior kept from battle.

"We shall have to dig if we want to hang those two swords with the others," he told me, looking at me but seeing someone else, long ago.

"With Mother's," I said, suddenly angry but not knowing why.

"That's why we use fae," Father told me, answering the question I hadn't known to ask. "They can withstand the death-bindings."

"Yes, Father, but why do they do it? You saw how sickly those two looked, how disgusted."

"They needed to feed. You saw them kiss the dying. They need the life that burns so brightly in humans, or in time, they fade away entirely. Just as your mother did. And as, in time, you will."

And he went out and left me standing there, tasting real horror for the first time in my life.

So that was why he'd never let me train with a blade.

NEW GROWTH

JAMES L. SUTTER

He comes carefully into the deep woods, as shy as a new lover. Broad shoulders and the big double-bitted axe give him no comfort, and he jumps at every cracked twig or sigh of the great trees around him, oak and maple shifting in the wind. He knows how deep he's pressed, how far from camp and cabin his way has taken him.

She watches him as she slips between the trees, sliding through them, inside them. A knothole opens and is her eye, judging how tall and straight he grows. A low branch trails across his face, its long fingers feeling the smooth, untwisted grain of him.

He can sense her but not with his eyes or ears. Only the finest of his hairs know she's there. They stand on end as his flesh prickles, feeling the still air. It's enough to set him spinning at every rustle, the axe coming up in both hands. Powerful hands.

She decides. Sap and bark shift and blend. She chooses a hollow tree, cracked and burnt by lightning, and emerges from its broken womb.

The woodsman screams, a bellow like a startled elk. He raises the axe high, then stops as his crude brain makes sense of what he sees. When she doesn't move, the axe lowers.

She steps out of the great tree's shadow and into a slanting shaft of sunlight, knowing that his kind see best with their eyes. She opens to the trees around them and sees herself as he does: a sleek parody of his own form. Blank eyes of hardened golden amber shine from a smooth-bald head. The grain of her honey-brown flesh runs in long lines and sweeping whorls, emphasizing the curves and crevices that speak fertility to his people. Her body is sleek, not bark but heartwood, as if stripped clean and polished by the rushing of a river.

She can feel his sap rising as he stares at her, yet still he places the axe between them. When he speaks, his voice is sharp and clipped by fear. "What do you want?"

Her own words are the creak of two branches rubbing together, the whistle of wind through leaves.

"Love."

His face twists into a grimace. He tries for mockery, yet she can see the hope hidden just beneath the thorns. "Right," he says.

He's correct to question. His definition of love is a warm-blooded thing: too fast, too frantic. His people bloom and drop in a single beat of the forest's great heart. But she steps closer. "Love. New growth."

The axe wavers. He can't take his eyes from the flowing contours of her face, the yellow tree-stones of her eyes. "You're a dryad. A forest guardian."

In fact, she is not the guardian. She is the forest. But she's long since quit trying to explain such things to his people.

"Yes."

"Have you come to take your revenge, then?"

She stops short and cocks her head to the side, as she has seen the little birds do, but finds the new angle brings no insight. "Why?"

He laughs bitterly, teeth flashing in a beard like thick moss. "Because we cut down your trees. Chop them up and burn them, or split them for lumber." The axe head gestures at her. "You do the same to men. I've heard the stories."

"I haven't," she says. One hand leads his gaze to the loam of the forest floor. "Do you know why there's no undergrowth here?"

The man looks confused. After a moment, he says, "It's too shady. Canopy's too dense."

She smiles at him, the moth-soft wood of her lips twisting up. "Once, this place was burned in a wildfire. If you had come then, you would have seen thousands of plants—fireweed and brambles no higher than your knee—covering a vast meadow. For a time, they ruled it. Then the trees grew taller. They jockeyed with each other for position, racing for the sun, always climbing higher, stretching branches farther. They covered the sky, drinking in all of it, and the shorter plants died."

The woodsman's axe wavers. "I don't understand."

The dryad ignores him and turns to a tree wrapped in thick twists of woody vine. She touches the vine's leaves. "This tree is dying. Once it was tall and proud, as mighty as any that came before it. But the vine, once so much smaller, has wrapped around it, climbed its trunk. In time, it will strangle it. The tree will rot away and only the vine will remain, twisted around the tree's memory."

The lumberjack's face is flushed, angry. "Why are you telling me this?"

She turns away from the dying tree, holding his eyes with the ones in her head.

"You fear reprisal for killing my plants. Yet all of them are killers. They strangle each other. They starve the newborns out of greed." She smiles and shakes her head. "Every forest is a battle."

"What do you want?" His voice is hoarse with desire and with anger at that desire. The axe lowers until its head rests on the ground.

The dryad turns and stretches, arching her back. She feels his eyes, his need. She looks back at him over one shoulder.

"It's spring," she says. "New growth."

✿✿✿

The first time he takes her is rough, on hands and knees there in the loam. The second is more tender, the third softer still. Her blossoms open to him, blooming full and red, and he pollinates them. His kisses leave fairy trails of moisture along the polished plane of her back, the smooth curve of her stomach.

Each time, he returns to town after only a day or two in her arms. Sometimes he's gone as long as a week, but each time, he returns once more, flushed and firm. He could live off game, off the sweet sap of her congregation, but still he leaves, and she does not press. He whispers things in her ear, unasked-for words of love and devotion, but she can hear the strain underneath them.

She knows why he goes home each time, even if he does not. She doesn't mind. A flower isn't jealous when a bee returns to its hive.

It is deep summer when the seed finally takes hold. She knows immediately, feels the first hair-thin tendrils of its roots spreading inside her, but says nothing. She feels it drink of her and smiles.

Soon, however, even he can see that something has changed. Still they couple, yet she no longer has the frenetic passion of their beginning. She moves slowly, gracefully, with half-lidded eyes and a beatific smile. He feels the new weight in her wooden breasts, the expansion of a belly that has never deviated in shape.

She feels the shift in him as understanding dawns. Confusion. Disgust. Excitement. He starts to withdraw, and for the first time, she denies him, bearing down on him, refusing to let him run from what he has helped create. They clutch at each other, and in the aftermath, he lies beside her on his side, one arm draped over her breasts, protective and possessive.

"So this is what you meant," he says. "Why you wanted me."

She smiles and weaves her fingers between his. Wooden lips press against his forearm.

"New growth," she says.

❀❀❀

The days shorten, faster with each that passes. As her time approaches, the dryad ceases to move about the forest as she once did. Instead, she lies inside the hollow tree where she first appeared to the woodsman, drinking from the roots of nearby trees, which burrow up through the soil to supply her.

The woodsman comes less often, now that they no longer make love. She feels the familiar conflict in him, the shame mingled with pride. She watches with the eyes of the forest as he stops for hours on his way to see her, sometimes even turning around and walking back toward the town before changing his mind once more and finishing his trek. She sees all of this but remains unworried. His kind questions everything. In his own way, he is as predictable as all the other animals in her forest—the sleeping bears and migrating geese. He will return at the appointed time.

And he does. As he enters the shadows of the hollow tree, she can see the surprise on his face, startled at how large she's grown. She's swollen as a water tree, her stomach a tremendous dome. She smiles and beckons him over.

He sits down beside her, and the contractions begin almost immediately. Skin as hard as mahogany ripples in great waves, sweeping downward. Her legs spread, her flowers tear. A crack splits and runs up her belly.

And then they are coming, pouring forth into the world in a wave of sap. Tiny things, as perfectly formed as their mother but no more than a hand tall. They have no eyes, for they do not need them, but all over the forest, leaves twitch and knotholes stretch wide as the children take in their new world.

With a last push, the tenth is expelled, and the dryad's body reseals, the yawning split knitting together. She grins in pleasure and exhaustion and squeezes the woodsman's arm.

He hardly notices. With one hand, he carefully scoops up one of the milling offspring and brings it close, marveling. Its shape is female yet not quite the same as her parent. Where the mother's skin is blank wood, the child's is covered in a dense coat of budding leaves, stretching and unfurling even as he watches. She makes no sound, but he feels her attention on him. He sets her down carefully.

The dryad is already standing. She extends a hand to help him up.

"They're beautiful," he says, and his smile is genuine. The dryad smiles back, pleased that he finally understands the wonder they've created, then lifts him and presses him against the tree's wall with her body.

She kisses him, and he returns it—then goes rigid. He tries to scream, but she covers his mouth with hers. Behind him, her hand grows wet as her fingers, now splinter-sharp, stab deep into his flesh, tearing a long gash down his back.

Hands batter at her, but the woodsman has long since left the axe behind, and his blows are like wind against an oak. She reaches out and grabs his wrists, lifting them and stretching until they reach the high thorns she's readied. The spikes slide in smoothly.

His lips part, and the woodsman's scream is one long note, a howl without words. The children gather around the dryad's feet, listening, as she begins to spread the flesh of his back in long strips, stretching them out around him in every direction. When they're in place, she splits him down the front as well, his skin parting as easily as ripe fruit.

More strips of flesh radiate out in a halo around him, his runny canopy now a brilliant autumn red. Beneath them, their children dance, his blood raining down patter-soft on their outstretched leaves. As trees drop leaves to fertilize the soil, so does his sap feed their children. One climbs up his shaking leg, burrowing into the nurse log of his torso.

She steps back and admires the fine blood tree they've made. She notes with approval that his noises have stopped, yet there's still a question in his eyes. She moves forward again, brushing carefully past the children that still dance around his ankles or hug his legs, showing their love and thanks and appreciation. It makes her smile to see them. She presses herself against the woodsman's body, feeling his love slick on her skin, his heart calming its pounding, then growing slower still. Cheek to cheek, she leans forward and breathes warm into his ear.

"New growth."

Volume Two

"... Run on the top of the dishevelled tide,
And dance upon the mountains like a flame."
—W.B. Yeats, *The Land of Heart's Desire*

THE GLITTERING BOY FROM NORIEDA

ERIN HOFFMAN

The glob of half-chewed orange rice candy hit the ground with a wet splat less than a handsbreadth from Satoshi's foot. A series of whoops followed from the lurking boys, a familiar mingling of glee and disappointment: cheering at the terribly clever idea to spit expensive rice candy at the yaro-boy, aww-ing that the shot had missed.

While his pals were still hooting, Kawamoto popped another piece of candy into his mouth, chewed, and spat again. This time his aim was truer, and Satoshi's arms wheeled as his feet tried to go one way and his body tried to go another, each valiantly seeking escape from the flying goo.

The lacquered box in Satoshi's left hand tilted, slipped, and dropped to the ground with a clatter. The rice that exploded out like a miniature white firework would earn him water duty, but it was the splash of color beyond that made Satoshi's throat twist up. The pickled eggplant and preserved daikon radish had come all the way from his uncle in Yasutori, and they were sublime.

He should not have stopped. The sight of the little splatter of purple and red paralyzed him. He wanted to dive after the fallen delicacies, try to stuff them into his mouth even flavored with dust, but the only thing more humiliating than Kawamoto spilling his lunch would be to be seen eating pickles out of the dirt.

The jeering from Kawamoto and the other boys had subsided into speculative silence by the time he raised his eyes again. Like him, they were wondering why he hadn't turned and run when he had the chance. Was he challenging them?

Did he need to be reminded of his place? He saw these cards slowly turning over in the nori-dark eyes of his five tormentors.

"Spilled your lunch, yaro?" the boy to Kawamoto's right asked.

"He wants to stick around. Perhaps he can make us a fine meal," Kawamoto sneered, "one fit for my uncle's table." Ichiro Kawamoto never lost an opportunity to remind them that his uncle was advisor to the daimyo.

"Even mice would not eat what he could cook," another boy added, and kicked dust from the road at Satoshi. The boys tensed to see what he would do—the first overture toward violence.

"It's true," Kawamoto agreed. "You'll be a sock-mender all your life, Satoshi, while we become samurai." His voice intensified with cruelty while Satoshi flushed at the insult to his father. "It will be like the story of Tsutomo and the water dragon. No matter how hard you swim, you are like the ignorant little pond slug." Kawamoto's foot lifted for a larger dust-kick.

"That is not an accurate description, per se."

The voice that interrupted—bright like green bamboo, subtly sharp—did not need volume to command their attention.

It was Chinami. She stood in the doorway to the bakery where she worked for Hiroko-san, Satoshi's aunt. With arms folded and her chin tilted downward, casting her eyes in shadow, she seemed—probably deliberately—a figure from a block-printed kami story.

Chinami's skin was like a fine baked sweet bun, soft and delicate, but her agile hands were a calligrapher's, clever as undetected deception. It was this charm that made Kawamoto hesitate, and for once, Satoshi did not envy him. Chinami had once talked him out of a whole sweet summer melon, and it was only when he crossed his family's teak threshold that he realized the gift had been not his idea at all.

With a sauntering twist of her foot, Chinami emerged from the doorway, her arms falling languidly to her sides, slender wrists powdered white with rice flour. She took their silence for invitation and sailed into the story: "In the time of our great-grandfathers, when the shogun was second cousin to the kami known as Eight Thousand Wisdoms, there lived a green water dragon in the Autumn Morning River—"

The boys' faces slackened from impending furor into grudging curiosity and then, slowly, into entrancement. Chinami spun the tale of stalwart Tsutomo, who navigated the water dragon's tricks and deftly turned the spirit's intentions toward his own with the help of a lowly slug who lived by the riverside and knew the dragon's secrets. The dragon proposed a test of wills when he recognized that Tsutomo was no ordinary tailor's son—

Chinami's eyes came up, caught Satoshi's in a hunting cat's stare, and then her eyebrows twitched up the road in suggestion.

Satoshi brought his hands together in a gesture of gratitude, then stealthily collected his lunchbox, cast one last mournful glance at the pickles from Yasutori, and fled.

He could not retreat the way he'd come without crossing in front of Kawamoto, so he worked his way through Norieda's small side-streets, winding west toward the river and its attendant warren of fish-drying shacks. He sniffed a little when his stomach growled at the scent of smoking sea-vegetable, and he turned north on a whim, wondering if he might be able to charm a bit of sweet grilled eel out of Kichi-san.

"There is another whose advice you could seek," a cracking voice said as he rounded the corner. Satoshi jumped, very nearly dropping his lunchbox again.

An old man he'd never seen before sat on the steps of one of the more dilapidated drying shacks. His nose was long, reddened with some affliction of the ancient, and he kept his hands hidden beneath an old-fashioned robe.

"I've never seen you here before," Satoshi said. "Did you come from the city?" It was hope more than genuine suspicion. The man had no ambiance of wealth around him that would suggest he had traveled far or well.

"I'm just a visiting uncle," the old man said. "An old taro farmer of no significance, visiting my brother Uyeda."

Uyeda-san tended rice fields on the outskirts of town. He had never mentioned a brother, but he spoke little since the sleeping sickness took his wife and son.

"You want to cook for the daimyo," long-nosed uncle said. Satoshi jerked, wondering how the old man could have overheard his embarrassment with Kawamoto, and then wondered if his aspiration was mocked by all the village. Before he could puzzle it out, the man added: "You've heard of the bakeneko who lives in the forest?"

It was an old village story. Chinami would have known it by heart. The old cat belonged to a widow whose husband was lost in the war. After much pampering, it grew old, ancient, and sprouted an extra tail. Then it fled into the forest, perhaps first eating the widow's niece, or else marrying her—the accounts were unclear. Satoshi nodded cautiously.

"Neko-san is said to have a marvelous palate, known and respected even as far as Torimachi. The shogun himself is said to employ a chef who proved himself by bringing Neko-san an original dish of his own devising and emerging unscathed from the forest."

A clatter in the alley behind him sent Satoshi jumping, thinking Kawamoto's boys had thrown off Chinami's spell and followed him, but it was only old Yuka banging her sandals on the threshold to shake them free of mud. "The bakeneko eats children—" he began, turning back around. The thought of confronting a monster made him question his ambition. Perhaps this would fade as his past aspirations had: castle-designer, rare bird collector, swordsmith. Time had withered them all . . .

But the old man was gone, his absence sending another chill up Satoshi's back.

"The life you want is not here, Satoshi-san," the man's voice came, muffled. When Satoshi turned toward it, toward the doorway of one of the drying sheds, a ring of ikayaki flew toward him. He caught it instinctively just before it hit his chest, then popped it into his mouth, hunger sweetening the tender squid flesh and overcoming its oven-fresh heat. The old man tossed two more sliced rings at him before shutting the shed door. "Think where it is, and go there. Ganbatte!"

❀❀❀

Satoshi woke gasping from a dream of gut-kicks from Kawamoto's gang, all of whom had turned to giant squid, and in that haunted moment, he determined that he would see the bakeneko. The pounding of his heart needed channeling, and so it was that his desire to escape Norieda for a bigger life melted from ore into iron. Still chased by shadow visions, he scrambled out of his blankets, shivering.

He dressed quickly, then raided the kitchen, filling an old rice sack with an iron pot, charcoal, chopsticks, vegetables. Clay jars of Uncle's Yasutori pickles went in also, and a measure of fine rice that his parents were saving for the new year. Part of him wondered if this counted as stealing, but he reminded himself that his parents would have wanted him to be prepared for the test to come, had he asked. He imagined his mother weeping as she wreathed his neck in a warrior's farewell garland made of garlic.

The sack was heavy and straining its fibers by the time he hefted it over his shoulder. Sweat crept down his forehead as he balanced his prizes as carefully as possible, fearing the betrayal of a clinking bottle or shifting rice. Once, one of the old boards creaked beneath his toe, but it was accompanied by the great sawing echo of his father's snore. For once he was grateful for that teeth-rattling rip and used it to sneak out the garden door.

Ikano-o, the white and brown stray cat his mother liked, wrapped herself around his feet as he exited into the cold. He cursed and swatted at her, and she gave him a quick swipe of sharp claws by way of answer. Satoshi stumbled away, gripping the heavy sack and willing it not to fall. Ikano-o, her fur bristled, brought her feet daintily beneath her crouched body and hissed.

"Baka neko," he muttered to himself, then chortled at the joke. The cat's green eyes followed him as he stole quietly up the empty streets.

Everyone knew of the forest where the bakeneko supposedly lurked. No one knew for sure whether it was still there because no one had risked visiting in years. Two summers ago, the potter's son had vanished. Some said he fled to the city to make his fortune, but others said the bakeneko took him.

Nonetheless, Satoshi did not hesitate when the time came to cross under the shade of the giant cedars that marked the forest's edge. Surely, the long-nosed uncle's tale of the shogun's chef was correct, and surely, that being the case, the bakeneko would see in Satoshi what no one else could. Even as the massive trees blotted out what little moonlight remained, Satoshi's conviction grew greater. This was his destiny.

If he had not believed in the bakeneko at all, the strange scent of the forest would have challenged his conviction. It grew stronger the further into the forest he went. By the time he was out of sight of the village, it was undeniable: the moldering aroma of decay and death.

The narrow dirt path continued winding deeper into the forest, and the scent intensified, a fetid thing that reached into the back of Satoshi's throat. Rude structures of crossed sticks marked the path at intervals, and above them hung papery streamers fixed to low-hanging pine branches. He passed a dozen of these decorated trees before he realized what they were: snakeskin.

And soon, not just skins: snakes, their ribcages split wide, jaws popped open and wrapped around branches like twisted hooks. The stench of their decay had become so rank that he instinctively opened his mouth to breathe, which only made things worse. Gasping, Satoshi clutched his hands tight around his rice sack, then tripped into an uneven run.

Satoshi could not have said how long he stumbled through the forest. Midnight had passed, but morning remained far. The air began to clear, only slightly, and then he stumbled into the smoke.

The bitterness of burning paper and just a hint of temple incense flooded his lungs, and he coughed, blinking tearfully. He stretched a hand out in front of him only to have it disappear at the elbow into the thick miasma. Strength left him, and he sank to his knees, lowering the sack behind him. Red sparks danced in the smoke, though at first he wondered if it was only delirium.

The breath rattled in his chest, nearly drowning out a soft sound—a whisper, a whoosh, as of furred tails whipping through the air. Gradually, the smoke began to clear.

He saw the golden eyes first, large as ripe plums and bright as summer lanterns.

Then, teeth: long, pointed, yellow beneath the curling black lip of a feline smile.

"How wonderful," the bakeneko said, his voice temple-bell hollow. "Supper delivers itself to me tonight."

"It does, great Neko-sama," Satoshi cried, desperation granting him a certain cleverness as he threw himself to the ground, arms outstretched in an attitude of worship. "But perhaps not as Neko-sama might reasonably assume," he said to the ground, not daring to look up. The smoke was continuing to clear, and his peripheral vision could just catch the rounded edges of two massive orange paws perched daintily on a tree trunk.

"Supper speaks," the great cat noted, and Satoshi was relieved that he seemed amused.

"O great Neko-sama!" Satoshi exclaimed again, touching his forehead to the ground, encouraged not to be already eaten, "I humbly come before you with the makings of a meal that I might prove my mettle as a cook by your palate as others have done before me. I beg your infinite wisdom and the honor of your judgment."

The longest silence of Satoshi's life passed then, followed by a most terrifying sound: the landing of four paws right beside his head, each as large as the hoof of a warhorse. All at once, the stench of gutted snake filled his nostrils again, and it was all he could do to swallow back his gorge. The cat's huge mottled-orange head descended, its lip lifting, black nose twitching, the pointed tips of its yellowed canines mere finger widths from Satoshi's neck.

"Cook, then," the cat smiled.

Satoshi rolled back onto his heels, then sprang toward his sack, redirecting the energy that told him to flee flee flee the monstrous creature's lair. With quick but careful movements, he emptied his sack, arranging all of his tools and pots and ingredients in an arc around him.

When he took up the small sack of fine New Year's rice, a realization dropped like a cold monk's stone in his stomach. But the bakeneko responded to his dismay: the cat exhaled, and a scrap of snakeskin paper fluttered up before him. He raised a claw and burned two symbols into the stretched surface: *fire* and *water*.

The dead snakes seemed to hiss all around them, and their breath rolled in thick, dry branches that crosshatched into a tidy hearth that promptly belched itself into red merry flame. When Satoshi set his iron pot atop it, the snakes hissed again, and a cloud of mist swirled in from the forest, then condensed into a potful of clear mountain water.

Satoshi could not be distracted by these wonders. He focused all his attention and will on the masterpiece. Vegetables were to be sliced just so, shoyu measured with perfect precision. Fine rice and dried saury and crisp young scallions—all together into his original Satoshi Stew.

At length it was there, bubbling and fresh. There was no more he could do. He presented it, arms uplifted, head bowed low, the bowl of stew and neatly placed chopsticks, the little dish of Yasutori pickles.

The bakeneko, who had remained silent throughout his cooking process, now lowered its broad orange head to the bowl. Its nostrils flared as it drew in a deep breath of the meal's fragrance, and then, to Satoshi's astonishment, it lifted a paw and proceeded to delicately transfer agile chopsticked portions into its mouth.

This lasted for perhaps three and a half bites. The great head tilted to one side, regarded him with a pale golden eye.

"Rudimentary," the bakeneko pronounced. "Lacking finesse or insight. I shall eat you now."

"B-but!" Satoshi stammered, terror slicing through him like sleet . "I can learn! I can cook for you as long as you like!"

"I'm afraid not," the bakeneko said, after a thoughtful moment. "Your flesh will be far tastier than fifty years of your cooking."

"I could bring you another," Satoshi said desperately. "I'd be but a snack for a creature of your size."

The cat paused, and Satoshi's breath caught. "Another supper? Like yourself?"

"Another," Satoshi promised. "Larger than I. Fatter, tastier."

The old cat's mouth drew wide in a smile that prickled his whiskers and bared a long bone-yellow fang. "I will let you do this," he said in his dried bonito voice, and Satoshi's heart surged with hope. "But I can't rely on you returning." Dread pulled Satoshi's guts down again, then panic sent them leaping into his throat as the cat raised a massive forepaw.

Sudden claws, dark and slick as fresh whale oil, slid from the furry paw, and just as quick slashed a gesture in the air. The passage of each claw-tip left a flash of red light in its wake, and a flutter of paper rose up from the cat's side to receive them. The markings burned themselves into the obedient white square as soon as they touched—and then the cat flicked its claws wide. The scrip, with its strange writing, flew birdlike toward Satoshi, flattening itself against his chest, and as it touched, it incandesced, jolting him with warmth that came and fled before he could draw another breath.

As he stood, shivering, waiting to die, there came a rattling sound that overcame the thundering of his heart: the bakeneko, purring with satisfaction.

When Satoshi ran his palms across his chest, feeling for injury or any sign of the burned claw strokes, the cat flexed his paws and yawned, unfurling a tongue red as temple ink between long, scissor-sharp canines. "That is a sleeping death spell," the cat said, heaving its great body up and turning away to curl itself on the rock for a nap. "Return to me before the next sunrise, or when you sleep you shall not wake again." The huge striped tail lashed once, as if to punctuate, and then wrapped itself around the furry body.

For three breaths, Satoshi stood in the glade, but the bakeneko did not stir. Satoshi's hands crept across his chest, searching for signs of the spell. A sudden terror of falling asleep shivered through him, and he searched the tree-line with darting eyes for some sign of impossible sunlight. It must be coming on evening already. Choking back fear, he fled toward the village.

❀❀❀

Satoshi's intent upon fleeing the bakeneko's forest had been first to figure out if there was a way he might escape the sleeping death spell. Possibly Yuka-san would know of some witch's way of foiling the cat, or he could find the old man by the drying sheds and ask him. Chinami might know of some story in which a bakeneko had been fooled or mollified.

As he ran through the woods, the terror in his blood melted away, chased by crushed pine needles, rising morning mist, and the dim light of dawn. With its fading came another idea: perhaps he could trick Kawamoto into coming into the forest with him. The more he thought on this, the better it seemed—surely his way of proving himself would be to deceive his greatest enemy into being consumed by the monstrous cat. He would emerge from the forest a proven master, and on top of it, Kawamoto would never mock him again.

There was no doubt that the boy deserved it. Satoshi was hard pressed to think of one single redeeming characteristic belonging to Kawamoto. If allowed to grow into a man, he would certainly become even more of a bully, expanding his terrorism to the daimyo's city. Surely it would be irresponsible *not* to feed him to the bakeneko before all this occurred.

As most of his interests tended to be, this one burned out fast, however. (Perhaps if this had not been the case, his stew might have passed muster.) By the time he reached the village, it seemed an awful lot of work to persuade Kawamoto to follow him into the forest. None of the other boys had ever once done something Satoshi suggested, so what made him think they would start now? The plan unraveled quickly.

In Norieda's main street, the first early morning fires were breathing their dragon-tongue smoke into the white dawn sky. One of them belonged to his aunt's bakery, and his feet carried him there, hoping for Chinami's advice and perhaps a hot steamed cake and a cup of tea.

Chinami answered his scratch at the door, looking down at him in surprise that rapidly widened into shock. "Where have you been?" she chirped, taking in the filthy mud that caked his calves, the stray pine needles , the lingering effluvia of desiccated serpent.

"I've been to see the bakeneko," he said, rubbing his arms to show more cold than he felt. Chinami stepped out of the doorway, allowing him in. He entered, managing a shiver, and noted with relief that his aunt was elsewhere.

"The bakeneko!" Chinami repeated, her voice rising further.

Satoshi looked longingly at the bamboo racks laden with sweet steamed buns, and Chinami silently responded to this barter, moving to set two moon-white pastries and a cup of tea on the rough plank working table. Satoshi set upon them with relish, though they were hot—the sweet red bean filling burned his mouth.

Between bites, he told the story of how he'd fled from Kawamoto, with her help, and then met the red-nosed uncle by the fish-drying sheds. Chinami's eyes narrowed cannily at this, and Satoshi wondered what she suspected, but she did not offer, so he continued, describing the gathering of his supplies and his journey into the dark forest.

But when it came time to describe his cooking—and his failure—the words stalled out.

Chinami stared at him expectantly. It was easy enough for her, he thought. She could talk her way out of anything. And that gave Satoshi another idea.

"You have to come with me," Satoshi said, "to see the bakeneko. He—he's asked for you."

"He what?" He must have truly had her. Chinami had never spoken so few original words in all the time he'd known her.

"I told him that you were the greatest storyteller for twenty islands," Satoshi said and saw by the gleam in Chinami's eye that his aim proved true. "He wanted me to bring you back." A flash of insight, just as her eyes began to narrow—"He wishes to eat the meal I prepared him, accompanied by fine entertainment. He promised to reward us both."

The slackening of Chinami's face then nearly caused him to confess all, even if it meant facing the bakeneko's sleeping death spell. He saw then that Chinami was as anxious to escape Norieda as he was. He felt foolish for not knowing this before.

"Very well," Chinami said, that moment of openness retreating behind her storyteller's mask. Had she said something else—had it been a murmured "all right," a nervous swallow—he might have deterred her. Instead, he gulped the remainder of his tea and stood, turning for the door. The sweet buns pressed together like lumps of coal in his stomach, and he did not trust himself to look back.

Neither of them spoke when Satoshi led the way into the dark forest. He could feel Chinami's eyes boring into his back, just between his shoulder-blades—surely she would discover his duplicitousness somehow, wring it from the bent bow of his posture, the hesitation in his footstep. Satoshi cringed with every footfall, sure she would unravel his plan, such as it was—and unsure whether this wasn't truly what he wanted.

The alternative was to think about the course of his own actions, culminating now in bringing perhaps his only friend in the entire village to be eaten by a decrepit cat monster. It was nearly unfathomable.

And yet . . . the breakfast turned over in Satoshi's stomach, and with it, his thoughts took a darker turn as well. Had Chinami really been his friend? She was more elemental than human, a strange girl who seemed to glory in the dramatic and actively enjoyed getting those around her into trouble. No, the truth was that Satoshi had never known a true friend, so Chinami had seemed the closest, but she was as blameworthy as the rest—if not moreso, for trying to convince him otherwise.

Behind him, Chinami gasped, and Satoshi nearly leapt out of his skin. He spun and found her poised with one hand over her mouth—gawking at the first line of snakeskins.

"He likes to eat snakes," Satoshi explained, reaching back to haul on Chinami's free hand. Listlessly, she began to move again, as he'd hoped she would—and his hand on hers would hopefully prevent any later attempts to flee.

Such caution proved unnecessary. The closer they got to the bakeneko's lair, the bolder Chinami grew until at last she was striding half a step in front of Satoshi, pulling his hand behind her. When at last they came to the clearing, she was first to throw herself to the ground, perforce dragging Satoshi with her. Together, they lay with their knees pressed to the ground, their heads bent low, arms outstretched.

"So this is who you've brought me," the bakeneko said. "She is not so much bigger than you."

The glare that Chinami leveled at him took only an instant but might have carried the weight of the entire shogun's palace.

When the cat saw the glare, his smile widened, baring pointed incisors. "Tell me, small one," the whiskered face turned toward Chinami. "Why do you believe you're here?"

Chinami did not raise her face. Nevertheless, the voice that she directed at the ground betrayed neither fear nor apology. "One was told that one's services as a storyteller had been requested," she began. "But one suspected one was being brought instead to be consumed."

Satoshi's back tensed with shock—she had known?

A sudden stillness from the bakeneko said that Satoshi was not alone. "You knew!" Raised, the bakeneko's strange voice invoked a grinding mill-wheel, brash and deep. "And yet you followed him here. How, and why?"

"One had read of the legendary and forgotten Tamaki no Kyoko, companion to Bakeneko-sama," Chinami began, and the cat's claws now clenched the wooden stump upon which he perched. "Kyoko-sama's storytelling abilities were legendary, yet the sad ending to her life made one quite certain Bakeneko-sama would not desire the company of but a humble apprentice storyteller. The explanation for this deception could be but one thing."

"This answers the first," the bakeneko replied, and his voice now had deepened into a solemn sawing of dry wood.

Now Chinami raised her head, boldly meeting the bakeneko's golden gaze. "One wished to experience the presence of such a legend, even if this should be one's final experience."

"A bold claim," the bakeneko said. The levity with which it had addressed Satoshi, even in discussing eating him, was gone. "Tell me—?"

"Maeda Chinami," Chinami said quickly, lowering her forehead once more to the ground.

"Tell me, Maeda Chinami: where would one go to seek out the summer lyric of the Snow Cedar Brotherhood?"

"Respectfully, Bakeneko-sama, there is no such lyric," Chinami replied, not lifting her head, "for the Brotherhood spends the summer in silent meditation in the caves of Kuonji."

"Ah, then," the bakeneko continued, "not being satisfied, where might one seek the plum wine favored by the kami of Amaya Mountain?"

"The wine is hidden in cold springs at the Amayamoto, but to partake, one must complete the study of six wisdoms carved into lanterns at the mountaintop or risk a lifetime of servitude to the kami."

"You are well prepared," the bakeneko concluded.

Satoshi's heart hammered in his chest. He hardly knew what to expect. Would the cat set them free?

Chinami bowed low to the bakeneko, her hands pressed together. "You honor this humble person beyond her deserving," she said.

"I have one final question for you," the bakeneko said, flexing its claws. "Shall I eat the boy?"

Chinami did not answer straightaway, and the gulf of her hesitation planted a new convulsion in Satoshi's ribs. She knew he had lured her here, and very likely, the monster would demand to eat *one* of them. He gathered his legs beneath him, preparing for a futile dash.

"Satoshi is foolish as a running stream in summer," Chinami began, "reckless as Goro in the tale of the nine-plumed pheasant." Satoshi felt his chest compressing, but she continued: "It is likely the flaw in his character that brought us here runs deep and indelible. But he is ambitious and capable of facing fear."

"You see some potential in him, then."

Chinami's face turned toward him, and Satoshi's cheeks flushed with mingled shame and gratitude. "I do."

"Very well. It appears he was not entirely unwise in luring you," the bakeneko said. "I will take a chance on him."

An itching sensation prickled up Satoshi's arms, beginning at his wrists and racing toward his elbows and fingernails. He staggered backward, watching in horror as each hair on his skin was replaced with a glittering silver fish scale. Ice raced through his veins, encasing him in cold as the scales locked him in a clammy prison, and his head reeled, not from the terror of transformation but from a sudden assault of light and odor.

Scent blinded him to any other sense: the musk of red cedar, the moldering bite of mildew, the reek of decaying snakeskin. Chinami exuded a fragrance of sweet rice flour and azalea soap, and the bakeneko gave off an ancient animal aroma, a hollow tang of stalking death. Satoshi's mouth dropped open, and the assault intensified: even his barely-eaten bowl of stew sent him a message, muddled and rude.

"You are fit now to cook for one such as I," the bakeneko purred. "I have given you enlightenment."

"My family," Satoshi stuttered, "the village—the daimyo—"

"You must leave that old life behind," the giant cat said. "They would skin you for a demon. You have a new life now." The long maw stretched in a quizzical, many-toothed smile; the voice deepened. "Isn't that what you wanted?"

Satoshi spun to his feet, then kept spinning, not by his own design but out of dizziness; his vision had all but left him.

"Your apprenticeship begins now," the bakeneko said. "Perhaps one day you will be fit to go abroad in the world as my student. But that day is far from this." He turned to Chinami, whiskers prickling outward in a sniff of approval. "And you, Chinami-chan. You are correct that I have little desire for a young storyteller that can but remind me of lost Kyoko-chan. But there is a river kami on the border of Yasutori who seeks a student." Once more, the cat lifted a bowl-sized paw, and this time the scrip it inscribed landed lightly in Chinami's outstretched hand. "She prefers cherries soaked in spring honey. Go, and embrace your destiny."

Chinami stood then but only to bow deeply from her waist. "Again you honor me, Bakeneko-sama. If you might indulge a final inquiry—" Her face, a pale blur, turned toward Satoshi.

"This glittering boy?" The cat thumped his massive tail against the tree stump, bemused. "He has years before he is fit to be seen. But let his legend go with you. A storyteller needs new tales as well as old."

Chinami bowed, and though he could not see them, Satoshi felt her eyes upon his wretched skin. "It is so, Neko-sama."

When she left the forest that day, never to return, Chinami was followed by the clank of iron and stone pottery and the millstone rumble of the cat's commanding voice: "Begin!"

A Brooch of Bone, A Hint of Tooth

Cat Rambo

The child ran clattering through stone-walled corridors and then, softer, softer, through the tapestry-lined chambers where the queen once dwelled. Princess Esmerelda was eight. Baby fat still clung to her limbs, but her face was a cherub's: blonde, blue eyed, pierced with a dimple that deepened as she continued, giggling, through the palace.

Courtiers and servants scattered out of her way. A few servants laughed, echoing the glee on her face. But laughter was scarce, or worse, only a crippled, forced version, as though most were scared to take much notice of the girl.

Only one person spoke to her. He stepped in her path deliberately. She collided with his silk robes with a surprised "oof." Backpedaling for balance, she stared as though confronted with a creature she had never seen before.

The smile on his lips was a withered worm.

"Softly, Princess!" he said. The tortured worm twisted. "Your Highness will injure yourself. It would be more suitable if you sent a servant running for whatever it is you are looking for."

"But I am looking for the wind, and I can only find it when running!" she chortled and was off again. The frown Sir Lyonel threw at her heels did not slow them. She grinned back at him, and he imagined a certain inhuman toothiness about her expression, like a dog that has scented something long dead or a fox picking morsels from a wire brush.

But the two court ladies that grabbed her hands and swung her along as she kicked her heels and giggled must have seen something different. Their laughter echoed hers, fair faces all alight.

Released, the child ran on. Sir Lyonel, advisor to the king, followed, slowly. He muttered to himself about bad blood and fingered the bone brooch at his neck. The coin-sized round was carved with a sword laid over a crown, as though to protect it from harm.

❀❀❀

In an echoing room, the king sat on his throne, listening to treaties. When the child ran in, he gestured to his court for silence. He lifted up his arms and caught the Princess and folded her against him in a rush of laughter.

"Have you caught the wind yet, my pet?" he asked.

She shook her head, making her fine blonde hair float in the air around her. "When I run, I feel it, and when I stop, it stops!" she exclaimed, having just made that discovery this morning. She had tried it at various spots in the castle. It was always the same, whether she tried it up on the roof along the parapets or down in the tunnels where no one but she ever came.

"She will tire you out, your Majesty," Sir Lyonel said as he entered.

The king stroked Princess Esmerelda's hair as she leaned against him, feeling it soft as silk under his fingertips.

"Nonsense," he said. "She is the best medicine I could have, full of life and sweetness, like her fairy mother." But dark shadows lay under his eyes, and a cough shook him as he set her back down.

"Run along, my fleet-footed one," he said. "Catch the wind and bring it back to me, and I will have it woven into a shawl to keep you warm in the deep of winter."

She was gone and left only laughter in her trail as he turned back to the kingdom's business. When had it grown so slow and oppressive, full of farmers arguing about the borders of wheat fields and foreign emissaries complaining of tariffs? When his queen had lived here, the castle was full of light and laughter, and no such matters had ever troubled him. Now the people praised him as they had not before, but he remembered those frivolous days fondly.

❀❀❀

Esmerelda went where she knew no one would follow her. Down, down, down, past the dungeons where a few prisoners lingered, and down further yet into the catacombs. They had been forbidden to her, but she knew them better than anyone else, for she came to this place every few days.

She did not tell anyone that she could see, down there, without candle or torch. Her father did not like her differences, the ones her mother had given her. Her uncanny elf-sight, able to see through darkness or smoke or lies, was only one of those.

Her slippers padded through the grime and dirt. The hewn walls gave way to others. At the end of a long, smooth tunnel was the room she sought, one whose edges hinted at a strange precision for such an unvisited place. Here, deep below the castle and the city surrounding it, there was a silence she could find nowhere else.

Others shared the room with her. Thirty-three man-sized shelves were carved into the rock in columns of three, holding bones that had been at rest for more than a thousand years. Frames like windows had been carved into the rock, but the art that had once filled them was gone, fallen to gleaming dust. The corpses lay in disarray, and skulls were stacked in piles. Most were unmarked, but a few wore red-inked glyphs that Esmerelda could not read.

The cold bit at her, but she chose to ignore it. She was tougher than any human child, but the palace folk forgot that and loved to coddle her. They missed her mother, missed the tall fairy queen who had gone away, leaving behind her husband and child. That was the way of fairies, they said, and they did not try to hide her mother's departure from her because all of them wanted her to love her father the best.

But that did not mean they did not miss the queen.

❀❀❀

In the council chamber, the king dreamed of his lost queen, the woman he had found in the wood one fine day when he was just a prince, out hunting. She had said she would always be with him. Always! And in the end, that had been a lie, for she had slipped away one morning, without even a word, and he still didn't know what he had done to offend her.

How beautiful she was in this dream! As beautiful as he remembered, skin whiter than the whitest rose in his garden, slim as a fleeing deer, laughter quicker than any prey. He had slipped down from his horse, so taken with her that he barely knew he was moving toward her. The knights held back, waiting to see what he would do. His father had thought fairies evil, had killed one, even, and they were rarely seen nowadays.

One knight, Lyonel, thought, "Perhaps she will kill him too!" Much later he would reprimand the princess for running too quickly, long after he had put away his sword and become a counselor, long after the fairy had failed to kill the prince, had even, improbable as he had thought it, married him.

That marriage had thwarted a long-laid plan by Sir Lyonel and his confederates, to render the king dissatisfied with any woman, so he would never marry. They had told him stories of beautiful fairies, never dreaming that one would come among them, and she came just as they were starting to think themselves safe, as white hairs were starting to show in his beard.

He had married, and proven himself a worthy king by siring an heir, who ran, motherless, through the palace, waiting to rule in turn.

❂❂❂

Sir Lyonel had entered the catacombs before but had never gone far. The castle had stood through three lines of kings and would stand for three more before it passed, like all things, into dust and legend.

When he was a child, Lyonel's nursemaid had told him terrible stories of what waited beneath the castle: great worms with teeth that would crawl after you faster than a horse could run, and rat-kings with their tails entangled and myriad rat-minions protecting them in swarms of fur and fangs. And ghosts and sorcerers and necromancers. Now he was old and no longer feared anything, but once, as he went down a passageway, he thought he heard slithering. He paused and listened but did not hear the sound again.

The torch in his hand showed the little princess's tracks, leading him along her path. He imagined her uncanny eyes gleaming in the shadows, and he paused again, thinking to hear her.

But by the time her tracks led him to the furthest room, she was long gone. He stood, feeling the cold creep up from the stone floor through the soles of his feet, and looked at the skulls. Paltry playthings for a child, and ones that betrayed a morbid cast of mind unsuitable in a ruler.

He stooped and picked up a skull. Red lines writhed on the bare white bone, red as blood, but the ink was long dry, even though it still shone wetly.

He touched the brooch at his throat. "Would you rather lie here, my dear?" he said and chuckled to himself. And then, looking around at the walls, he thought, *No one ever comes here. No one would ever find this place.*

This time he smiled fully. The worm splayed as though in terror and delight.

❀❀❀

In the days that came, Sir Lyonel watched the princess closely. As though she sensed his scrutiny, she played in the gardens and the great hall, in the attics among the maids, and in the stables, where a new batch of kittens had just arrived.

Meanwhile, he planted seeds. In the kitchen, he mentioned the princess's flightiness, so like her mother. To the other knights, he spoke of fairy blood and how prone to whim it often proved, emerging after decades of ordinariness— and none would say our little princess was ordinary, would they, he chuckled. He mentioned the princess's disappearances in the hearing of the king and said worriedly, "What if something should happen to her? She is the heir, after all."

At the same time, he made people vanish.

People had always vanished from the castle. It was a very large place, and servants came and went—usually as they pleased, rather than how its officials pleased.

The princess had known before that maids might decide to marry or return home, now that they had enough to buy a new comb or a teapot. Soldiers stayed longer, but even they were not permanent—some went off to other lands or other fights and some simply went to beat their swords into implements of farming, now that they had seen the wide world and had some of it see them.

But now some were vanishing with less word than ever, not even a note, and sometimes they left their belongings behind. Perhaps in emulation of the queen, it was said, who had returned to her homeland clad in nothing. She had abandoned all her jewels and silken dresses, even the lace-trimmed night shifts the king had bought for her, the delicate shifts made of white silk that seemed sallow when placed beside her skin.

It seemed to the princess that her friends were the ones vanishing so, but she could not figure out how to tell her father this. He was prone to patting her on the head and telling her to run along. "There will be time enough to worry about learning matters of state when you are older," he said. "Run along now and continue to be a child."

And it seemed to Esmerelda that Sir Lyonel, whom she found watching her too often, like a snake watches a mouse that might make a particularly good meal, smiled in a little, "You may think so, but I know better" sort of way, an expression that was wiped away before the king could turn and look at him.

✸✸✸

How inevitable that the king should try to curtail his child's wandering. He set a nursemaid to following her, and when that proved inadequate, he appointed other servants to watch over her.

Her father took her aside and tried to reason with her. He did not want to frighten her. She was such a sunny spirit, like a little canary that sang all day long. Her mother had sung too, and the sound had delighted the king's heart so much that he did not want it to fade away, for his child's voice to be lowered in fear.

He said, "Do you love me? You must always be honest, my child, always straightforward."

"Of course I do, Papa." The little girl laid her cheek against his, and he closed his eyes, feeling her warmth, smelling her lavender soap. It made him feel young again to be so close to her, this perfect thing that was the last thing that reminded him of his lost wife. So all he said was, "Then look after yourself, my dear, for it would break my heart to not have you here."

She peered up into his face. "Can hearts break like that?"

"Yes," he said. "They can. Don't test mine!"

"I will not break your heart," she said and smiled at him, and danced away.

✸✸✸

It was only a little work to lose the servant following her. Esmerelda thought to herself that it was the kindest thing, perhaps. Her guardians were prone to vanishing. She did not want whatever stole them to take the latest: a pleasant, cheerful maid named Lia, who brought the princess fresh baked pasties from the kitchen and didn't mind fierce hugs or being teased.

So Esmerelda left Lia calling to her in the garden and ducked through a stone archway, and soon, as though it were inevitable, she was going to the catacombs.

She did not sense the man following her, so intent was she on picking out her path. Or perhaps it was the way he took care to muffle his steps, to follow with inexorable slowness. He carried a hooded lantern, which he could shutter in an instant if need be, and he paused often, cocking his head to hear the child's footsteps far ahead. He knew the route she followed, and he went there too.

In the room of the skulls, Esmerelda stacked skulls into pyramids and spoke to them. Outside in the corridor, Sir Lyonel tried to make out what she was saying. Singing a nursery rhyme, perhaps. Or some other nonsense verse, the kind that adults filled children's heads with, not realizing the dark nightmares in the tales. It was only the work of a moment to swing the door shut, to bar it.

He stood outside, still listening.

He heard Esmerelda step to the doorway, heard her test it unsuccessfully. He expected a cry or shout at that point, but none came. He listened harder, even pressed his ear against the door, but there was no sound.

He thought that he had always thought her an unnatural child, too perfect, too enchanting. Her mother had not been human, after all, even though she resembled one. With his eyes closed, as they were now, he could almost see her slim, menacing form, close to him in the darkness, waiting for him to open his eyes.

He opened them with a start, half-expecting to see her there, but she was not. He wondered again if he heard the distant rustle of scales slipping against stone. He had never feared ghosts, but here in the lantern's flickering light, he found it in him to imagine them, and he shuddered to think of what they might say

He went away, padding as quietly as he could. He didn't fear Esmerelda—she would not be able to identify who had locked her in there, in the unlikely event that someone stumbled across the room in the inevitable search. Rather a part of him, a mean and ignoble part, smiled to think of her there, still listening, wondering whether or not he had gone.

He played fantasies over in his head as he went along the corridor. The king, bereft and in need of support, would turn to him, and he would comfort the old man and continue gently leading him to the place he had yearned for so many times in his life: being appointed the king's heir.

He would make a good king, he thought. He would not meddle much in the affairs of others, and he would see a barrier built so no fairies could come into this kingdom without being noted and discouraged.

When he came to the courtyard, Esmerelda was there. Lia was watching her as she played a game in the dust with a rubber ball and a set of jacks.

He stopped, stupefied. How was this possible? What did it mean?

Looking up, the child smiled at him. It was not a pleasant smile. Rather, it was a smile that made his blood run cold. He reached for the brooch at his neck as though to reassure himself. As his fingers caressed the touch-worn bone, the child's smile grew.

"Where have you been, Sir Lyonel?" she said. Her voice was clear and bland, and he sensed deep in his heart that she knew who had stood outside the doorway after closing it. Somehow, she had read his thoughts. The blood rose to his cheeks as though she were rummaging through his mind, exposing hidden things to the light. His thoughts skittered like insects living beneath a stone, never having seen the sun.

He stammered something.

She pursued the topic. "Your boots are all dusty and covered with cobwebs. Perhaps you should have your valet brush them."

He turned away, confused, to do just that, when she added, "After all, don't you want to look regal?"

He could have stammered something else at this, as though she had exposed his ambitions to all the courtyard, but instead, he fled. He heard the child laughing as though at her game, but he knew she laughed at him.

✵✵✵

That night, he dreamed of the skulls and the red writing that covered them. He woke with a thought: witchcraft. Had her fairy blood made a witch of the princess? If so, surely he could denounce her, surely she would betray herself.

But no, she had shown herself too clever for that. He would have to wait and see, would have to lull her into a sense of false security.

In the library, he read everything he could find about fairies. There were not many books about them and almost as many disagreements as there were books.

One book said that they were just like humans, just another race, with no powers at all. People had ascribed magic to them because they were strange and unknown. But, the author concluded, it was a case of hysteria. He set that book aside quickly, for it was full of lies.

Others said they were angels, or demons, that they tempted humans to do wrong. Another said they kept to themselves but would always rectify wrongs done to them. That was nonsense, he knew. The king's father had put a visiting fairy to death, and how had he suffered? One of them had even appeared to be his son's bride! Perhaps fairies were like children and only required a strong hand to keep them from running amok.

He read that they could be defeated by iron, but he had seen the child set her hand to the metal with no apparent harm or pain. He read that they could be defeated by the pure of heart, but he knew of no one in the kingdom who would qualify. He read these words: "If you have angered a fairy, the best thing to do is vanish. But they will come looking for you, no matter what."

He set the book down. For the first time in many years, he felt the urge to cry, tears of fear and despair, but he set that aside. It would do him no good. It would do him even less good than the books.

The thought of the skulls burned at him. He touched his brooch. The bone was not human. Its fellows lay deep in the garden, where he had lured the queen one midnight. He had come up from behind and crushed her head with a stone, knowing in his heart of hearts that what he did was for the kingdom, removing this threat.

Others thought she had disappeared, dissatisfied with the king and life among the humans. He knew better. She was gone, gone for good.

But she had left her daughter behind.

❀❀❀

The next day, he went down to the chamber in the catacombs. The door stood, still barred. With shaking hands, he lifted it and swung the door open. The chamber was empty, but he could feel the skulls watching him, watching him. Only the red-marked skulls, though. He could change that.

Inside the chamber, he smashed the skulls. Bone chips flew, white and red bits that filled his senses. He never saw the door closing. When it shut with a thump, he spun, heart racing. He went to the door and called out, "Who's there?"

No one answered him. He could picture the child standing as he had stood, listening. His heart hammered in his chest so loudly he was not sure he could hear her, even if she did reply. He beat his hands against the door until they were sore, but everything was silent.

His lantern flickered, and he wondered how much fuel he had, how long it would last. And how long the darkness would last, once it failed. He thought that perhaps when the lantern was gone, he might hear slithering again, and this time he had no way of beating it back.

In this last thought, he was correct.

❀❀❀

Sir Lyonel's disappearance was marked with sorrow but not surprise. Too many had already disappeared for that.

His disappearance did not stop the vanishings. Indeed, it seemed to increase them. Servants disappeared, and councilors, and visitors, until the castle seemed more like a great ghost ship, floating on deserted waters, with only Esmerelda's singing as evidence of habitation.

Esmerelda did not mark his disappearance much. She was occupied with her dreams, for lately, a beautiful lady had appeared in them, kind and loving as Esmerelda's mother was said to have been. She would not say her name, would never speak to the child, but she held her and comforted her, and her arms were as warm as the king's.

In the mornings, Esmerelda thought she could hear the woman whispering. But no matter how she listened, she could not make the thoughts out.

But as though the whispers stirred something in her, she began to know things, began to know where lost things were. She found Lia's lost necklace and the cook's keys, and when her father could not find an important treaty, she led him to the correct desk drawer.

She had never shown him such powers before, and they made him a little afraid. He reckoned up the numbers of the disappeared, and their size frightened him further, but he did not know what to do. Instead, he waited in his throne room, at first attended by a few, then less, then none.

One day when he heard his daughter come up the stairs, singing a nonsense song, love and fear struck him like a blow.

She entered the room looking more like her mother than he had ever noticed.

His father had feared fairy beauty, had destroyed it in the act that had brought this all upon them.

His child settled on his lap and put her arms around him.

"Do not break my heart," he pleaded, stroking her hair, as she nestled closer.

"I will never break your heart, Father," Esmerelda said. Then added, for she had always been taught to be honest, "I will eat it instead."

FAMILY TIDES

MINERVA ZIMMERMAN

Jory hooked her feet in the ratlines and leaned out over the water. She closed her eyes, thrilling at the warm wind caressing her bare arms. She'd finally been able to pack away her oilskin rain gear and woolen clothing when they'd passed the thirty-sixth parallel six days ago. Now she wore a gray vest with silver buttons, which she'd convinced a continental sailor to trade her in exchange for his life, over a pair of her father's old breeches. She absently rubbed her fingertips over the red, black, and yellow beads on the belt that had been her mother's.

There was a pull in her heart like a compass needle. Jory turned her face where it pointed and opened her eyes. She blinked against the glare and lowered the slitted bone goggles perched on her tight braids. Their narrow opening protected her eyes. The goggles were the only good thing to come out of their time in the polar north.

"Jory, what do you see?" called her father from the deck.

She pointed to the southeast. "Port Fortune, Captain." A smile made her lips tumble wide. "Home," she whispered.

✵✵✵

Jory stood at the bow laughing and pointing at the long-necked scarlet birds settling to roost in the mangrove trees where streams entered the sheltered bay of Port Fortune. Glimpses of a freshly harvested sugar cane field in the distance invoked the smell of hot syrup straining through burlap from her memory.

No more cold Northern winters. After twelve years, they were finally going home.

Jory stood at the prow looking for sandbars and debris as the ship approached dock. "Hard port," she called back to Xavier. "We're pulling starboard in the current."

Xavier, the tall helmsman, leaned hard against the tiller and the *Water Maiden* and her crew straightened toward the dock. Jory jumped to a piling and then again to the dock to secure the lines.

"I want everything secured before anyone leaves this boat." Jory's father walked up and down the deck. "We leave for southern waters in two days."

"Aye, Captain," chorused the crew, except Jory.

She could feel a storm approaching from further than the sharpest-eyed sailor on the tallest ship could see. A bad storm. The kind of storm that had taken her mother. They would not be leaving port in two days.

Jory said nothing.

❀❀❀

Jory went to retrieve her bag from her bunk in the main cabin. Her father followed.

"I want you to take the first watch."

Jory whirled, eyes flashing, her hands balled in fists. "Don't need a watch. No cargo. No fear."

Her father buttoned his shirt back to the top and unrolled his sleeves. "Can't be too careful. Someone might be looking for us."

She put a fist against her hip and flipped her other hand in her father's direction. "For what? When was the last time we took a ship, Captain Bartram?"

"Jory." He made her name an admonishment. "Countries have long memories where money is concerned."

She made a noise of disgust and threw herself on his bunk while he rummaged in a trunk. "You just don't want me to go off the ship."

"Not alone." He pulled out an emerald-colored coat and tricorner hat and set to brushing them clean.

Jory made pistols with her fingers and fired them toward her father. "Old enough to fight." She sat up. "Old enough to be a full-share sailor on a navy ship."

"Jory." He expelled her name in exasperation. "The navy doesn't take girls, and if you put down your years of experience aboard the *Water Maiden*, they'd hang you as a pirate."

"At least then I'd have a better view of Port Fortune," she snapped. "And how would they know? I'm stronger and a better man than half their midshipmen."

"Jory," he pleaded. "It will take more than vests and breeches to hide your beauty."

She fluttered her eyelashes and pitched her voice high and feminine. "I could be the prettiest middie."

"Jory." Her name became a shared joke between them. He smiled and shook his head. "I am an old man."

She nodded. "Nearly dead."

He sighed. "I have business I must do alone. When I return, we will go wherever you want to go."

"Even market?"

He pressed his hat against his heart. "Even there."

"Fine. I won't leave the dock."

His lips twisted in irritation, but he accepted it with a nod.

Jory took the clothing brush out of his hand and exchanged it for a comb. "Your hair."

He set down his hat on the bunk and pulled out the leather thong holding back less than half of his long, gray-streaked hair. She watched him vainly comb at wind-twisted knots for several minutes before taking the comb from his hand.

"I can—"

"Stand still."

Her father held still while she combed out the tangles and then braided his hair. It still had golden strands among the gray and curled neatly against his collar after she tied it in place. His deeply tanned skin was just as dark as her own, but hers had never been pale.

She helped him into his coat, brushed off his shoulders, and handed him his hat. "How long?"

He turned toward the door. "Not long." He paused, but Jory left the next question unasked, and he left without turning to meet her eyes.

Jory waited until she heard his footsteps fade down the dock. She slipped out of the cabin and slung herself over the side of the ship, hitting the dock with a muted thud. She kept her eyes fixed on her father's emerald coat as she slunk down the dock. He turned to look back near the end of the dock, and Jory ducked behind a rum barrel waiting to be loaded. When she looked again, she saw no sign of emerald among the colorfully dressed crowd. She scrambled up on a pile of fishing nets to get a higher vantage.

"Off my nets!" yelled a gruff voice from an adjacent boat.

Jory turned. The old man looked startled and brought two fingers to his lips then lifted them in her direction. He said something in rapid pidgin. She only caught the word for "mother."

"He wants you to bless his nets," said a man in the shadows of a nearby canopy.

"I'm no one's mother," said Jory.

"Couldn't bless it if you were."

Jory looked back at the fisherman, then crouched down to put both hands against the pile of netting. She could feel the sea still clinging to the strands.

"Be full," she whispered, then rose and nodded at the old fisherman. She jumped down from the netting and poked her head under the canopy. A thin man sat on a tall stool smoking a long clay pipe, giving him the appearance of being all limbs. Around him, small bundles of brightly colored cloth stacked up like a merchant stall, but this was not a marketplace, and he'd not been hawking his wares.

"Why you dressed like that?" He waved his pipe at her breeches. "Pretty lady ought to have pretty clothes."

"I'm a sailor."

He leaned forward, half-stepping from his stool, and in a trail of smoke, said, "You're of the sea, but that doesn't make you a sailor."

"Who are you?"

He laughed, white teeth flashing against his skin. He grabbed a bright blue bundle and unrolled it to show a simple dress as he glanced at Jory's face. "Of course not that one." He shook out a crimson bundle into a short sleeveless dress, never once looking away from her eyes. "No?" He tossed it aside. "How about this?"

He seemed to pull the dress out of nowhere. It had bright red sleeves, a striped bodice and a full white skirt. He put it in her hands. "I know who I am. The question is, who are you?"

The fabric was cool and crisp under her fingers. She could almost feel the skirt swishing against her legs. Knew how it would fit against her curves. Knew the stunned looks that would fall in her wake.

She wanted it. Wanted the life that went with it. But that was a life without her father.

Jory laid the dress back down. "I am a sailor." She caressed the striped bodice one last time.

The man caught her hand. "It is yours."

"How much?" asked Jory.

He placed her hand on the dress. "It has always been yours."

The tang of salt air overwhelmed the smell of ships and cargo, stronger than the smell of dye in the clothing arrayed around her. Her heart shifted beat to thrum in time with the waves. She felt her legs draw together and heard voices among the seabirds calling her name.

Jory snatched her hand away from the dress and pressed her fingernails into her palm until the dock steadied beneath her feet. She shook her head and looked down at her toes. Just a bad case of landlegs.

The man sat back on his stool, limbs akimbo as he puffed on his pipe. "Your way is now open."

A cold chill ran up Jory's spine. On shaking legs, she turned and ran back to the *Water Maiden*. She found herself at the bowsprit of the ship. She slid out and dropped down into the space above the fish-tailed figurehead and rested her chin on top of it. The sun reflected off the growing waves pushed ahead of the still-unseen storm. The familiar rocking of the ship lulled away the last traces of anxiety, and Jory closed her eyes.

✵✵✵

A storm raged. Mountains of water rose beneath the ship and then dropped out from beneath it. With a groan and then a splintering crash, the mast broke. Lines snapped and slingshotted across the deck.

A sudden cry turned Jory around. Her mother leaned out over the railing, screaming. Part of the rigging swung and caught her mother in the back, knocking her over the railing into the roiling sea.

Jory screamed, but no sound came out. She swarmed over the railing and ran to the spot but couldn't feel the wet deck beneath her feet. Her father was already at the railing. He scanned the water. Jory's mother reached out of the waves toward him.

He dove, not toward her mother but away.

Jory watched in horror as he surfaced, clutching an oilskin bundle, and struggled back toward the ship. She stood at the railing and watched as her mother sank beneath the waves. She leaned over the rail to scream at her father and found herself falling.

❀❀❀

Jory flailed, managing to catch the figurehead around the waist, and found herself staring at the flaking green paint of the mermaid's tail. Her fingers found a grip just above the mermaid's waist. Jory looked up at where her hands clung to a snake carved around the figure's middle.

She pulled herself up and placed her feet on the hull, straddling the mermaid. She shifted her hands to the second snake around the figurehead's neck. This wasn't a carving of just any mermaid.

Jory hauled herself back on board the *Water Maiden*. The waves in Port Fortune's bay rose higher now. The water looked milky with churning silt. A dark smudge on the horizon blocked out the setting sun, turning the sky a sickly color. Several ships headed out to sea, hoping to outrun the storm. Sea birds had ceased their raucous calls. The air felt like a thick blanket, swallowing sounds.

As the wind rattled the rigging and whistled past the mast, Jory could feel it whispering her name, heard it echoed by the slap of water against the rudder.

Jory turned to face the wind. A branching design denoting the crossroads was drawn on a rain-speckled piece of paper tied to a red and white bundle at the top of the gangplank. Jory picked it up and went inside the cabin.

She paced back and forth, her muscles jittering for movement. A storm rumbled inside her. She unbraided the five braids that held her long black hair tight against her head. Her fingers rippled through hair as it spread and cascaded over her shoulders.

Jory untied the salt-tight knots of her mother's belt, feeling its comforting weight slip from her hips. She lay the belt across her bunk in a sinuous wave. She peeled off her vest and breeches, tossing them to the floor. The string on the cloth bundle snapped beneath her strong fingers. The dress slipped over her head, its crisp cloth smoothing over the curves of her body. She tied her mother's belt back on over the dress.

The door to the cabin opened. Her father held fresh mangoes and a single red hibiscus flower.

He stared at her. "No."

Anger swelled, heightened by her nightmare vision. She would make him tell her the truth. "How did my mother die?"

He set the mangoes on Jory's bunk and carefully laid the flower at the head of her bed. "She was knocked overboard in a storm."

Jory straightened to her full height and advanced, skirt swishing around her ankles. Her father took a step back toward the door.

"You could have saved her."

He raised his hand to protest.

"Do not lie!"

He stepped back through the doorway and onto the deck. "Please."

"I saw! You dove after treasure."

He backed up against the mast. "The greatest treasure."

"She died!"

His face was wet with rain and streaked with tears. "She made me promise."

Jory could feel the sea swelling with storm and anger. The belt around her hips began to writhe, curling on itself into the body of a snake.

"TELL ME!" demanded Jory in a voice like crashing waves.

"I was to love no one but her." Tears streaked down his weathered cheeks faster than the rain fell. "But I could not leave you to the sea." He sank down, falling to his knees on the deck. "I'm sorry, so sorry."

The snake that had been her mother's belt slithered up her torso and laid its great weight over her shoulders. "It was you he chose to save," hissed the snake in her ear before curling around to stare into her eyes.

In the snake's eyes, she saw the end of the vision. Her father pulled himself hand over hand out of the stormy sea, her younger self bundled in the waterproof sling around his neck.

The seas calmed and her mother reappeared from beneath the waves.

"You were sworn to love no one but me yet chose to save her."

Her father clutched little Jory tight against his chest. "She is our child! You are . . . a spirit of the sea."

Her mother gestured, and the sea rose in a giant hand reaching for the bundle around his neck. "She is also of the sea, but you have kept her from it."

"Please. Do not take her from me too."

"If you can keep her from learning the truth, she can stay with you above the sea." The hand of water withdrew. "But she is mami watu, a woman of the water. When she learns the truth, she must join us."

The snake broke Jory's gaze and left her looking at the heap of her father lying on the deck.

"I'm . . ." Jory looked down at her dress and the serpent around her torso and knew she would never be a sailor again. That she might never see her father again. Regret twisted cold and sharp in her belly. "I'm sorry."

She dove over the railing, her legs already joined into a scaled tail beneath her skirt before she touched the stormy sea.

Star Performer

Amber E. Scott

Half Moon

Agate's routine was fixed even in the furnace of summer. She rose at dawn, careful not to wake Jheryl and Lisette, and dressed in a pair of old tights and a loose tunic belted around her waist. The belt had eight holes. At her thinnest, she had used the first hole. Then a sprained ankle had thrown off her routine for several weeks, and she'd slipped down to the second hole and then the third.

She tried for the second this morning, but the metal tongue wouldn't quite go all the way through the hole. Agate's rules were "no straining, no tugging." She adjusted the clasp down to the third hole and slipped out of the tent.

Even this early in the morning, Agate wasn't the only one awake. Melindy, the halfling knife-thrower, sat sharpening her blades. Two clowns sketched new chalk faces on paper. Agate passed the staging ground ringed with benches, which they were using in lieu of a big top—the heat made indoor crowds unbearable. Beyond the staging ground sprawled the horse corral and the caged animals: two lionesses, a muscular but gap-toothed lion, six trained parrots, and a juvenile owlbear they'd found injured on the road.

To the north stood a town. Its name escaped Agate, but all the towns were more or less the same. To the west sprawled an old forest. Its trees were as thick around as Agate, Jheryl, and Lisette put together, and the branches grew into a gnarled canopy. Agate found a birch-ringed clearing, the perfect size for practicing.

She began with a series of stretches. She folded until her forehead touched her knees, then walked her fingers forward and hovered over the ground on knuckles and toes. Handstands and headstands followed. She kept her eyes on the trees that now stretched from the sky down into a blue void.

By the time she finished her somersaults, cartwheels, and handsprings, the glade had grown uncomfortably warm. Her back and thighs quivered. Agate's mind drifted to breakfast. Then she remembered the third hole on her belt, did twenty backflips, and walked on her hands until her wrists screamed.

When she righted herself, dizziness swept over her. She had to rest against a tree, despite the gnawing in her stomach. The smell of her sweat lingered in the clearing. When Agate felt sufficiently recovered, she headed to the mess tent.

The mess was always packed in the few hours between the afternoon and evening shows. Chickens, some purchased, some traded for admission, roasted over a pit fire just outside the tent, while their eggs fried on butter-soaked skillets. Cheese wedges, crusty bread, chard leaves, raw carrots, dried apples, and fresh berries sat piled atop a trestle table in the center of the room. Agate's stomach groaned.

Before she could talk herself into a pile of greasy chicken pieces or a wedge of acrid yellow cheese, she piled her plate with carrots, a single egg, and a small piece of bread. She was eyeing some dried apples, curled like scraps of parchment, when Jheryl's voice knifed through the din.

"Aggie—Aggie! Over here!"

Agate picked her way through the crowd and slid onto the bench next to Jheryl. Jheryl was so slight that she seemed to leave a hollow of space next to her, a space Agate filled to overflowing. Lisette sat across from them, sky-blue eyes unfocused and distant. The cousins were almost identical with their sunny hair, oval faces with high, sharp cheekbones, and primrose-pink lips. Agate stood out next to them with her rough, dark hair and freckled face.

Kalem sat next to Lisette. Agate's heart sped up at the sight of him. The circus wizard had a magic act in the show, but he also used his incantations to enhance the other performances. One of Kalem's tricks, a shower of shivering colored lights, trailed after Lisette when she took center ring in the aerial show. He was only a few inches taller than Agate, with dark skin and hair cut close against his scalp. The clowns painted runic tattoos on him before each show.

Agate nodded hello and fell to cutting the ragged edges off her fried egg. One of her rules was to cut the egg into a perfect circle before eating it, leaving the trimmings on her plate. If her knife slipped or the circle was lopsided, she had to try again, cutting the circle ever smaller.

She trimmed in silence for a few minutes, listening to Jheryl and Lisette discuss last night's performance.

"You were sparkling!" Jheryl gushed to Lisette.

Lisette played down her talent. "Oh no, I was positively wooden."

Neither of them mentioned Agate's performance. Agate said nothing and tried not to stare at Jheryl's hands as the woman tore her bread into quarters. Acrobats, especially trapeze artists, required strong wrists and calloused hands that could suffer abuse. Jheryl's hands were small and delicate, the blue veins showing through her skin. Lisette joked that Jheryl had bird bones.

When the egg was perfectly round, Agate cut it into quarters and nibbled methodically on each one, stopping as close as possible to the yolk, which she saved for last. She felt Kalem's gaze on her and kept her head down, unwilling to risk eye contact. He might say something about her routine, and she wasn't sure how to explain her rules. The rules made sense to Agate, but she had developed each one individually from year to year. Out of context, to an outsider, the rules seemed strange.

She finished her egg and began dicing the carrots into tiny cubes. On her best days, she could make three carrots last a full hour. She wasn't done dicing even the first one when Lisette said, "Is that all you're eating?"

"Yes." Without thinking, Agate looked up and accidentally met Kalem's eyes. She blushed.

Jheryl sniffed audibly. "Practicing again this morning? You are a dedicated soul, Aggie."

"I wish I had your discipline," Lisette added, tearing a strip of meat off a glistening chicken bone.

Agate stood abruptly. "Yes, well, some of us aren't lucky enough to have an elven grandmother." She stepped over the bench seat and marched out of the tent.

She stopped outside, blinking against tears and the dazzling suddenness of the sun. The tent flap rustled behind her. She turned, ready to lay into Jheryl. Instead, Kalem stood before her.

"Oh—uh—"

"Everything all right?" He put a hand on her shoulder and guided her out of the path of three jugglers.

"I'm sorry. I didn't mean to snap like that. I should be used to it by now."

"Used to what?"

"The teasing." Kalem looked blank. Agate spread her hands. "Twitting me about all the practicing I do. I have to. They have elf blood. They're naturally that thin and strong. I have to work for it. I have to keep to my routines. If I don't . . ."

"If you don't?"

"Bad things happen."

"You look great to me," Kalem said.

Agate flushed. "I wasn't fishing for flattery."

"I'm not trying to flatter you. I'm saying that you're as talented as they are." He brushed a lock of hair from her face then dropped his hand to rest briefly on her upper arm. "Plus, you're strong enough to be a catcher. Not everyone is."

She jerked away. "I'm not staying a catcher forever." She hugged herself, rubbing her arms briskly as if cold. As if she could rub away the muscle that kept her arms so thick. "If I keep to my routines, I'll be a flyer someday. Just watch."

Before Kalem could reply, Agate turned on her heel and stalked back to her tent.

❀❀❀

At midnight, Agate lay motionless in her cot, listening to Jheryl and Lisette whisper outside.

The afternoon show had gone well. They began with a floor show: tumbling and handsprings. Then they moved to the tightropes, dancing across wires almost too narrow to see from the ground. Last was the trapeze act, where Jheryl and Lisette threw themselves headlong into nothingness, turning over like dried flowers blowing in a breeze, and Agate caught them. The girls were dazzling, flashing through the air, and Agate was the solid presence with her legs pinched around a wooden dowel, ready to clasp them in her arms and drag them back to reality.

In the evening performance, though, she'd felt dizzy climbing the scaffolding. Colored lanterns that burned with heatless light, courtesy of Kalem, lit the staging area. The ring was open to the stars pulsing above. Jheryl's and Lisette's costumes, sewn with sequins, gleamed in the lantern light and left trails like fireflies in the dark. Agate, swinging from her bar, blinked near the end of the routine and saw double. She grabbed at a soaring Lisette, hoping she'd picked the right image.

Agate's fingers closed clumsily over Lisette's forearms. The murmured "gotcha" that signaled safety was slow coming from her lips. Lisette tightened her grip and made a sound of concern.

"Gotcha," Agate had whispered quickly. But she was shaken.

Now, in the darkness, she could think of nothing but the abandoned food on her plate that morning. She had gone back for carrots and bread between performances, but the ritual had been ruined. That was why she'd fumbled in the evening.

Agate slid her hands over her hips in the dark. Her hip bones curved up on either side of her stomach like blades. She liked those curves of bones. Her thighs, though. And her waist, wrapped with muscles.

She was so thick.

Jheryl and Lisette crawled into their cots. They practiced every day, but only once a day, and never minded what they ate. Agate lay still and tried not to think about how hungry she was. She was used to being hungry, of course, every day. But the routine kept the pangs manageable.

The cousins finally fell asleep. Agate dressed in the dark—belt buckled in the third hole—and stole outside.

Not a breath of breeze stirred the humid air. Voices and laughter drifted from the staging area, where the performers celebrated another successful show. Agate turned away from the merriment and picked her way to the edge of camp.

I'll practice until dawn, she thought. That will help.

Then she heard music.

The sound was faint. Agate thought for a moment she was imagining things. The camp was behind her now, and all that lay ahead was a stretch of fallow field and then the forest. She stopped and held her breath.

There it was again, just on the cusp of hearing—high-pitched and lilting. She followed the music across the strip of grass and stepped cautiously into the forest.

Agate's cotton tunic clung to her skin like a damp blanket. Leaves hung limply from the trees around her, bathed in the silvery light of the half moon. For a moment, Agate worried about forest creatures, but the music gripped her. A wailing note soared higher and higher before tumbling into a jangle of bells. Low notes thrummed out as the bells quieted. There was nothing now but the low, quivering tones, like a heartbeat. A flute sighed into the stillness between beats.

Agate saw a spark of light up ahead, a brightness that flickered and died and then flared up again. She crept forward until she reached the edge of the light. She knew where she was now. This was the clearing where she had practiced at dawn.

It was greatly changed.

The birch trees looked spectral in the moonlight. A harlequin fire leaped and crackled in the center of the clearing. Motley sparks snapped off the fire and flitted through the dark, twining like garlands along branches. The music came from nowhere and everywhere, the notes springing up from the ground like grass.

Creatures twirled on the green. Bare-chested men with shaggy legs and golden horns that curved from their temples. Women no taller than Melindy, jewel-toned gossamer wings stretching from their shoulder blades. Men that would fit in the palm of Agate's hand, hair made of water and eyes like river stones. Androgynous figures leaning down from the trees, skin rippling like birch bark and hair tangled with leaves.

Agate crouched in the shadows and watched, breathless. The dancers danced on. It could have been minutes or hours later when one dancer stopped right in front of Agate.

The dancer's skin was shadowed like twilight, and her eyes glimmered green. Silver hair clouded around her lean figure, concealing and revealing as if stirred by a wind.

"You look hungry," she said.

The music stopped. The dancers stopped.

Agate found herself on the receiving end of countless alien stares. "I'm sorry, I didn't mean—I heard your music, and it was so beautiful—"

The silver-haired woman studied her. "The forest knows your face," she said. Her voice sounded like the wind in the trees and those jangling bells and the aerial silks falling to the ground. "You danced here as the night waned and the sun took to the sky."

"I was practicing," Agate said. Her tongue rasped in her sandpaper mouth. "My routine. I'm an acrobat."

The woman clasped her hands together. "Show us, then! The movements of mortals are beautiful to behold."

"Oh." Agate stammered. "I don't know."

"When mortals dance . . ." The woman trailed off.

The creatures in the glade began to move. They picked up their dance but gently, silently. The woman swayed in place.

"When mortals dance," she murmured, eyes closed, "it is as if they will never die."

Agate hugged her knees and dared not move. She had heard stories about the dangers of a faerie revel. Men and women who joined in the moonlit dance and died on their feet from exhaustion. Others who danced with the fae for a night and returned home to find a hundred years had passed. She rose from her crouch, preparing to flee.

The woman's eyes opened. "Will you not stay? We could teach you many things. You could learn the grace of the rill and the strength of the reed. The trick of falling from the sky like dandelion fluff."

Agate straightened but didn't run. A new kind of hunger whined in her gut.

The creatures danced even more slowly in the glade. Their exaggerated movements cast creeping shadows on the ground. A lone violin began playing a sweet, simple melody. The silver-haired woman spoke more quietly. "We could teach you to step as lightly as a sylph, to grow as slender as a shadow. All for a single show, here in the moonlight . . ."

The stories of lost mortals flashed through Agate's mind. She swallowed and forced herself to speak. "I can't. I'm sorry."

One of the winged women stepped forward and proffered a hand. In the center of her miniature palm sat a square of yellow cake topped with a ruby-red berry. The smell of warm cake and sugary berry hit Agate like a fist. Her mouth erupted with saliva.

"If you cannot stay," the silver-haired woman said, "you at least can eat before you go."

The scent was overwhelming. Before she could stop herself, Agate snatched up the cake and popped it in her mouth.

Sweetness exploded on her tongue. The berry was so fresh and intense it made her teeth hurt. The cake melted away like a dream on her tongue. She closed her eyes without meaning to, lost in the flavor. The music soared, drums and flutes joining the violin.

Agate opened her eyes. The dancers were moving faster now, too fast. They blurred together in a smear of light. The harlequin fire blazed up, a bonfire now. A gentle hand tugged on her arm.

Agate moved forward, lost in the music and yearning for another taste of cake.

✖✖✖

"Aggie! Aggie!"

Agate came awake with a start. She was on her cot in the tent. Her head felt fuzzy, and her mouth was dry. She felt like she'd spent the night drunk.

She sat bolt upright as she remembered.

Jheryl tugged fretfully on the sheet. "Aggie, do wake up. It's almost time, and you're not even dressed!"

Agate tumbled out of bed, pushing away the fractured memories from the night before. There had been wonderful music. She had refused to perform. The fae had attempted to coax her into a somersault, a single backflip. She had held firm.

There had been no more cake. But the silver-haired woman had taken her to the fire and fed her one of its sparks. The spark had burned on the way down and filled her belly with quivering energy.

"What will this cost me?" she remembered asking.

The silver-haired woman had replied, "Are you afraid we will demand what you are unwilling to pay?"

Agate had tried to think of what she wouldn't pay and came up blank.

And then it had all blurred together and gone dark.

"Hurry up! Here, I brought you lunch. We couldn't wake you for breakfast. You slept like the dead."

Agate changed out of her sweat-soaked tunic and into her tight sequined one. While Jheryl fixed her hair, Agate took a bite of toasted bread. She almost spit it out but forced herself to swallow. The bread tasted like sawdust.

She tried a slice of dried apple, but it had no flavor either. It might as well have been parchment.

"Not good enough?" Jheryl said waspishly, seeing the abandoned breakfast.

"I'm not hungry," Agate said and realized it was true. She felt satisfied and strong, full of energy. She stretched and glanced at herself in the glass.

She looked thinner today.

✾✾✾

That day, Agate was spectacular. Her floor show was perfect. The tightrope was solid ground under her feet. The movements came easily, the way she'd always seen them in her mind. Applause rang in her ears.

Kalem was watching. When she skipped off the staging area, he caught her eye and gave her a nod.

She passed up dinner. The feeling of satiety remained, and the bite of cheese she tried tasted like putty.

That night, she felt stronger than ever. She added an extra tumble on her dismount, and Lisette frowned prettily at the sight.

After the show, Jheryl gushed, "You were sparkling tonight, Agate! Truly!"

By the end of the week, she was down to the second hole on her belt.

FULL MOON

They pulled up stakes and rolled on to their next show. As the days slipped by, Agate made excuses to avoid meals. She never felt hungry for food anymore. Instead, a craving to practice and perform filled her. At every show, she felt lit from within, strong and limber and slimmer than ever. She often dreamed of rehearsing among the trees in a moonlit glade.

After one evening's show, on the way back to her tent, Agate looked up at the darkened sky. It's happening, she thought. I'm going to be a star.

Was that a shuffled step behind her? Soft laughter in the underbrush?

She turned, but there was nothing there.

Agate went to sleep, and when she woke, Jheryl was gone.

✾✾✾

"Who?" Kalem asked, his brow furrowed.

"Jheryl. You know. The other flyer."

Kalem raised one eyebrow. "Lisette's our only flyer."

Two single cots stood in the acrobats' tent. Two boxes of face paint stood on the dressing table. Two sets of clothes hung on the line.

Am I going crazy? Agate thought. *Or is everyone else?*

Agate sat on the edge of her cot, rubbing her hands together. "She was real," she said out loud. "She was here."

Blue veins showed beneath the skin of her arms and hands. Her wrists had slimmed down, slender as saplings. She flexed her strong, delicate hands and thought, *Bird bones.*

She'd woken feeling particularly radiant. Sparkling, as Jheryl used to say. Her stomach had felt warm and full but remained delightfully flat. Her lips had tingled as if she'd been eating something tart. She'd wiped her mouth, half-expecting a sticky red smear. Berry juice, like the berry atop the fairy cake.

But her hand had been clean.

✪✪✪

The circus followed the trade road towards the capital. Though the larger, more practiced troupes were the ones to play in the city, there were plenty of villages and towns along the route happy to trade for entertainment.

Everything Lisette did hypnotized Agate. She watched Lisette covertly as the woman dressed and painted her face. She watched her eat, watched her rehearse, even woke at night to watch her sleep. Watching Lisette became one of the rules.

One night before bed, Agate said, "We did a good job today, the two of us."

"Yes." Lisette stood, brushing her hair before the mirror.

Agate stared at Lisette's willowy legs. The woman could press her knees together and her thighs wouldn't touch.

Lisette frowned, as if trying to grasp a fleeting thought.

"Something wrong?" Agate asked.

"No. I was thinking about my grandmother."

"The elf?"

Lisette nodded. "I haven't seen her in years, and for the last few weeks, I keep feeling . . . well, homesick. It's strange. I was never homesick before."

Agate's mouth went dry. "Do you have a large family?"

"Not really. Just my parents and grandmother, and . . . and one aunt. Still, I miss them." Lisette shook her head as if coming out of a dream. "Silly of me. I'd much rather be in the show than wasting my time back home. I was thinking this afternoon about our handsprings. I believe we could do four instead of three and then cartwheel back to the center. What do you think?"

"Sure, we can practice in the morning."

"Practice, practice. That's all you do." Lisette set down the brush and climbed into her cot. She said no more of her family tree or any missing leaves on the branches, but Agate could think of nothing else all night.

The next evening, she sought out Kalem.

They sat on a bench next to the staging ground, where the other performers made merry, Lisette among them. Agate tracked Lisette with her eyes as she told Kalem about the fae. Kalem listened without interrupting. He lit his fingers with purple flames and then snuffed them out again as Agate spoke. When she finished, he said, "And you can't remember what bargain you struck?"

"I didn't strike one," she said. "I'm sure of it. I refused to perform. That's what traps you, isn't it?"

"There are many ways to make a bargain." Kalem leaned forward, elbows on his knees. "The fae don't give up their secrets for nothing."

"Am I stuck, then? What if . . . what if they ask for something bad?"

"Bargains are easily struck, more difficult to break. I'm not an expert on fae by any means, but I've read a few stories." He turned his head, met her gaze. "If you want, I can look into the matter. Try to find something in one of my books."

Agate broke the look.

Lisette trilled a laugh that floated above the noise of the crowd.

"Yes. Please," Agate said.

The next morning, Lisette was gone.

NEW MOON

The scaffolds had been raised for the tightrope and aerial silks but not the trapeze. Agate couldn't do a trapeze act by herself.

She dressed for the evening show, muscles aching from the morning's practice, followed by the afternoon show, and then a shorter practice. Agate practiced three times a day now. Every day she got better. Every day she performed for bored country folk, farmers who needed a break from the fields, and wives who had never set foot out of town. Small towns that had never seen like of her talent before and therefore had no idea how talented she was.

They laughed heartily at the clowns who came after her and applauded just as loudly. They left when the show ended.

Agate smoothed her hands over the perfectly flat plane that had once been a more rounded belly. Her belt buckled loosely in the first hole.

"Knock, knock." Kalem poked his head through the tent flap. Agate turned and nodded to him. He stepped inside. He held a thick book bound in blue leather in his arms.

"I found something," he said.

Agate's stomach gurgled. She sat down on the edge of her cot. "What is it?"

"There are ways to break a bargain with the fae." Kalem sat down next to her. He opened the book to a sketch of a woman with light pouring out of her mouth. Her features were twisted in agony. In the background, two eyes peered from the shadows. "You said you ate a spark that looked like a star?"

Agate nodded.

Kalem said, "It seems that spark created a link inside you, between you and the realm of the fae. The Eternal Twilight."

"A link?" Agate frowned. "In my stomach?"

"Well . . . it's not literally a portal. Everything you eat doesn't fall through into another world. You'd starve to death, right?"

Agate said nothing.

Kalem continued. "The fae are drawing something from you, though, and feeding you with whatever you asked for. Talent, you said?"

"Something like that."

"Well, you're certainly the most talented acrobat I've ever seen. And you always have been." He shut the book. His shoulder brushed hers. "I've always admired you, and not just since the bargain."

Agate stood up. She hugged herself, feeling the long bones in her arms. "That's kind of you to say."

Kalem stood up and stepped around to face her. Their eyes met. "Agate . . . I'd like to help you. There are ways to sever the link, to purge you of the connection."

Agate glanced down at the anguished expression of the illustrated woman. "Not very pleasant ways, it appears."

"I told you, bargains are more easily made than broken. And remember, the fae never make square deals. Whatever price they're asking, it's not worth it."

"Will everything go back to the way it was?"

"Maybe. Whatever they gave you, they'll try to take back."

"And what if I gave them something not easily returned?" Agate pressed her knees together. Her thighs curved around empty space, like a wishbone.

Kalem took her chin in his hand. She started but didn't pull away. "Is there something you're not telling me?"

She tried to speak, but the words caught in her throat. She pulled away from his touch and dropped her gaze. "No."

Kalem bowed his head. He left her standing there, next to the single cot. She thought she heard a whisper from the shadows beneath the cot, but when she bent to look, nothing was there.

❀❀❀

Agate sparkled again that night. The audience oohed and aahed at the right moments. They showered her with applause when she landed. She walked off, and no one followed.

I want to be a flyer, she thought. But there was no one who could catch her. *Maybe we could have auditions*, she started to think, but then she remembered what was likely to happen to anyone who joined her troupe.

I'm still the star, she thought.

She slipped her hand into the space between her waist and her belt. There was room to wiggle her fingers.

She was hungry.

Kalem waited next to her tent. Agate stopped before he saw her. She imagined trying to tell him what she suspected her bargain was. Who had paid the price for her stellar talent.

She turned and crept away.

The night was pitch black. Agate picked her way carefully in the dark. She was exhausted and hungry. She hadn't done her third practice yet. When you break the routine, she thought, bad things happen.

Soft grass stretched before her. The sounds of the circus had faded away. She did a forward roll, sprang to her feet, did two back handsprings, and then somersaulted again. She couldn't see her hands before her face.

Agate unfolded into a handstand. The stars swam around her feet. She walked forward on her hands into a patch of moonlight.

Wait, she thought. *There's no moon tonight.*

A crash of applause shattered the silence. Agate almost lost her balance. She flipped forward and righted herself, staggering with the rush of blood from her head.

A full moon hung heavy in the sky, swollen larger than any moon Agate had ever seen. The sky glowed a dim silver-gray, as if caught between day and night. The field had vanished, and she now stood in a forest of pale trees with jade-green leaves. The goat-legged men, the tiny jewel-winged fairies, the tree folk, and the water gnomes sat arrayed around her.

The silver-haired woman stepped forward. "You found your way."

"Where am I?" Agate spun a full circle. "What happened to the circus?"

"It continues on, as it always has. One small town to another." The woman's green eyes caught Agate's and held them. "You have practiced with starlight in your blood. Have you learned what you sought to learn?"

"Where are the others? Jheryl and Lisette?"

"They are here, with you." The silver-haired woman brushed her fingers across Agate's stomach. "But you are the star. And we hunger for a show."

She looked up, and Agate followed her gaze. Two trees grew taller than the rest. A trapeze hung from one. Two tree-folk with gnarled arms of oak waited to catch her.

The fae and the forest both were utterly silent. Agate stared at the trapeze for long moments. Music bubbled up from the ground.

She began to climb.

BLIGHT

JEFFREY SCOTT PETERSEN
& CHRISTIE YANT

Melora was only eight years old and not yet a hero on the day that her childhood came to an end.

The sky above the hills was pink and gold, and her shadow stretched out in front of her like the tallest clown in the puppet show. She and her best friend June skipped back toward the village walls, holding hands and singing:

> *Pay the tithe at circle stones*
> *Tinkling bells and weirdling lights*
> *Past the Queen of Fairy's throne*
> *The woods of bone belong to Blight . . .*

Their song faltered, and their steps slowed as they approached the gate. Where only the young guard Rory should have stood, polishing his armor and looking bored, there were now four men, armed with swords and pikes.

"You two," shouted one, "get inside the walls. Quickly, now."

The girls did as they were told.

Something was wrong. Melora could tell, the way she could tell a storm was coming by the dark smudge above the hills and the rich smell of wet grass on the wind. They went to June's house first. Her father, a carpenter, was still at work in his shop, sanding shields instead of chests and window frames. A cluster of adults stood around his shop, talking urgently. They all fell silent when the girls walked into the room.

June's father smiled, and so did some of the others, but they only smiled with their mouths, not their eyes.

"I better go," said Melora. "Bye, Junebug."

"Yeah. Bye, Mela."

❀❀❀

Melora's mother brushed her hair for bed even though the sun had barely set, her strokes hurried and less gentle than usual, tugging so hard that it hurt. She sang their bedtime song as she brushed, but her voice was wrong—rough and sharp as if she'd been crying or trying not to shout.

> *To bed, to bed, now hide your head*
> *The dark belongs to Blight*
> *From deep within her forest dead*
> *She carves the bones at night.*

"To bed now," her mother said, "like the song says, or Blight will come in the night and spirit disobedient children away."

"Blight's not real," her brother Tomas said. "She's a made-up story, everybody knows that." But Melora wasn't sure at all.

"Not another word," their mother said. "Upstairs, now."

Melora crawled into her bed and listened to Tomas toss and turn. She stared up at the thatched ceiling and wondered if she would hear anything when Blight stole into her room to carry her away.

❀❀❀

The bang of the front door startled her out of troubled dreams. Angry voices carried up the stairs. Melora crept on silent feet to the landing to eavesdrop on the frightened adults.

"Nine feet tall if it's an inch," a man said. "I only got away because Hammond didn't."

"The wall will keep it out," a woman said. "It held the Northmen for a hundred years. It can stop this mountain lion, no matter how big."

"It weren't no lion," the man said. "Hammond stabbed it, and it didn't bleed.

It stood up on two legs, his sword still in its gut, and killed him with a single blow. Gods help me but I ran. I fought a mountain lion once, but you can't fight what won't be killed."

"We've strong men and sharp swords," said June's father.

"Hammond was strong, and his sword was sharp, as were the dozen other men we've lost. It's not enough."

"Then attack it where it lives," said Melora's mother. "Kill it while it sleeps. All things must sleep, even monsters."

A chair creaked and the floor shook with the familiar thump-thump-thump of her father's pacing.

"I haven't slept in three days," he said. "I sit up all night with my sword in my lap for all the good it will do. We've naught but words. The monster hungers. Our swords do it no harm. It kills our best every night, and tomorrow, it may be one of us disappears in the dark."

Melora crept back to her bed. She wondered if June knew that her father was here and if she knew about the monster. Her parents had always told her that monsters weren't real. *Nine feet tall and doesn't bleed.* Monsters were real—real enough to kill Hammond, the smiling shepherd who loved dancing and named every one of his sheep. She would never see him dance at the harvest festival again. A tight knot in her chest wouldn't go away.

Melora pulled her covers up over her head and told herself that her father and mother would keep her safe, like parents always did. The men would kill the monster, and someday, it would be nothing but a song for children to sing while skipping rope. She thought of songs about how they defeated the Northmen and of songs about how to trick the spirits at the bottom of a well. For the first time, she wondered if all of those songs and stories were true and not just playful rhymes and tunes to dance to.

If they were true, well . . . she knew lots of stories and songs about Blight.

✹✹✹

The men that came to the door the next day looked ashen and sick with worry. When one started to speak, Melora's father shushed him and stepped outside, closing the door behind him.

Melora lingered by the door, straining to hear what was said.

"The chirurgeon had to take Marc's arm," a voice said, "but he'll likely live.

Monster tore right through the wall of his house. Half the roof caved in. That's the only thing that saved him. It couldn't pull the wood back fast enough to eat him before the guard came. It took ten men to drive the beast back over the wall, and only three of those are fit to walk."

Blood pounded in Melora's ears. It had come over the wall. It had broken into June's house and hurt her father. They just lived down the road. She ran to her mother.

"Mama—" Her mother gave her a sharp look that silenced her for a moment, but she felt as if she might burst. "Is Daddy going to kill the monster?" Melora whispered.

"Someone will," was all her mother would say.

The door opened with a bang, and her father hurried in, his face set in a determined scowl, and headed straight to where his sword hung on the wall.

"No," said her mother. "You have a family."

"I am thinking of my family! And Marc's, and Emon's. We have to end this now, whether it takes a dozen swords or a boulder dropped on its head. We'll call up the devil himself to take it to hell if we have to."

Melora ran to him and hugged him. He kneeled and hugged her back, smoothing her hair as she cried into his shirt.

"Don't go, Daddy," she said.

"Be good and help your mother. I have to go, but I'll be back soon."

She followed her mother to the kitchen without complaint, fighting back tears and sniffling into her apron. If only they knew how to kill it, how to trap it and starve it, or poison it—a new thought struck her.

"What do fairies like best?" she asked as she carefully put away the wooden bowls.

"I don't know," her mother said. She'd been washing the same plate for some time now. *Don't worry, Mama,* Melora thought. *I have an idea.* "Milk and bread, I've heard. The same things children like, I suppose."

Maybe some fairies, Melora thought, but not Blight. Milk would sour, bread would mold.

"What would Blight like best?"

"Why? Do you want to take her a birthday present?" her mother teased. When Melora didn't answer, only looking at her mother with a silent plea, she creased her brow in thought. "Well, doesn't she like bones?"

"She already has a lot of bones."

"That's true. She would probably want something she doesn't have."

That night, listening to the sound of her mother weeping in the next room, Melora thought about her plan.

> *Pay the tithe at circle stones*
> *Tinkling bells and weirdling lights*
> *Past the Queen of Fairy's throne*
> *The woods of bone belong to Blight.*

What doesn't she have? Blight in her dark forest of bone trees—what would she like best?

❀❀❀

Walls weren't strong enough, swords weren't sharp enough, and men and women were too few to keep them safe, to keep June and her father safe in their own house. But there was one thing that nothing could survive, not even a monster.

Melora knew it was dangerous to bargain with fairies. They were tricky and untrue, and the one she needed to bargain with now was the most dangerous of them all. But she thought she knew what Blight would want most in the world.

She crept out of her silent house, its bright red walls black in the moonlight. Down the street, June's house was in ruins. The front wall was staved in, the door split like kindling. All the fine woodwork lay in pieces, scored by stone claws.

In the wreckage near the back, she found them: smashed pots in the shadowed moonlight. Only five were miraculously unharmed among the shattered pieces. She packed them into a wooden box and added it to the contents of her thin, patched sack. She slung this over her shoulder, along with the water skin Rory had given her when he'd seen her and June come home late one too many times, and made her way to the village wall.

Melora kept to the shadows, avoiding the few men who patrolled the base of the wall with torches and pikes. She'd expected a phalanx of glittering spears, but maybe the soldiers had gone home to guard their families or gone off to hunt the monster.

She waited near the breach where the monster had torn through, her heart beating as fast as a rabbit's. She waited as a guard walked past, then scrambled over the pile of stone and threw herself face-down into the tall grass. She lay motionless, the cold seeping through her shirt, but no one called out, so she picked her way forward from bush to tree, until at last, her feet were on the well-worn road.

Melora ran as far and as fast as she could, ignoring the ache in her feet, until the biting in her side made her slow. She sucked at the water skin to soothe the ache in her throat. How much farther? She ran on through chill clouds of her own pinched breath.

Eight smooth stones poked up through the goat-cropped grass. They came up to her knees and were almost as long as Melora was tall. On each stone was the mark of a different guild: the hammer and chisel of the stone workers, the crossed saws of the wood workers, brush and paints of the artisans, bone saw and leeches of the chirurgeons, and several that she didn't recognize, including a jar with a long, thin neck hovering over a fire and a bear holding a feather.

The circle stones. She walked around them, wondering where she should pay and how much, when the soft sound of chiming bells behind her made her turn. Through the thorns that lined the road, lights winked like pyrite in a streambed. She remembered the words of the song:

> *Pay the tithe at circle stones*
> *Tinkling bells and weirdling lights*
> *Past the Queen of Fairy's throne*
> *The woods of bone belong to Blight.*

She warily approached the thicket where the bells tinkled. With one hand, she rubbed the iron ring she kept on a red ribbon around her neck, and with the other, she carefully pushed aside the brambles. Inside lay another, smaller circle of stones, ancient and worn smooth by wind and rain. The twinkling lights scattered into the brush, and the bells stopped as she stepped through the brambles and into the circle. She could feel eyes upon her as she produced a muffin and three pennies from her sack. She left them in the center of the circle and waited expectantly, hoping it was enough.

The silence grew deeper still. The lights winked out.

Taking this for permission, she almost forgot the ache in her feet. Pleased with herself, Melora walked on into the territory of the fey.

Past the fairy stones, the air grew colder and the stars disappeared. The road narrowed until it was barely more than a deer track. She had walked an hour, maybe more—it was hard to tell here in the endless twilight—when she came to a wall, impossibly high, blocking the road. It was old and crumbling, held up by creeping vines.

Against the wall stood a marble slab carved with the figure of a tall woman, draped in leaves, her face worn flat and featureless. A square of stone lay by her feet. Long ago, this would have been an impressive throne for any queen, but time and weather had stolen its glory.

> *Tarry not to breathe the air*
> *Pile the stones the devil's height*
> *Twelve spans high or ill you'll fare*
> *When o'er the wall comes Blight.*

Melora's small feet found easy footholds. *The devil must be very tall.* From the top of the wall, she could see the road widen again on the other side, lined with dense and thorny brush. She dropped to the ground and fell, skinning her knees on fallen stones.

Black, twisted mushrooms sprang up alongside the road, and shriveled fruit clung reluctantly to sharp branches overhead. The ground, littered with skeletons of birds and mice so numerous she couldn't avoid them, crunched beneath her feet.

Somewhere in this dead forest was the blight fairy, who poisoned everything she touched and turned the world around her into dust and bone.

Except the trees weren't bone at all, Melora realized. They were just dead, their bark scoured away, leaving only smooth gray wood. And the curves and crevasses weren't teeth or knuckles but intricate carvings: blooming flowers and snaking vines, an imitation of life where nothing but death remained. Some were stained a faded rusty brown, as if painted long ago in blood. The air was still and dry and smelled like nothing. Not soil, not dust—emptiness.

> *Tarry not to breathe the air—*

She should go no further. She twisted the ribbon around her iron ring nervously between her fingers as she slowed.

"Blight!" she called, her voice shaking. "Blight, we need your help!"

HELP?

The voice came from everywhere, a scratching whisper that made the chill air colder, the dead forest darker, and raised the hairs on her arms and neck. Melora bunched her shoulders. She searched the branches for the source of the sound, and even in this endless gloaming, she thought she saw movement, something darker than the tangled trees. A twisted shadow, thin and ropey. The voice came again.

HELP?

Was it answering or just repeating the word?

"A monster is killing us. It's nine feet tall and doesn't bleed. Swords can't kill it. It comes at night and takes people. I think it eats them."

MONSTER.

"Yes," Melora said and wiped her nose with the back of her hand. "You're a kind of monster too, aren't you? But maybe one monster could beat another. I brought you something. I hope that maybe if you like it, you'll help us. Like a bargain. Please?"

She pulled the box from her pack and set it among the tiny bones in the road and backed away until she thought she was far enough for safety.

"If you like them," she said. "You have to come with me. You have to save us from the monster."

❀❀❀

Blight skittered down from the treetops on thin, precise legs, her head darting from side to side, her shoulders swaying the way the brittle trees in her forest once did. She circled the box, examining it from all sides. With one sharp finger, she traced the carvings across the hinged lid. Crude. Not as elegant as her own but cut into shapes she recognized—leaves, petals, vines.

She snatched up the box and scurried back to her hollow tree before the girl could change her mind and take it back. Her eyes grew softer as she turned the box slowly, walking her fingers over the carved images, black travelers leaving dead, gray footprints in the wood, until the whole box had gone from a rich burgundy to cracked ash.

She turned it over and over, listening to the rattle inside of something hard and substantial. Her head bobbed slowly as she lifted it to her ear, making it clink, clink, clink, then brought it down in front of her again and flicked the tarnished latch open with a knife-sharp nail.

Inside were five small, glazed brown pots, each stoppered with cork. She picked one up and turned it carefully, holding it up in the dim, diffuse light. She sniffed at it, and her lips peeled back at the mellow tang of earth and minerals. She pried the stopper out of the jar and dropped it, only at the last moment snatching it, tumbling, from the air.

Blight reached into the jar with the tip of a withered finger and withdrew it slowly. Green. She stared at her fingertip and waited for the green to turn to brown, to black. Waited for the shining liquid to dry into ash and blow away—but it did not.

GREEN.

She rubbed it on the back of her hand, admiring it. She rubbed her thumb and finger together, spreading the paint.

She began to dip her finger in again and hesitated, then carefully replaced the stopper. It had been so long since she had seen green. She placed the jar back in the box, and something else caught her eye. The side of one pot had something on it, a drip down the side from where the stopper met the lip of the jar—

YELLOW.

She snatched it from the box and held it up in the faint light before her eyes darted back to other jars.

On another, a drop of red. There, a splatter of blue. The last one she saw was white—true white, chalk white, not the dirty gray of her trees that matched the always-overcast sky above. Not the fading gray of old bone.

Her fingers danced back and forth across the jars. The mineral colors stayed true. She snapped the lid shut, then opened it a crack to peer inside before snapping it shut again. She pressed the box tight against her chest and climbed down to the forest floor.

She imagined her forest above transformed by her new treasure, the gray leaves and vines painted a vivid green, the petals a yellow that would never turn to rust, to soot. She raised a hand, her fingers pinched together in a crude mime of holding a paintbrush. She stared into the distance, still as stone, caught up in her fantasy, then scurried back up her tree to secret her treasure away from the girl who would bargain with Blight.

MONSTER.

Out on the road, Melora waited until she was sure the creature wasn't coming back. She dropped her head, defeated, and turned to go.

Blight followed at a distance, nodding, rubbing green across her fingers, where it dried and flaked away, leaving a faint trail of color reaching out from the heart of the dead forest.

BARGAIN.

❀❀❀

Leaving the gray forest was even harder for Melora than entering it had been. Where she had hope before, there was only grief at her own failure. It had seemed like such a good plan—she had thought herself so smart. Now her feet felt heavy, and her heart ached. The climb over the wall seemed even longer than it had before.

At the circle stones, she could see how far she'd come the night before. The town lay in the distance, hills and rooftops bathed in golden light, white-painted windmills turning lazily in the breeze. Stretches of green sprinkled with wildflowers, orange, purple, blue. After a single night among the dead, silent trees, the riot of colors were spears thrust into her eyes, and the sounds of the birds and insects were a painful din.

She pinched her eyes shut, peering at the over-saturated world through fluttering eyelashes, and for a moment, she considered retreating back to the shadows with her failure.

She turned, and over the wall came Blight.

❀❀❀

Blight shielded her sensitive eyes with her hand, the slick membranes that slid over them not enough against the sun. She scrambled over the wall and came down on all fours in the grass. The wind blew up a dust devil, pulling black flakes of dead grass high into the air, spinning across the wide circle of bare, cracked ground that spread around her. She stepped through the pillar of rising air, cocking her head in the direction of the town. Saliva pooled at the corners of her mouth. She watched a single drop fall, shining with the reflected colors of wildflowers before the ground drank it up.

❀❀❀

Melora's heart leapt at the sight of Blight coming over the wall. Her bargain had worked! She imagined the mayor pinning a ribbon on her chest as the whole village cheered her cleverness and bravery.

Blight crouched low in front of the wall, her wasted body all twists and angles, and blinked at Melora, unmoving. Of course, she was waiting for Melora to stand clear, or she'd be poisoned herself—the grass around Blight turned black and brittle as she watched. Melora's stomach hurt. Blight mustn't kill all the grazing land or their crops. She needed to show Blight where the monster was, but she realized then that she didn't know. Someone in town must. She'd just tell Blight to wait here while she went to find out.

This wasn't working quite the way she'd hoped.

✸✸✸

As Blight followed the girl out of her forest and out of Faery, the eternal dim twilight lifted, and the sky turned to fire—fire that burned her eyes that had seen only gray for an age, until the girl came and gave her GREEN. And green, too, was everywhere. It covered the hills and made Blight's heart hurt, the pain of a long life of sorrow and loneliness.

But the pain turned quickly to anger. She could taste the acid in her throat as she realized that this was always here, just beyond the wall. Green hills and skyfire—it was here. It could have been hers, and only now that they wanted her help did they let her know what they'd kept from her.

Pots of green were nothing. Pots of green were lies.

✸✸✸

Blight ran across the field toward town, and Melora ran after.

"Wait! I have to find out where the monster is! You're going the wrong way!"

✸✸✸

Blight heard the screams but paid them no heed. It always started with screams. It would be quiet again soon enough.

She ran easily across the fields, ignoring the winding road in favor of a direct path to the town, its brightly colored houses aglow in the warm morning light.

She came to a small shack, nothing but three short walls and a thatch roof that sheltered a lone sheep. She stopped to stroke the soft white wool, which crumbled under her fingers and fell away to reveal the skin beneath it. The sheep bleated in confusion and fear, but Blight blocked its way—at her touch, the supple skin turned brittle and peeled away from bones that sprouted from the husk, shining and smooth.

She plucked a rib from the pile and carved a curling vine into it with one sharp nail. She smiled at her work and placed it reverently back into the jumble of bones. She trailed her hand absently along the painted blue wall of the hut as she set out once again toward the town.

❊❊❊

"Please! Oh Blight, why aren't you listening? The monster isn't in the town!"

Melora ran then. Ran faster than she ever had, ignoring pain, tears streaked back, tickling her ears.

"Stop, you have to listen to me. I gave you the colors!"

❊❊❊

The colors were all around her, and she touched them all. The armor and swords of the guards sparked and flashed like fish scales, then dulled to rust. Blood burst in carnation red sprays and sputters from split skin before pooling black in the streets of Blight's new home.

She ran from house to house, stopping here to watch corn burst gray and swollen from its husk, there to hear the pattering rain of a hundred bruised apples splitting open against the ground.

Ahead was a red house. So bright. She reached out for it as she ran. A man stood outside, his clothes an assembly of colors even more varied than her new paints! She knocked his sword aside and embraced him, stroking his soft, blue shirt as it fell from his wasting body.

Forward. Ever forward, toward new colors, new sounds. Behind her, all was silent, black, and still.

❊❊❊

Melora stood by the breach in the village wall that would never be repaired, sickened by the silence. From here, she could see the tops of trees within as the leaves curled and died, marking the path of the blight fairy. No dogs barked at her passing, no children shouted for their mothers, no men rattled swords or rallied their neighbors within. Nothing made a sound, her home now as dead as the bone-white forest of Blight.

A gust of wind caught dry, red leaves and blew them off the dying branches. They rained down on her, catching in her hair. She managed to take a step forward, and then another, afraid to look up and see what she had done. But there was no avoiding it—her foot came down beside the body of a bluebird, stiff and cold.

Her family. Her friends. Everyone she'd ever known. It was her fault. Melora should find Blight, so she could die like they had, poisoned by the fairy that she had brought here to save them. It's what she deserved.

A sound in the distance made her stop—the whisper of a song carried on the wind. There, coming out of the hills, brightly colored specks, which grew in size until they were clearly men, jubilant men, men singing a victory song as they returned to town with the head of a monster hanging from a pole carried between them.

The hunters were headed to the main gate at the other side of town. They were flushed with victory, unaware that the city had fallen.

Melora ran, her eyes and nose streaming, trying to yell through hiccupping sobs. She had to stop them. She had to save someone.

"Stop. Oh, please, stop!"

They were too far to hear, but a man at the back of the group must have noticed her because he stopped and waved. Melora sniffed hard and wiped her eyes.

It was her father. He had gone out with the hunters. Gone to kill the monster and survived. Now he was going to his death.

He patted one of the other men on the shoulder, motioned him to go ahead into the village. The hunters walked through the gate, her father waiting behind them, beckoning her to join him. His smile was so warm in the morning light. She broke into sobs again and ran faster.

He had his arms spread, waiting to catch her up, but he must have heard something within the walls—a muffled gasp or the heavy fall of limp bodies because he turned, his face fell, and he sprinted into the city, drawing his sword as he ran.

Melora screamed and pushed herself even harder, stumbling, falling forward more than running.

A pair of birds had fallen dead just outside the gate, their jeweled feathers twitching in the faint wind. The city was so still. Why hadn't they stopped?

She tripped and fell just inside the gate, her hands smearing through the rotten remains of blackened fruit spilled from an overturned basket. The men lay all around her, faces shrunken and dry. The monster's head dropped on the stones, bloodless but still pristine, untouched by Blight's pestilence.

A rasp behind her, she turned. Her father was backed against the wall, his face pale, breathing labored, but alive. Blight stood across the courtyard, perched on the side of a wagon newly carved with flowers. She was studying Melora's father, her head cocked to the side. She crept down from the wagon and took a step toward him.

"No!"

Melora flung her iron ring at Blight. It struck her cheek, and Blight flinched, turning to Melora with pointed teeth bared.

"No! I paid you to save us. We had a bargain! You just killed everyone. Why?"

Blight raised her hand, a smear of green streaking her palm. She bobbed her head once, climbed the wagon, and resumed her carving. Melora ran to her father, and together, they left their home for the last time.

❀❀❀

Melora sat, silent as the dead village, alone beneath the stars. Her father slept in a pile of dry leaves, the only shelter she could manage. She had slept outside the walls only once before, when she and June had gotten turned around in these woods while pretending to be knights.

She and June had used sticks for swords then. She had her father's sword now, dragged away from where he lay. The leather wrapping on its hilt had cracked away. She wrapped it with strips of cloth torn from her father's shirt. Blight's magic had blackened the fabric, hardened it.

She had taken the red ribbon with its iron ring from around her father's neck to help him breathe more easily. It matched her own. She wove it into the new hilt, adding its color and softness.

Stars danced along the blade as she strained to hold it up. It had kept its edge.

Her father had taken good care of it. It was heavy, but she held it—held it until her fist ached, held it until her muscles burned and her arm shuddered.

The sword was heavy, but one day it would be light. Light as a song.

Under the Dreams of the Gods, We All Weep

Jaym Gates

Sand crunching between my teeth, catapults thumping, men screaming their death-songs, the stench of blood and woe. Oh, I know these things. I know why you've called to me, desperate for something to hold as you storm Death's citadel.

A thousand, thousand times before I have seen men like you, dying, desperate, holding to their freedom at the cost of their lives. I have sat on the battlements of empires, waiting to collect king and slave alike. Your weapons have evolved, your political boundaries changed, but the result is still the same. Your broken souls still come to my arms, your empty eyes still haunt my endless dreams.

This is your final night. Tomorrow, your enemies will overrun you, pound your bones into the sand of your homeland. They do not care if your cause is right, if your soldiers are children or old men, or if your culture is dying. You are stones beneath their feet, to be crushed and swept clean from the path of conquest.

It is your right to make a final request of me, one last kindness, at the price of your souls. Mercy or vengeance, a death peaceful or glorious. If you wish stories of what comes behind that last bright splash of blood, I will oblige, but there is no mercy in that.

Some have asked for the story of my becoming, but such requests are of no use. If I told you all the stories of my life, the walls would fall to the sons of your enemies, and your bones would crumble, stories still untold. My lives were endless before my final death, and my death is eternal. And do not think you can use that to put off your own death, your time is etched in the Book of Names.

You wish the tale of my death? Brave, foolish mortals. There is no story more grim, more terrible in its repercussions. I shook the roots of fate, and I will pay for my audacity. Why must you ask for that story? It is foul, and fills my dreams with darkness, and when my dreams are dark, your kind die. But—as you wish.

❀❀❀

Long were my years of adventure, and only some of them are told in song and story. The tale of how I laid down with the Sea King and learned his tongue is told in every sea-tavern from here to the Silver Sands. My exploits in the golden halls of Niroji, my years with the Immortal Army, the years of my life wasted chasing the gates of Paradise, all of these things are common knowledge, even now. I was a hero, a mighty woman in an age of legends, the toast of warriors and the goal of princes. The price on my head was greater than the ransom of a king. A lofty pedestal for a simple witch from a small mountain holding.

A pedestal I happily relinquished to return to my home, far to the north of my glory. I renounced my titles, my lovers, my lands and turned my face toward home. Riding a white stallion won in combat from a djinni warlord, my retainers leading mules laden with things I could not bear to part with, I wrapped my veils about my face in defiance of the late-winter cold, and left my old life.

So much had changed. Gone were the goat-trails I had come south on. Wild fields were now tilled, hills covered in wheat like golden velvet. The tiny towns I passed through were new. The little towns my family had traded with when I was younger were now bustling sprawls or wild ruins. I dredged their names from my memory. Halla, with its rose-colored temple. Babilah, surrounded by almond orchards and smelling of the harvest. Pila, nestled into the cliffs high above the river, her towers crumbled and covered with wild red poppies.

I had not marked the passing of years as well as I thought. The weight of age never touched my shoulders. Maybe I had become blind to what was around me. My people were long-lived, but few lines marred my face, even though tavern gossip spread the names of kings whose grandfathers I had bedded. Perhaps

I had indeed found the fountain of youth, or perhaps the Gates of Paradise were not so mythical after all. Now I wondered if my parents still lived, if my brothers' children were grown, if the castle still stood. Breathless with fear and anticipation, I pushed the caravan hard through the last passes.

At last, the remembered vista spread beneath me. A wide green valley, the afternoon sun turning the lazy river to gold and throwing rainbows from the falls. White cattle grazing in the reeds. Herds of sturdy mountain horses higher on the slopes, where the herbs and clover grew most sweetly. And the white stone castle, its slender minarets cloaked with blue tiles, and the eerie cry to afternoon prayer ringing from the valley walls . . .

It was brighter than I remembered, but it was still home.

Scouts had shadowed me for half the day, perhaps thinking I was a rich trader. I had dressed as a foreign man, and their suspicions had most certainly been roused. My horse was different than anything that would come this far north, his fine bones and thin tail strange against their strong, shaggy mounts. They stopped us, finally, and accepted my plea for sanctuary within the city's walls.

They settled me at the inn, next to the wall, but were suspicious of my claim to relations within the city. The older guard announced that he had lived long enough to know someone as young as I, so I could certainly not be who I claimed. I shrugged and asked him to call my brothers.

My brothers were indeed older than I could have imagined: not only fathers, but grandfathers. Their white hair and shrewd eyes unnerved me. We had always been long-lived—some said we were descended from one of the mountain gods—and to see them old was strange.

They were wealthy, respected men. Kopos was the judge of the city, Kando was a prosperous farmer, Haralambi, master of the city guard. They were solid men, married to fair women, all with strong sons and grandsons. It did my heart good to see them.

But they did not know what to do with me. Kopos had become something of a fanatic, enforcing rigorous worship on his people, saying it kept the dark gods away. Kando supported him, and even Haralambi seemed less open with me than he had been.

They did not welcome me to their homes as I had dreamed but gave me a small house in the poor section of the city until I could arrange lodgings for myself. I dismissed my retainers, sending them with a great portion of my wealth off into the world to enjoy their freedom. I hired two widows to keep house for me and began writing my history.

For a while, I was content. A life of great and glorious deeds is tiring and empty, and the comforts of stability and home are beguiling. I rested and meditated, coming to terms with the darkness that dogged my footsteps, the ghosts and the demons of my past. I had evaded them for years, distracting myself with adventure. Peace brought regrets nipping at my heels.

Too soon, the gentle haze of peace began to wear thin. Winter was coming, and with it, the hungry gods would be stirring. They had descended from the mountains for centuries, hunting hot blood to warm their frozen hearts.

The city was not a fortress only out of pride. It was built high in the mountains, near a valley no one would name, guarding the bleak passes where monsters roamed. When I was child, not a family in the city had been untouched by the fell beasts that came from the valley.

Even our darkest stories held no clue to what lay within that place. Conjecture ran wild. Some spoke of a rogue sorcerer or a monster-king lost from his homeland. Others said that it was the mouth of hell, the underworld, that white bone dust lay thick and undisturbed before a mighty wooden gate, that dark goddesses walked forth with blood on their tongues, seeking the souls of men. We called it the Valley of Tears when we were forced to speak of it.

We had lived prepared and strong, holding the pass south. But the flood of monsters had slowed, and the city had grown soft in the years I was gone. As the first winter moon began to wane, I took up my sword and rode out with the men.

I had fought many beasts and gods before, but here, so close to the valley, it seemed that they were stronger. We hunted them by day, always making sure to return to the city well before dusk. We stalked the weak and desperate ones. Even so, we lost warriors. The carcasses of these monsters provided bones and fur much prized by collectors and sorcerers. It was the wealth of the city. When the snows thawed, the merchants would take them south. But we had to survive the winter, first.

It was a long, bitter winter. Mad with cold and lust, the beasts were desperate. Twice, they nearly breached our walls. We lost many men, and as spring drew near, we found ourselves short on warriors, supplies, and courage.

I flattered myself that the city still stood because of my aid, that I would be honored for my service. Instead, the old women began to mutter about my youth, my strength, my lack of husband, family, and respectability. My brothers began urging me to take a husband, to prove myself harmless. But I was not harmless, and I had no desire to become so. So I redoubled our patrols, and I wore myself ragged, riding with all of them.

It was no use. Winter clung to us, and then the giants woke from their long sleep, hungry after decades of slumber. We put them down one by one, wasting arrows by the score as we fought to find weak points in their thick hides.

A band of trackers from the next city became lost in a snowstorm and found their way to us, half-dead. They spoke of a foul voice in the wind, a breath that struck men dead from the walls. They did not believe that their stronghold would last until spring, and they warned that ours would be next. The next morning, they were not in their rooms. We found them, their fingers worn to bone from clawing at the walls .

They were right. Something had shifted that night. The monsters sought shelter with us, pressing against the walls, pounding at the gates. Their weeping drove us mad, rising over the howling wind. We could not patrol the walls for the winds, and the snow packed doors shut. For two days, the storm raged. On the second evening, silence fell.

We fought our way out of our houses into a world soft and white. The silence was deadly, carried on bone-crushing cold. We made our way to the walls, intending to drive away the beasts outside, but it was too late for them. A pack had huddled in the lee of the city, their hunger put aside in a bid for survival. They were frozen stiff, empty eyes fixed upward, seeming to track our every move. Elsewhere, blood painted the walls where they had battered themselves in an attempt to break through to safety.

Most chilling of all was the northern wall—and the people. Perhaps they had fled from another city or were a lost party of foolish travelers. Whatever they were, they had sought a last, desperate refuge. Children huddled against scaled bears, a fellwolf lay curled over a blue-faced woman. Men and beasts ringed the mass of corpses, not a wound to be seen. Yellow stained the snow under them, their faces were frozen in the same rictus of the corpses found on our walls.

As we stared, their killer came, beautiful in ruin, riding a white stag with silver antlers. His tattered robes were white as the snow, his skin the pale blue of the corpses beneath our walls. He halted at the foot of our walls and sat, watching us in silence. It seemed that he weighed each of those around me, dismissed them, and passed on until he came to me. I met those storm-ridden eyes and knew that my tale was not yet over.

I had met him before. And his kin—dark demi-demons with power over the physical world and a vile sense of superiority to mortals. They often hunted humans, or enslaved cities, becoming leeches on the land, draining it of life. I had fought them on the banks of the Blighted Sea and in the gilded halls of Karkasos, even in the steaming jungles of the east. I had fought this one, known as gyathok—"teeth of ice"—in a brutally cold mountain pass years ago, struggling to save a tiny village from annihilation. I had won my glory against them. I had triumphed then, and I would triumph now.

He smiled, and I staggered. His power was terrible, a whirlpool at my feet. Every moment of grief, of weakness and death wish washed over me. I wanted to throw myself into his arms, to let his cold lips pull the warmth from my soul. I felt the embrace of snow, soothing my life away, ending the nightmares and dreams. I tasted the bitter glory of a death wound, the cold steel of a blade pressed against my throat, the hot gush of blood, the throttling hands of a river monster.

⊛⊛⊛

The memories were beautiful, beguiling. I had always wondered at what came after. All the things I had discovered, the wisdom I had achieved, that was nothing compared to that great mystery. But I would not gently fade to nothing.

My soul was chilled, much of its strength already gone. I fought the urge to blaze with sorcerous power, to scald his chill from my soul. I saw in his eyes that most patient of hunters, unaffected by time or lust or need. Flame would gutter against him, the earth would heave uselessly without displacing his feet.

The only escape was greater patience. One at a time, I pulled in little memories, warm and welcoming, pitting them against the great cold. Picking flowers with Haralambi as children. The warmth of a tavern after a long cold journey. The triumph of surviving the Battle of the Seven Dragons.

Bit by bit, I forced his fingers from my heart, warming him with my own returning heat, as slowly as a frostbite victim. His power was immense, but mine was as deep as the sea, and I had only ever tapped the foam. Now I began to drink deeply, and I summoned brighter memories. His face was not visible to me, for we warred in another place, but I could feel his form beneath my hands. He was melting, putrid ice water sluicing from him. I was winning.

Abruptly, he withdrew, shrieking, and his cry brought all those around me to their knees. I, too, almost fell but held my ground and met his eyes again. He was no longer beautiful but a rotted corpse unfrozen after a long winter. The ground around him, too, was wet with melting snow. Hatred poured from him as he raised a trembling hand and pointed at the city.

I require an offering, an apology for this grave insult. His words eddied like snow on our ears, pale and cold, melting away when we tried to grasp them. *A soul bright as the sun to warm my Master's chilled lips. We have seen this one in many stories, and she will be a fitting bride for him.*

Send her to the Valley of Tears on the next full moon, or I shall bury your city in ice. It will seal a pact of peace between us, between the gods and you mortals. Bring her alive and dressed for the marriage bed of a god, and your lives will linger for eternity.

A gust of snow blew from the walls, and he was gone, and my doom was sealed.

❈❈❈

If they had waited, I could have fought free or left before they could act. But I had been blind, and the knowing smile on Kopos's face told me everything I needed to know. Even Haralambi, with his deep sense of justice, turned his eyes away as his men laid their hands on me. Weak from my battle with the gyathok, I could only scream in betrayal as they bound my hands with silver chain.

Mortals weren't meant to war against the gods, and my power was nearly ruined. The full moon was three days off, and I thought I could, perhaps, regain my strength in that time. But again, they anticipated me. Bound in a lightless room, my mouth filled with wet clay and silk tied over my eyes, I had no power, no movement, no hope. I had felt fear before but nothing like this.

For three days, I lay in my own filth and hatred, strength sapped by my indignity. For the first day, I could only struggle against madness. On the second, desperate, I played with what little power I could summon, shaping it with the thin streams of air from my nostrils. It was all I had, and it kept me from fading. In those breaths I mended my will, forging the pieces of my heart into something sharp and cruel, touched with the strange madness of a trapped animal.

On the third, they led me forth in ropes and chains. The women poured buckets of water over me, cut off my clothes and scrubbed me clean as the men watched to ensure my compliance. I could only bear it in a furious silence when they ransacked my house and anointed me with my own scented oils.

Fresh white clay was packed into my mouth. Reeking of southern jasmine and orange blossom—scents that did not belong in the icy north—I was dressed in red silk and silver jewelry, my face painted white and hidden behind a pale blue veil. A heavy silver crown, and my bridal dress was complete.

❀❀❀

I was shoved onto my stallion, jingling like a court jester, ready for my wedding.

Twenty men escorted me, holding chains from my wrists and neck and ankles. Even my mount was collared with silver and led by heavy chains. We were their blood sacrifice, and they were glad of it.

I will not speak of what happened next, for that is a grief even my dead heart cannot bear. Suffice to say that when it was over, I opened my eyes on the realm of the dead and my new husband.

I knew something of the gods and had guessed who I would be brought to. What I found was not a grim specter, rotted and ragged like an old corpse. He was tall and beautiful. His garments were as fine as mine, white silk embroidered with gold and red, tiny bells tinkling in the hundred braids in his thick white hair. Thoughtful eyes assessed me, long fingers wrapped around his staff as he waited for me to speak.

I had come prepared to fight, to sell my death dearly. His peace threw me, left me unsure. I felt his stillness stealing into my heart, banking the fire that sustained me.

"Who are you, lord?" I asked, wary.

He smiled, slightly, the tiny movement triggering a waterfall of sound from the silver bells in his hair. "Slaves do not have names."

"You are a god."

"I am a god who is slaved to my duties, forgotten by my decadent siblings."

He shrugged, another whiffle of sound from the bells. "But you may call me Death, though some call me the Exquisite Ghost or the Caller."

I had guessed correctly as to my fate, and yet . . . he was not what I had expected.

The gyathok materialized next to me. An oily smile split his jagged face as he bowed low before his master.

"Lord, I bring her for your bed. A fitting bride."

Death raised one elegant eyebrow. "And why have you done that?"

The gyathok looked suddenly less sure. "It has been a long—since her—I thought . . . you seemed to miss her, lord. This one is a match even for the Lady of the Lost!"

"I will be a match for you, gyathok, and the end of you," I snarled. My stallion's teeth snapped a few inches from the creature's bald head as the winter specter lunged at me, radiating rage.

Death snapped his fingers. "Enough. You had her killed for me?"

The gyathok nodded, throwing another sweeping bow. "As you can see, she is perfect. Her legend is great on the earth, and she was given years beyond that of her people. Her deeds are many, and her beauty great."

"Is she kind? Did she love someone there? Can she bear the weight of endless years, knowing she cannot die?" Death's tone was still gentle, honeyed, but I could taste the razors beneath. "You seek to curry favor from me, worm, but you have instead created trouble for me."

He turned to me. "Come, child, and let me see what might have been."

I had no wish to dismount—the gyathok's claws were growing visibly as he watched me—but I trusted his master already. The heavy silver pendants on my crown slapped against my face as I swung down. I was not used to acting as a woman. I caught the thing and flung it aside before Death took my hand and drew me forward.

His elegant fingers traced my cheekbone and jaw. His eyes were like the endless night, pin-pricks of light at their very center. He took me into his arms until I had no choice but to turn my head or stare into those deadly eyes. Trapped, I slipped into his viper's gaze.

I saw immediately what danger I faced and tried to turn away, but his hands were iron. "If you can return from my embrace," he whispered in my ear, "then we shall speak further of your future. But you must pass that test first."

I had never shied from a challenge. His forehead rested against mine, and I fell into darkness.

❀❀❀

Of what came next, I cannot speak. It is different for everyone, and you will find out soon enough. Suffice to say that, when it was over, he crowned me his successor and retired from the mortal realm. I now linger, nameless, the blood-stained mistress of the dying.

They are here. The thump of the marching soldiers vibrates in my teeth. Your souls already flutter nervously, ready to flee their prisons, knowing that death will be fast and terrible. Your dreams of glory will not come to fruit, but that is no evil thing. I, too, dreamed of glory, and look what that brought me. It is better to die too soon than to linger as I must.

I have ceased to be myself, my own. I belong to Death, to murderers and kings, to the hopeless and the dying. My name is what you wish it to be, the shape of your last, desperate thoughts. Is that glory? I do not even have the freedom that you do, the power to choose my way.

Stand and laugh with me, my children, and we will face the end together.

THIS IS RED

SHANNA GERMAIN

Annan's late, and the city smells like blood-blades and tidal breaths, like three-day-old war.

No, that last part isn't true. Annan only wishes it was.

She is late, that much is true. But the city doesn't smell like war. It smells like safety and peace and honeysuckle. Like coddled babes and sweet fruits and clean linen. The scent of it makes Annan's stomach go in knots—the bland of it.

As she runs along the city's outer wall, paws soundless on the grass, her black form little more than a shifting shadow, she reminds herself that she has chosen this. This life, this city, the smell. For Gemelle. All for Gemelle. She tells herself she would choose it again if asked.

She reaches the gates in the gloamed half-light, still panting slightly from the run. The city has already shut the wrought-iron gates against her. No, not against her. They don't know that she is what she is. The gates are shut against all bad things that slink in the dark outside the perfect city. Of course, everyone knows but never says that bad things don't always take a form that can be shut out by physical things. So the iron of the gates is molded into words of protection, invocation, harmony.

Behind the gates, watch guards stroll, unnecessary but for the way they make people feel at ease.

The guards don't see Annan. They never see her. Not when she's like this.

She slips through the wrought iron—the words are new words, without power, and mean nothing to her—then follows her nose although she doesn't have to. She comes to the city every evening, winds her way past the watch towers, slinks along the edges of taverns and lower courts, the stables and fish markets, and makes her way to the Glass Tower.

It isn't really made of glass, of course. Glass is precious these days, even for the kings. But it's made of something that is known only to the kings. In the daytime, at certain times of light, the tower's surface shimmers and reflects just enough to fool those who would ask. It is the tallest building in a city of tall buildings, square at the bottom and round at the top. The lanterns are lit already. They glow orange in the tallest points of the tower through the latticework windows. She's even later than she thought. Somewhere up there, Gemelle is waiting for her. Impatient, impetuous, impulsive, ever planning. Annan must hurry.

One of the court guards strides by behind the tower's latticed doors. He's not entirely human—Annan can see his godblood, the crimson aura, flowing around him. She wonders if he knows. So few do these days. Someone certainly chose him for this rank, so *someone* knows.

Annan skulks into the shadows and exhales slowly to steady herself. Changing was easy once, when she was young and war was everywhere. The bloodbaths powered her, gave her everything she needed. Then, she could have flown here as a crow and entered a room as a wisp of smoke, all without having to face the guards' questioning expressions, without having to get into the lift that makes her feel sick to her stomach. Without having to play at being human.

But the kings are kind and generous, and there is no more war. Annan uses the waning bits of her energy every time she comes here to see Gemelle. This is why she must go into the woods every day. It is not, as she has told Gemelle, that she has an ailing family member outside the city walls. It is not, as others who think they see her more clearly might think, for food. Not even for blood. It is to pit the tiny woodland creatures against each other, to gather what power she can from their snarls and bites, their ripping anger and fear. Their delicious war.

Annan closes her eyes, remembers who she once was, and with a ripple of exertion, she *becomes*. Black hair lengthens and cascades down her shoulders and back. Her form stretches from wolfish to human, skin pale as bone, covered in a dress the hue of blackening blood. Her many cerise tattoos—one tiny dot for every death in every war—re-form over the surface of her skin. Only her eyes stay the same, blue as veins.

Changing leaves her vulnerable, and she must rest a moment, despite her need to make up time. She watches the guard walk by. He's no threat now. Godblood or not, he can't see past this form.

She walks into the tower, pushing the door before her with a quiet strength, like any other woman who belongs in a place. The guards recognize her as Gemelle's . . . what? Tutor? Handmaid? She doesn't know what Gemelle has told them, but somehow, Gemelle has given her permission to be here.

Just the thought that she needs permission to be in a place, that she has accepted that as her new life, makes her feel small and angry. She pushes that small ache aside. It won't do.

When she smiles, she remembers her teeth are flat and soft now.

"Evening." Her tongue works fine. Its soft form makes the transition easier than the rest of her.

They don't trust her, but they want her. They also know that Gemelle will be their queen one day, and Annan is in Gemelle's favor. So they say nice things to Annan and let her pass through to the lift without trouble and, probably, wait for the day when she is no longer under the protection of the princess. Annan can feel their gaze on her backside. There was a time when no one would have dared look at her, front side or back, but these men want to eat her alive with their gaze. They salivate over her. This is her life now. This is what love has brought her to.

The rise to the top floor makes Annan clutch the wall with one hand and her stomach with the other. Flying as crow feels free. This? This feels like dying. Every time. She thinks on the difference but can't put her finger on it. Something about control, she guesses. Something about being able to see what's coming.

Annan steps from the lift , through the open door, and into the hallway.

She must knock—her! She must *knock* on Gemelle's door to be let in. The thought nags her lightly even as she does it, rapping her knuckles quietly against the wood.

Gemelle opens the door. Her hair is blue today, short-cut with only a long, thick braid down the back. Her augmented eyes are purplish, a flower that Annan once knew and can't quite picture anymore. She's wearing a shimmery copper dress covered with spinning gears and boots that look like they're made of wrought-iron but are actually made of lamb's wool and doe's hair.

Gods, Annan thinks. *A lifetime of wars and this is what brings you to your knees?*

Yes.

"Annan," Gemelle says, joyous. She pushes forward in a rush, touches her mouth to Annan's. In that soft touch alone, the journey here every night, the change, the weakness, even the stomach-lurch in the lift, is all worth it. "I was hoping you'd come."

As if Annan has not come here every night for the past months. As if Annan could stay away.

"Quick, come in," Gemelle says, pulling her inside even as she speaks. "Who knows what creatures the daddies have wandering around tonight to keep an eye on me?"

The daddies. Only Gemelle could get away with calling the kings such. Gemelle doesn't know which one really belongs to her—and they won't tell her—so she claims them both as hers. It doesn't matter in the end. Once the kings are gone, Gemelle and her chosen will go on to rule the world. This safe, quiet, calm, godless, warless world. This is why Annan must spend all the time she can with Gemelle now before she chooses her other queen and fully becomes the quiet, peaceful creature she's been groomed to be.

Gemelle's bedroom is the only room in the glass tower that isn't white, but pink. It's not red, but it's close enough that it makes Annan's mouth water. She swallows and sits on the chair next to the bed, unsure what to do with herself, as she always is. No one makes her feel like Gemelle does—uncertain, out of her body, hesitant, and submissive. She hates it, and she loves it, both.

Gemelle comes toward Annan, letting her dress drop away. Where Annan is lean and muscled, Gemelle is soft arcs and lushness. Pale skin that swings out in curves, then swings back in to a waist so narrow you'd think the girl had grown up in corsets instead of crowns. She waxes everywhere—one more thing that Annan doesn't understand entirely—but she does like the slippery feel of Gemelle's skin against her fingers and tongue.

"You're late," Gemelle says.

The accusation is teasing, yet Annan feels oddly stung by it. It wasn't, after all, like she was dallying, doing nothing. Life lies in the forest, in the blood and gashes. But this is not for Gemelle to know. Never for Gemelle to know. Annan would give up her own life—if such a thing were even possible—before she let Gemelle see her true self.

"I know," is all Annan can say.

"I've been so bored," Gemelle says, settling herself in Annan's lap, straddling Annan's waist Petulant, pouting. "Waiting for you."

Annan can't hate the tone of her voice. For one thing, the kings keep Gemelle locked here in the tower day and night in an attempt to preserve her. Sometimes, it makes Annan laugh to think that she, of all dangers, has breached the king's walls. Although, truly, she is powerless now. Hardly a threat—except to their daughter's innocence, which, Annan would bet, has been gone a long time now.

For another, the pouting means that Gemelle will not ask where Annan has been. And Annan will not have to lie to the one she loves.

Gemelle's mouth touches Annan's, her big violet eyes still open, rimmed with black, her fingers in Annan's hair. Here, it doesn't matter what the world looks like or smells like. Only that there is the soft press of Gemelle to her, the gentle tug of her fingers, the teeth that nibble fishlike at her lips.

Gemelle has her arms around Annan, and Annan inhales the scent of her; it is not as staid as the world around them, not as bland. Gemelle smells, at least slightly, like blood and passion. There are moments when Annan worries that this is the reason she's fallen in love with the princess, because she's the only one in this entire world who reminds Annan of what she is.

"I hate it here without you," Gemelle says. She bites Annan's lip softly, a nip that draws a groan from somewhere deep inside Annan. "The daddies never let me out. And they keep it so . . ." Gemelle makes a noise that sounds like boredom incarnate.

Sometimes she sounds like such a girl, a child. But she's not. She's just younger than Annan in worlds and ways that can't be described.

"I don't want to stay here anymore," Gemelle said. "Nothing ever happens."

"Come away with me," Annan whispers against the depth of Gemelle's mouth. She feels stupid even saying it. She's lived a thousand years, she once held court on battlefields while men clawed and begged at her feet, she was revered once as war itself. And here she is, begging this girl-child, this lush creature, to run away with her. And knowing full well that she won't. That she can't. And that Annan couldn't take her anyway, couldn't show her who she really is. It's just a silly dream.

"Silly Annan," Gemelle said. "You can stay here instead."

Before Annan can answer or even breathe, Gemelle brings her lips back to Annan's, pushes her waxed cleft against Annan's fingers. And this is where Annan knows what to do, where she feels herself returning to the creature she once was, the hot-blooded goddess of war that she was born to be.

This is passion, she thinks as she brings her mouth to the pale, lush curve of Gemelle's breast, bites at the side of her neck. This is close to red. This is enough.

✵✵✵

Gemelle, who never dresses after sex if she doesn't have to, sits on the window ledge, twirling something silver and sharp in one hand. At first Annan thinks it's a forbidden coin, but it's longer and leaner. Gemelle is always coming up with things from the beforeworld. Smoking pipes, darning needles, bone bowls. Annan has no idea where she gets them.

"The coronation ceremony is just three weeks away, you know," Gemelle says.

There is hair in Annan's face, a pillow half over her head, and Annan brushes both away so she can hear more clearly. She's heard. She knows she has by the roar of jealous blood that fills her ears. Still, she can't help saying, "The what?"

"Coronation ceremony."

Annan swallows. She knew that Gemelle needed to choose—and soon. This is part of why she's felt such pressure lately, such a need to be here as much as she can. Soon, Gemelle will choose her queen, and Annan will be alone. Too far gone to return to what she was. But she didn't think it was going to happen yet. Not yet.

"I've chosen my queen," Gemelle says.

"Who . . ." Annan manages, mad at the humanish throat, mad at the things that rush her and choke her. This is jealousy, this is pain, this is grief, this is her heart splitting, shattering. This is why she was always the goddess of war and never of love. Whoever said the goddess of war is the stronger knows nothing. She realizes that all these eons she has been weak, hiding behind others' pain. She can't even finish the question.

Gemelle twirls the silver object in her fingers, and Annan sees that it's a knife—or rather, a knife blade. She wonders, briefly, if Gemelle even knows what it is, what power she holds in her impetuous fingers. Doubtful.

Gemelle slinks across the room to sit on Annan's body, hip to hip, Gemelle's hands on either of Annan's shoulders. When she looks down, her eyes are violet-hued, violent-hued.

"Do you not know?" Gemelle asks, laughing.

Annan misses her former rage, her power. She wants to eat the violet-eyed creature who's laughing at her, to draw blood and pain and make war against her. But there is nothing left in her, so she makes the only gesture she can. She shakes her head. She doesn't know what Gemelle does all day, whom she sees. The kings keep her among the best-of-the-best, present company excluded. Every woman in the kingdom and beyond would kill to be Gemelle's queen.

"Sweet Annan," Gemelle says. "You. You are to be my queen."

This heart, this silly thing of blood that is in her chest, it opens. Winged like a thousand crows. Rising like smoke through the air of her throat.

Oh, so this is that thing the others always spoke of while she was out waging war. She didn't know. She didn't know.

✸✸✸

The gates slide closed just as Annan reaches the city wall.

Late again. Today of all days. Annan dreams of the world where she controlled time and was not controlled by it. Fittings, introductions, people wanting to do things to her hair, to her skin, to measure her waist and try out makeup colors. She's agreed to most of it, only fought the hardest battles, the ones that might reveal her. The tattoos, of course. Her teeth, which mostly flatten, but not always. No makeup on her eyes.

She slides through the gate on all fours, panting. There was little fighting in the woods today. The creatures are few for a reason she hasn't discerned. It's full summer, and there is no hunger, no war, no reason for them to be scarce. But she finds she needs them less and less. Love makes her soar better than rage, better than war. Gemelle has chosen her. Her. Not her as the goddess of war, but herself, as she is now. This is enough. She will be Gemelle's queen. She will become a goddess of love.

It takes a great deal of effort for her to change outside the tower. She can feel the blood in her teeth, the sharp edges of her nails in her skin. Even her dress is losing its crimson hue.

For Gemelle, she thinks. *For love.*

She nearly throws up in the lift, her stomach looping when the contraption lands on the main hall floor. The main hall is closed already—these doors are just as ornate as the city gates, scrolled with safe words and omens—but she can't slip past them in this form.

She knocks. Her knuckles have gotten used to the rasping for permission, so she barely notices anymore. The drapers slide the doors open—ghosts of the past, see-through things of little worth. This is part of the way the kings keep their peace. Let the ancestors live among us, silent as sheaths. Let them see every move you make, every thought you think.

Annan steps into the main hall. It is the only room she ever feels at home in. The domed ceiling is a membrane so thin one can see the rain through it, almost see the dots of the stars. Trees grow around the edges of the room, touching the ceiling as if holding it up. And maybe they are. She's never been able to fly up and look.

Her dress moves against her ankles, and she's aware of the gazes. There is no music yet, nor dancing. A few young boys dart about with food. Among the royals and those who are lottery-invited—your random chance to be royalty for a day—Annan is something for everyone to look at. She is many things—or will be many things—but right now she has no power, and she is late, and they have had to wait for her. Her dress is not in style, certainly not the right colors. No one wears red or even pink. White, yellow, pale blue: these are proper colors.

She is an irritant in their quiet calm although no one can say just why. She can see them checking it off their mental lists. The dress? No. The hair? Maybe? The demeanor? Possibly? Perhaps it is because, if nothing else, they love her despite all of these things, flock to her as though she herself were one of the kings, bow lightly as she passes them.

The kings, of course, think otherwise. Sitting on their dual-seat throne high above the crowd as she approaches, they frown as if in unison and furrow their salt-and-pepper brows. If not for Gemelle's protection, if not for Gemelle's claim on her, Annan would not be allowed here, a clearly open danger, a sharpened knife about to be held to the city's calm, expressionless face.

The kings deepen their frowns as Annan draws near. They had, of course, hoped their daughter would choose her queen, but they had not hoped, not even imagined on their darkest of days, that it might be someone like Annan. They neither hate her nor fear her. Such things are not allowed in a kingdom built of peace. But they certainly can question their daughter's choice of consorts, at least behind the masks of their faces.

She wishes she could tell them the truth. She has lost her desire for war. She lives only for love. Only for Gemelle.

Dropping her gaze as the ritual requires, she watches her feet move forward across the pale path that the crowd creates in their parting. When she reaches the end, she bows and kneels, surprised at how easy it is. At last, when she is low enough, she looks, finally, at Gemelle, who sits in front of the kings, at their feet.

Annan gasps. Gemelle's hair is blood-red, her dress the same color as Annan's was once. Her skin is painted with tiny scrolls of red. Even her eyes flare a bright, bold crimson, so dark the pupils don't show. Her crown is the only non-red thing about her, its glass-like shine reflecting everything else.

The sight of Gemelle in bloodstain makes Annan falter, her breath rushing out of her on black wings. She realizes it wasn't herself that makes the crowd restless. It was their blood-coated queen. Annan has a million questions, but she can't ask them, not here. Not now. She can't stop looking at her love, red-rimmed, blood-colored. Dark as death against all the white.

"Come," Gemelle says finally, holding out her hand to Annan.

Annan, on her knees, crawls toward her love. This is the way it is done. Gemelle has told her the ritual. Annan's knees burn against the fabric of her dress, her palms ache against the wood.

When they are face-to-face, Gemelle leans in and kisses Annan, long and deep and open-mouthed. Her hand goes in Annan's hair, tugs and holds. The crowd around them stirs, fabric on skin. Annan has lived a thousand years, had twice that in lovers, started a thousand wars, killed a million men, and yet this open display of lust sets her face aflame.

"Rise," the kings say in unison. They are still in control, will be in control until they choose to give up their posts or until one of them dies. They exert their control now, strongly, but Annan senses a fear behind their words. Is it her they are afraid of, still?

Gemelle takes Annan's hands, pulls her to her feet. Annan's head spins from heat and passion and love and something else that she can't name. She thinks it might be a kind of fear. But of what? What does a war goddess, even an ex-war goddess, have to fear?

From the pillow beside her, Gemelle picks up the second glass-like crown. She settles it on Annan's head. It is heavier than Annan expected, sharper at the edges, as though it really were glass. As though it isn't the well-honed illusion she believed it was after all.

In unison, the rest of the room holds their miniature versions of the crown up in the air, above their heads. They all have them, even the smallest child. It is a promise of their loyalty, a literal standing beneath the rule of the crown. Around the city, everyone is doing the same.

The councilman comes forth and joins Gemelle's and Annan's hands together with big, wide ribbons. White, of course, written upon with black ink. Despite Gemelle's dress, there should be no red here. The councilman says words that Annan mostly hears. The words are new words and cannot bind her, but no one else knows that. She binds herself by her own choices. That is the strongest binding of all.

"You are mine," Gemelle says. "And I am yours."

Annan says the same, right after. As she says it, she feels the final war goddess bits of herself slide away. She becomes the thing that Gemelle has come to love. Calm, peaceful, a quiet city in a quiet reign.

"You may kiss your queen," the councilman says to both of them. He steps back slightly. Gemelle leans in, her red-red eyes, her red-red lips, and takes Annan's mouth to hers. Annan closes her eyes, hungry for Gemelle's touch, for her sweet kiss. She could stay here forever—the world shut away, the taste of Gemelle's skin, the way her fingers work against Annan's waist and pull her closer. Body to body, mouth to mouth, Gemelle's hand leaving Annan's waist, but the rest of her pressed against her. *Peace*, Annan thinks, having a true understanding of the word for the first time.

It is the noise of something breaking, something that sounds like glass but isn't, that rouses her from this closed-eye dream of love and stillness. Annan whirls, still caught in Gemelle's kiss, but catches the end of the movement from her sliding gaze.

"What?" Annan asks. She smells blood on the air, fear and panic thrumming through the room.

Gemelle laughs but doesn't let Annan go, their hands still bound by ribbon and words. "A celebration, my Queen," Gemelle says, her red eyes shining dark with bloodstain. "For you. For us."

Annan can smell blood, cloying and thick. Her teeth ache at its sweet tang. A sound next to her, a sound that Annan remembers from a hundred wars, a thousand years. Annan turns to see the councilman has fallen. He is wearing Gemelle's crown upside down, the glass-like points buried in his head. Gemelle's free hand is blood-covered, dripping. She raises it in the air, a move of triumph that Annan has seen too many times to count.

The kings have risen, are coming toward them with their stern voices, making gestures to the guards at the doors. The crowd has stopped in their white-white dresses, stuck like windup toys without a forbidden hand to wind them.

"Don't . . . don't do this, Gemelle." She is pleading, begging. It is, it turns out, hardly different from knocking. It burns her skin the same way.

"Take out the daddies," Gemelle begs, pleads. Petulant, wanting. That bloodied mouth, those bloodiest eyes. "Take out the daddies, so we can rule together in blood and war and chaos."

Annan pulls from Gemelle's grip, the white ribbon streaming to the floor.

Gemelle catches Annan's hands and tugs her back, touches her mouth to whisper, "I know what you are, what you crave. I will give it all to you. Morrigan."

The old name from Gemelle's tongue is too much, too harsh. It splits Annan in three, sends her breath and heart and mind into separate places of confusion.

"No," Annan says. "No, no." Gemelle's love, not for her after all but for what she is, what she can become. How stupid to have believed in a child's talk.

"My Queen," Gemelle says. She lays her palms to Annan's cheeks. Bloodied palm, war palm. The scent of her desire overpowers Annan's heart. Pleasure can be held off. Love too. But there is no stopping this, what comes on the breathing promise of blood and rage and war.

The blood calls to her, the rage, the war that simmers just below. Annan refuses, closes her eyes against the pull. To take it on is to have them kill each other, all of them, down to the bitter end. "Oh, child," Annan says. "You do not know—" Already her teeth grow longer. They cut her tongue, slice her words off at the end.

The power of the blood slides through her, splitting, sending her memories. The men who had eyed her, who'd watched her knocking on doors, seen her crawling the floor like an animal. They are small animals, every one, put here for her purpose, for her power. They have just been waiting to be released from their prison of peace.

Annan opens her mouth, the transformation sliding her from wolf to crow to woman and back again, and in that gesture, war begins as so many others have before. Annan—no, she is Morrigan now, Morrigan again, and she must claim that name as she has not for a hundred lifetimes. She has not begun this end-of-days—she never does—but she will stir it and eat from it, and she will not be around to see its end.

She roars, a soundless dangerous thing, and the world responds around her.

The flash of crowns against skin, teeth and fists and nails unsheathed. Annan becomes the needle in the middle of it all, rooted amidst the killing. Gemelle holds Annan's hands, laughing. The white ribbon between them is stained red.

Something jostles her. It is Gemelle, falling, tugging on the crimson ribbon. She is saying something, but her mouth is blooming red, her words are dying even as they leave their birthplace. Their hands come apart. Annan feels something small and still break open inside her, and then it is gone.

It is the god-blooded guard standing over Gemelle, a sliver of steel in his palm. So someone did know, someone did suspect. The daddies? But little use, now. The guard turns to Morrigan, bloodied crown in hand. He has been waiting, too. The whole world, biding time, and here she was, growing soft. Believing.

Morrigan succumbs to crow, flies up to the treetops upon which the ceiling does rest. Below her, her worshippers fight and fall until the world is crimson. She breaks the ceiling with her beak and claws and climbs ever higher. The world circles as she circles, spinning and spun.

It is days before she comes to rest outside the city's gates. Dead guards and new words and the silence of after war inside its walls.

She becomes woman again—so much power wrestling in her now that it takes mere seconds and barely a thought—and slips in through the hanging gates.

The city smells like blood-blades and tidal breaths, like three-day-old war. And in its center, walking, the red-dressed goddess who has become its bloodied, beating heart.

BY GOLDEN STAGS AND FIRE BRIGHT

NATHAN CROWDER

Even the cursed weather outside the Blue Rooster couldn't convince Densin du Mer to overlook the promise of easy money. The stranger's desperate offer of employment was certainly timely. If not for the conspiracies against his family back home, Densin would no doubt be a merchant prince of the Azure Islands by now. Instead, the young captain scavenged along the coasts of the Vale Land, accepting what jobs he could find. Some were more legal than others, and even then, he barely scraped by. Densin's quick wit when navigating trouble, his moral flexibility, and his truly horrible character judgment ensured him a long line of newfound friends not unlike the rain-soaked stranger.

This one wasn't even asking him to do anything illegal. In fact, he seemed to desire nothing more than a speedy departure.

Densin understood. He had only been in Craver's Bay for a handful of days himself, and the small town had little to recommend it other than good crab and passable cheese. Work of any kind other than crab fishing had failed to materialize, and his purse was feeling light.

"You have your own boat?" the stranger asked, hard, brown eyes shifting to the door like he was expecting the devil himself to come in any second. Densin smiled inwardly, knowing from experience that nervousness was a poor business partner. A rational, even keel, free from the storm-tossed seas of emotional influences was the safest bartering position.

"And an able crew," Densin added, tilting his scruffy, ginger chin toward Mike and Peety. They were busy trying for a third thus unsuccessful day to talk the barmaid out of her skirts. Listening to the rain pounding on the slate roof of the Blue Rooster, Densin was confident not many townsfolk would venture out for watered-down beer and bitter wine. If he didn't take this job, Peety could actually stand a chance. As lumps of sod went, he was the more charming of the two.

"How much?" the stranger asked, his knuckles white against the black wool purse. "Provided we leave immediately?"

"A hundred gold stags." Densin expected a hasty counter offer of some sort. The stranger dressed as if he had money. In his experience, those with money tended to negotiate harder than a beggar, but this man appeared to be in no mood to haggle for long.

The man flinched at the price. He had every right. It was ridiculous. It was supposed to be. He glanced down toward his purse, acknowledging he wasn't carrying that amount of coin on his person. His voice shook, a ghostly whisper below the clatter of the rain. "Done. I'll collect my things and your payment and be at your boat momentarily. Be ready to cast off as soon as I get there."

"Trousers up, boys," Densin shouted to his men. "We have work."

The two mutton-heads were good enough sailors, strong backs and naval trained by choice rather than pressganged into service in some backwater. But both were a damned liability on land. They looked at each other, at the barmaid (who had the temerity to bat her eyelashes), then back to Densin with a look of betrayal.

Densin knew he'd get nowhere by bullying, or even by merit of being their employer. Not when they got this intractable. They'd drag their feet like petulant children and eat up valuable time that he didn't have. "I suppose you'd prefer the glamorous life of crab fishing then? I'm sure you'd be right at home here. But which one of you gets to shack up with the missus here?"

Mike looked hurt, realizing like they all no doubt did, that he'd be the lone sailor at the Crab Town Ball if they stayed. "Ava says only a fool would set sail in this weather. It's a warning from the doonda sidhe."

The doonda sidhe. The idea almost made Densin laugh out loud. He hadn't given the fae spooks a serious thought since childhood. They had been the monsters under the bed, the vain and wicked creatures of night and shadow, with skin like alabaster and helms of fire. When a boy did something wicked, it was said the sidhe wrote their name down on lambskin and that every further act of wickedness earned them another mark. When the child was judged sufficiently wicked, the sidhe would ride through the night on their golden stags to claim the child as their own.

By Densin's estimation, that threshold was pretty damned high. He had been plenty wicked growing up. The life of privilege he had been born into afforded plenty of opportunities for a creative child to test his boundaries. He had stopped believing in the sidhe by the time he plundered his first cargo ship of Yerban spices at the ripe age of fourteen. Cautionary tales of vengeful spooks were for the children and fools, not for men hardened by commerce and the world.

"Mike?" he said pleasantly. "Peety? If you have ever seen a sidhe, I give you permission to stay behind. I wish you nothing but the best of luck finding a new employer who tolerates your superstition. Otherwise, get your sorry carcasses on the boat and prepare to cast off. I've sailed the *Shanna's Kiss* alone before, I'll do it tonight if I have to."

He went straight for the door, adjusting his hat. It was true that he had sailed his ship alone before but never in a storm like this. Still, he was always up for a challenge. Mike and Peety scurried out after him, even rushing ahead on the slick mud streets of the provincial town to beat him to the boat.

As storms went, the strength of this one didn't trouble Densin. While it brought pounding rain thick enough to turn the late afternoon sky into twilight, the wind was mild. He was more concerned that it had come out of nowhere. The sky had offered only a scattering of wispy white clouds when he had entered the Blue Rooster mere hours before. This much rain with no warning . . . superstition almost seemed merited, and against his will, his thoughts returned to the warning of sidhe-cursed weather.

Like the rain, his new employer had not been in town earlier in the day, either. Densin vaguely remembered seeing him coming ashore with a handful of companions, well-armed and meant for business three days earlier, not long after Densin had tied *Shanna's Kiss* to the weathered mooring. The ship that brought the strangers took on cargo and left with the next tide, and the strangers rode out on newly purchased horses the next morning.

He eyed the customer, who was huddled within his dark cloak, two satchels down at his sides, a small and lonely figure in the rain. He wondered, despite his best business instincts, what had happened to the man's companions from days before. The thought was as troubling and unexpected as the storm. Densin waved at his client and detoured to the small shack the local harbormaster used for her office.

"Wanting to rent out the slip for a few more days, I take it?" the grizzled old woman asked when Densin stepped through the door. The two of them had shared a few drinks since coming to the town. Martha had a history almost as spotted with trouble as his, and they had become fast friends.

"Setting out, actually. Just stopped in to say goodbye," he said. He paused, realizing his real reason for making the unnecessary stop. "Martha, what is there inland by a day or so from here?"

"From here?" She sucked on her remaining teeth and sized him up. "Darbyshire," she said slowly. "They make our cheese. Lovely people in Darbyshire."

"That's it?"

"Well," she glanced nervously out the window. "There's the matter of the hills."

"What's the matter with the hills?"

"Quite lovely. Very scenic. But folks have been known to wander into the Doonda Hills and never come out or, worse, come out changed."

Densin felt his tongue go dry in his mouth. It had never occurred to him that *Doonda* was the name of an actual place. He stuttered out a thanks and goodbye and backed out of the tiny office as Martha quietly sang, "The queen judged them strong as man may be. Two hundred souls rode out that night, and vanished like the doonda sidhe . . ."

. . . by golden stag and fire bright, Densin completed the lyric in his head as he retreated through the rain. How long had it been since he had heard that song, drunk in a tavern somewhere? How far away? Did it matter? Here, tonight, it sang in his blood, gave haste to his step. He saw Mike waiting for him on the deck and urged him to cast off the line with a crisp wave. Densin leapt the gap as retreating waves pulled *Shanna's Kiss* from the docks.

Mike was waiting to catch Densin's arm and help steady him as he landed. "Why the hurry?"

Densin clapped his mate soundly on the shoulder and hissed above the clatter of the storm. "On the off chance your barmaid was right about the sidhe, and I don't mean to say that she was, we should make haste away from these shores. Peety has the wheel. Tend the lines while I speak with our employer."

Mike jumped into action, and he and Peety struggled to move the boat deep into the bay, away from the sweeping, wooded bluff that curved along their port side. The wind was not cooperating, and Densin recognized he'd have to keep his conference brief to try and correct course.

"You," he shouted to the stranger above the rain. "Hand over our fee, or I'll have my boys turn right back around to the dock."

The man began to fumble within his luggage, frantic. "No. No, please. I have it." He removed a leather pouch from the depths of his bags and handed it over. Densin tested the heft and judged it almost exact. He teased it open and removed a single coin, turning it between his fingers. It was gold as promised but a rough oval rather than round. And instead of the familiar interwoven stag antlers of the Vale Land coins, he saw an older symbol—a sword crossed by two daggers. Densin pocketed the coin and cinched the bag closed with a trembling hand.

"Your gold, as promised," the stranger said.

"I said a hundred stags."

The two men locked eyes: one weighing whether the captain would turn the ship around over a technicality, the other wondering if he should raise an objection on principle. The only reason he had specified stags was because that was the coin of the realm. The gold coins from the Caliphate of Dust to the south were smaller, worth only two-thirds as much, while the gold coins of neighboring Yerba Kolo were smaller still. But he had judged the weight and found it good. His judgment of people was lacking, but when it came to coins, Densin du Mer had the touch of a born merchant prince. If anything, the stranger had overpaid him by a coin.

But the age of the coins and the desperation in the man's face troubled him.

At that point, Densin realized that the stranger was not even watching him. His eyes were on the port shore. Densin turned to squint through the gray curtain of rain and saw only the fires of the town of Craver's Bay behind him. No. The town was further still to the side, and the firelight was too bright for a town that small. And it was moving, racing through the trees. Densin felt a chill and offered a silent prayer to Aleph the Wanderer that the lights which blazed through the trees were merely torches.

"Come with me," Densin grabbed his employer by his elbow and dragged him toward the wheel. The captain took the wheel from Peety's uncertain grip. "Go help Mike with the sails. We need to tack out to deeper waters."

Peety backed away, torn between insult at his implied inability and panic at the urgency on Densin's face. "The wind . . ."

"I know," Densin snapped. "The fae-cursed wind. We'll make the best of it."

Peety raced to his post, and together, he and Mike fought the sodden sails, trying to eke a miracle out of a sky determined to drive them toward shore or nowhere at all. Densin plied the tiller with a deft hand, but it was all he could do to keep his course parallel to the shore. He knew, not too far out there, the coastline curved to a rocky point where there had once been a lighthouse in more prosperous times. Now, it was an intractable set of teeth set in a muddy sandbar ready to hold *Shanna's Kiss* tight if he couldn't find the course.

They would survive the beaching. He suspected that they wouldn't survive what was racing through the tall pines along the shore. As the fires raced closer, he felt his stomach tighten, knowing to his core those were not torches which blazed. There had not been enough horses in Craver's Bay to amass even a fraction of the forces which pursued them. He had asked the stranger for a hundred stags. He feared he had gotten that and more: a doonda sidhe war party mounted on fantastical stags as they blazed between the trees in pursuit of the stranger Densin was trying to spirit away.

"Tell me! What did you steal?" Densin shouted to the passenger. The captain's voice shook as his understanding of what was real and what was mere fable crumbled around him.

"Not stolen! Reclaimed!" The stranger clutched one of his bags tightly to his chest. "Family treasures lost in the hills generations ago, now to be returned to their rightful home!"

Densin fought the urge to take a hand off the wheel and point. He needed both hands to save the ship, and he was damned certain the stranger was watching the pursuing war party just as closely. "I don't think they see it that way."

"I don't care how they see it, you damned pirate! You have your fee, now do your job!"

There just isn't reasoning with some people, Densin thought. He understood the man's fear and frustration. He could only imagine what he must have come through to get this far, what must have happened to the companions who rode out with him not to return. He had raced to Craver's Bay with a war party on his heels, and here he was, on the edge of the sidhe's domain. Freedom must taste like honey.

But at the same time, he had sacrificed those who had ridden into danger with him so that he could live. He had led a war party of angry fae down upon Craver's Bay. And it didn't matter how crappy of a town Craver's was, or how bitter their wine. Densin found himself wondering if Martha was safely tucked away in her little shack, if Ava had watched the golden stags blaze past from the shelter of the Blue Rooster. The unwavering menace of the rocky point and ruined lighthouse was a shadow with clear sky and open ocean behind. His time was running out, and the wind was determined to drive him into shore and an unpleasant fate.

Densin set his teeth, calculated the odds. "Mike! A hand up here, please!"

The burly seaman abandoned his post to join his captain at the wheel. "Captain, the sails . . ."

"Leave them," Densin said, his voice tight. "Our passenger has a bag that is very precious to him. Separate it from him, please."

The stranger tried to put up a fight, but he had spent what little true fighting spirit he had just getting to this point. Mike was a bigger man, fresher, and had a little something to prove after his inability to coax angel wings out of the sails. Separating the bag required little more than a hard cuff on the jaw and a wrench of the wrist. Mike offered the bag to Densin, who declined with a tight shake of his head.

"Open it and tell me what's inside," Densin ordered. He saw the stranger open his mouth to object. His lip was bloody. "And if our guest objects, hit him again."

"Gold, Captain du Mer," Mike said. "And a jeweled music box, and a few little statues, and, oh . . . this looks like a little princess crown!"

Densin didn't take his eyes off the ship's imminent grounding. This was no time for sentiment, no time for emotion. This was business, and in his business, that meant survival. "Throw it and our guest overboard. Portside."

Mike didn't hesitate, catching their now-former employer by surprise. Both bag and cloaked figure hit the icy waters with a rousing splash. The wind didn't change.

"This, too?" Densin asked the not-too-distant line of flaming sidhe under his breath. There was no time to wait for an answer. He took the bag of gold coins from his belt and hurled them after the rest of the ill-gotten loot.

The rain stopped and the wind immediately shifted direction. Peety and Densin let out a whoop of relief and cranked the sail and till to take advantage of their newly purchased luck. *Shanna's Kiss* shuddered lightly as her bow scraped the sandbar on their way past, and then they were free, out into the open waters beyond the bay.

They turned to look behind them before the ruins of the lighthouse stole their view of Craver's Bay. Densin got his first clear look at the doonda sidhe, and he feared that glance was enough to stay with him until his dying day. They rode huge stags, pelts tinged golden in the firelight. The sidhe themselves were glorious, tall and regal, dressed in ornate plate armor chased with shades of red and gold. Their helmets were high, sweeping backward like the fang of a wolf, and blazing like bonfires. Bristling with swords and spears, the war party rode into the churning surf towards the dark shape of the former client. And then the ship was around the point and gone.

"Do you believe, now?" Mike said.

"Oh, I believe," Densin said. "I also believe your payment is washing up in that surf back there."

"Frankly, Captain? I'd rather be poor."

Densin nodded in agreement and sent his crew about setting course for the next town down the coast. They might get lucky and find work. They might even find enough of value in the poor, fae-damned bastard's other piece of luggage to make some kind of amends. But as they slipped through the azure waters farther and farther from the doonda sidhe, Densin couldn't help but wonder if he could ever run far enough. When he had inspected the oval gold piece, he had neglected to put the one coin back in the pouch. He felt it sit heavy in his pocket, but when he moved to throw it overboard, his fist closed about the coin instead.

No. I earned this much at least, he thought to no one in particular. *Call it bounty. Call it blood money. Or better yet, call it an important reminder that some stories from childhood might have been more than just stories after all.*

THE WHITE TUNIC

ELAINE CUNNINGHAM

They called Ma a Wise Woman, mostly because she had a knack for telling stories folks wanted to hear. People would come worried and leave hopeful, thinking maybe they could handle whatever came their way. To hear Ma talk, you'd think a clever lad could deal with dragons and nobles and suchlike and end up safe and smiling. That didn't sound much like real life to me, and I told her so more times than I like to remember. She'd always laugh and say, "What's the harm? If trouble is everywhere, there's no sense in fretting over its coming."

I can't say I agree. Seems like some troubles merit a thunderstorm's worth of fretting or, better yet, a horse fast enough to outrun them. The only horse on the farm can barely stay ahead of the plow, but I should've started running on my own two legs the day the new midwife let Ma and her babe die in childbed. I should've run before the wench took it in her head to replace Ma in Da's bed. I should've run before her swelling belly announced a son meant to replace me.

Well, I'm running now.

My last day on the farm started out peaceful enough. Da led our two cows out of the barn while I hauled water for the trough and set up the milking stools. Too nice a day to work inside, he said, but truth was, he didn't miss many chances to moon over his new young wife.

She bore watching, all right, but I was less interested in Cindra's pretty face than what she might slip into my morning ale—or for that matter, between my ribs. She was a mite too handy with that knife of hers, an odd curved blade as pale and sharp as a crescent moon. Early as it was, she wandered through the herb garden, singing to herself as she cut sprigs of this and that. I didn't know the half of what she'd planted in Ma's garden, but I do know that all the rue and fennel and red verbena—herbs said to keep away fey and witches and suchlike—had died with Ma, and Cindra hadn't seen fit to replant them.

I'd no sooner settled down to milking Brown Berta than a red-haired girl child comes running out of the barn, shrieking like someone was beating her with a rock. Berta danced a step or two and flailed at me with her tail. I caught the pail before it tipped over and grabbed ahold of that tail. This calmed Berta down some—there's no logic to cows, and that's a fact—but she kept those big eyes of hers fixed on the girl pelting toward us.

Cindra's girl was five, maybe six, with wild red curls and a scream any banshee would be proud to claim. She wasn't sparing with it, so when she let loose, we'd look her way to check for blood, then just let her be and hope she'd return the favor. But wee Tamsin had her own ideas, and she wasn't shy about making them known.

Da kept at his milking, shoulders hunched up like he was bracing for a strong wind. Don't know why he bothered. It was generally me the girl pestered.

Sure enough, Tamsin caught hold of my sleeve and started tugging at me. "Hemli, you've got to come! It's Tom! He's caught a pixie!"

Now, that got Cindra's attention. I can't say she smiled, exactly, but whatever thoughts she was having didn't seem to displease her.

If it was up to me, I'd pluck the girl off me like a tick and get back to my work, but that wasn't something I could do, not with Cindra watching me like a cat trying to guess which way a mouse will run.

So I pointed to a stand of red flowers by the garden gate and the butterflies fighting over a turn to light on them. "Old Tom must've caught himself a butterfly," I said as kindly as I could. "It's a sad thing, them being so pretty and all, but you can't fault a cat for hunting."

From the way she huffed and rolled her eyes, you'd think I'd just mistook the soup kettle for a chamberpot. "It's a pixie," she said. "You've got to come *now*! You've got to save Tom!"

Now, that last bit made no kind of sense. Tamsin's old yellow tomcat was a big, one-eared brawler who could run off foxes and kill weasels. He faced off against a badger once and gave more damage than he got. Even the dogs we took boar hunting knew better than to trifle with that cat.

"Now!" shrieked Tamsin.

Da flinched, then sighed. "Go see what your sister wants."

My tongue itched with the need to remind him that Tamsin was no kin to

either of us, but Da sent a stern look my way and Cindra gave me a sweet smile.
Doubly warned, I moved the bucket out from under Berta and followed Tamsin
to the barn.

She scrambled up the ladder to the hayloft, which, this being midsummer,
was empty of everything but one yellow tomcat and a whole lot of cobwebs.

Old Tom looked no worse than usual. There was blood on his ruff and more
on his paws, but no more than you'd expect from a mouser at work.

I caught the beast by the scruff of his neck and handed him to Tamsin. She
slung him over her shoulder and hurried over to the hay chute, singing a weird
little tune that lifted the hairs on the back of my neck.

As I was scrubbing one hand over my hackles, a flash of color caught my
eye—yellow and green, bright as jewels, but misted over by a tangle of old spider
webs. The butterfly that had got Tamsin so worked up, most likely, though I
never saw one quite that color. There was no sense in trying to free it—once
caught, a butterfly could no more fly than could a bird whose pinfeathers had
been ripped off by the handful. So I resolved to kill it quick, like I would any
other creature that's too hurt to live.

I took a hayfork down from its hook on the wall and swept the webs out of
the corner. The butterfly flopped about on the floor, getting more tangled by the
moment. Before I could lift a foot to stomp some peace into the bug, something
grabbed ahold of my hair and tugged.

I knew a moment of pure panic. Letting out a yell that would've done credit
to a scalded cat, I spun around, both arms flailing the air. Bats lived in the barn
rafters, but they slept days—unless they were too sick to know day from night.
Having put down a dog that went mad, I knew what a bite from a rabid bat could
mean.

Bright wings fluttered as the creature dodged, then stretched out wide to
frame a tiny lass, no taller than my little finger. Her mop of long curls reminded
me of Tamsin's, except for being the color of summer leaves. The pixie wore a
green tunic and tiny green boots, and her wings were the same yellow and green
as the "butterfly" in the web.

My jaw hung slack as I stared at the impossible thing floating just beyond my
reach. Ma had told stories about the Fey Folk, and I suppose I believed them,
after a fashion, but I'd never expected to see one.

"Free my brother, and I will let you live," says she, haughty as a queen.

Now, if this were one of Ma's stories, the clever farm lad would say, "For how long?" This would be a sensible thing to say, what with fairies being so good at lying by telling half a truth. But it was marvelous strange that something so tiny could talk loud enough for me to hear, and I'll admit that a breath or two passed before my head caught up with my ears. Even then, I wasn't inclined to follow the path Ma's tales blazed. A man grown, big and strong, I saw no need to dicker with a green-haired bug.

Neither was I one to let any creature suffer needlessly, so I pulled my knife from my boot and went to one knee to take a closer look at Greenbug's brother.

Tiny as he was, I could see that he was in a bad way. Tom's claws had shredded one bright wing and drawn deep furrows across the pixie man's chest.

"The spider's web is poison to our kind," said a voice near my ear. "Release him, and hurry!"

Seemed to me that the web was the least of the little man's worries, but I obligingly cut through the strands.

His sister fluttered down to his side. She picked up a bit of straw and used it to scrape off as much of the web as she could. He peeled off his tunic and leggings and tossed them aside.

The red wounds on the little man's body began to fade and close, but black rot crept across one wing, fast enough for me to see it move.

Greenbug placed her hands on her brother's shoulders and looked him square in the face. "You must lose your wings or die."

"Then I will die."

The pixie girl took one faltering step back, her breath hitching in a broken little sob. When her brother turned away—maybe from shame, maybe out of respect for her grief—she balled up her fist and planted a haymaker on his jaw.

Down the little man went, and down he stayed.

Greenbug looked up at me. "You must do it. I have no blade, and Obin spent his to kill the cat."

Could be we had different notions on what a dead cat looked like, but more likely the pixie's knife had been poisoned. I resolved to check on Tom later and set my mind to the task before me.

Careful as I could, I cut away the broken, rotting wings. The little man jolted awake with the first cut, but he didn't make a sound, nor did he bleed. A single drop of fluid, like from the stem of a cut flower, rose from each stump and then just as quickly disappeared.

"You pixie folk heal fast," I said. "At this rate, new wings will be coming back quicker than weeds in a corn patch."

I meant this kindly, but the silence that followed chilled the air like a winter wind. After a spell, I cleared my throat and tried again. "Where should I take him?"

Two tiny faces turned my way. "*He* can hear you just fine," said the little man. "You cut off my wings, not my ears."

He made it sound like it was my idea. Not wanting to argue with a fellow who was having such a bad day, I just laid my hand flat on the floor, palm up. Greenbug helped her brother climb onto it.

She fluttered after me as I climbed down the ladder, but as soon as we left the barn, she lit off for the forest. Not far into the trees, she stopped by the creek and settled onto a half-fallen tree Da meant to cut up for firewood.

"In here," she said, pointing to a big knothole.

Hoping no snakes had made a nest there, I obliged. The little fellow scrambled off my hand quicker than you'd think possible. Most likely he was as glad to be shed of me as I was the two of them.

Greenbug paused at the edge of the little tree-cave. "No further service is required." A long moment of silence passed before she added, "We owe you thanks."

I noticed that she wasn't actually *giving* thanks, but that came as no surprise. Ma's tales made it plain that the fey folk didn't like to be beholden. In general, I didn't much care for high-nosed ways, but from a thumb-sized girl, it was kind of amusing.

So I gave her the sort of bow I fancied a lord might give a queen and said, as grand as I could, "My lady, it was an honor to assist in this—if you will pardon the expression—small matter. Please call upon me any time."

Fey folk are said to be prideful, and I figured Greenbug had taken about all she could handle for one day. So I didn't expect her to say what she said:

"I accept."

A faint gong followed her words, so soft it was more like the shadow of a sound than something you'd hear with your ears. Telling myself I didn't hear anything at all, I set off for home.

The yard was empty but for a few chickens. Da was probably out past the cow meadow, sowing late turnips. Since he'd put Tamsin at the top of my list of chores, I went into the house to check on her.

She was sitting on the kitchen floor, her hands bloody to the elbow. A big kitchen knife lay on the floor beside what was left of Old Tom.

Now, I'm not one to be squeamish. You can't be, not when you work a farm and hunt for what meat you don't raise. But butchering hogs don't come close to what that girl had done to the tomcat.

Tamsin looked up at me with strange, ancient eyes. "I couldn't save him."

A dull sickness filled me, something that went deeper than fear. I shook it off as best I could and spoke like the big brother Da expected me to be. "You picked a strange way to try."

"Oh no, this is the way," she said without a scrap of doubt. "You have to dig out a heartseeker before it finds its way home. I was too late."

She held out a lump of bloody meat. It took me a moment or two to figure out what I was looking at.

"Did you kill the pixie?"

Her voice was so fierce that I was tempted to say yes and have done with this. But I wasn't in the habit of lying, and today didn't seem a good time to start. "No, but he's hurt bad. I cut off his wings."

That seemed to please the child. "He'll be back, then. And when he returns, you'll kill him with his own knife."

Now, I'd had just about enough of being ordered about by small people. Something in my face must have told her that because Tamsin rose to her feet slowly, like an angry queen.

"You will kill the pixie with his own weapon." Her words came out soft, for once, but I could feel the power of them in my blood and bones. "You *will*. Swear it."

Cindra chose that moment to come to the kitchen door. She took everything in without so much as a blink and then turned that smile of hers on me.

There wasn't much I wouldn't do to get out from under that smile, so I gave Tamsin what she wanted. "I swear."

Again, I heard that distant gong. I looked from the bloody child to her mother, and suddenly I understood more than I ever wanted to know about the two of them.

If Cindra noticed the fairy chime, she pretended not to. She plucked an old sack from a basket on the floor and held it open. Tamsin dropped the cat's heart into the bag, which her mother handed to me.

"Bury this under the elm tree in the clearing near the stream. You know the place?"

I ought to, since I just took the pixies there not an hour before. It troubled me that Cindra named the very spot, but I couldn't bear to stand under the same roof for another minute. Off I went like a fox with its tail afire. In no time at all I was back beside the half-fallen tree.

The tree leaned against the elm Cindra spoke of. In my hurry, I'd forgotten to fetch a trowel to dig a hole, but my knife would serve well enough.

I'd no sooner pulled it from my boot than a ring of mushrooms sprung up around me, quick as a blink. The light in the clearing changed, as if deep green shadows rose from the forest floor, and the air pressed in on me until I was pretty sure I knew how an apple felt when it was going through a cider press. The pain drove me to my knees. I clung to the moss as the world whirled around me, spinning me away into a darkness deeper than sleep.

I woke up to the feel of someone's boot in my ribs. Two fairies stood over me—tall, fearsome warriors conjured straight from Ma's darkest tales. One was a woman in a white tunic and leggings. A thick braid of green hair fell nearly to her knees, and wings of green and gold rose from her shoulders. The other was a man, also dressed in white, with short green hair and a stub that looked like a plucked chicken leg poking out of a slash in the back of his tunic: Obin. Both held swords, which were pointed in my direction.

"You pledged service to me and mine," the woman said in Greenbug's queenly tones. "Rise, and fulfill your oath."

I got to my feet and took a look around. The mushrooms that formed the fairy ring were as big as cottages. A cow-sized beetle ambled by. And if I needed any more proof that the damn pixies had shrunk me down to their size, there lay my knife, big enough to serve as the keel of a ship.

Well, then. Looks like I had some adjustments to make, starting with what to call the pixie woman. "Greenbug" didn't fit anymore, not when she stood tall enough to look me square in the face.

"How shall I address my liege lady?"

I used my grand tone of voice, but this time, I shoveled on a pile of respect, like I imagined a bootlicking sort of lord would give a warrior queen.

She stared at me with the kind of surprised look a farmer might give a pig that just stood up on its hind legs and took to spouting poetry. This went on for longer than I liked, especially seeing that she still had a sword aimed my way.

Just as I was starting to worry that I should have added another shovelful, or maybe dropped to one knee or somesuch, she gave me a short nod.

"You may call me Adeesh."

I bowed a little to let her know I understood what an honor she'd just handed me. "Whatever you want me to do, Adeesh, seems to me I could do it better at my usual size."

"Does it?" the fey man said coldly. "*Seems to me*, the tunnels leading to the dragon's lair are too slender and subtle to accommodate a blundering meat mountain."

That was a pretty good insult, and normally I wouldn't be inclined to let it pass, but he'd given me something more interesting to think on.

"We're going to fight dragons? Like this?"

"Oh no," Adeesh assured me. "We will be protecting dragons."

This was sounding worse by the moment. "What from?"

Their faces turned grim and solemn. Obin leaned toward me and whispered, "Squirrels."

I busted out laughing. There was no helping it, for the notion of a squirrel offering any sort of threat to a dragon was rank foolishness.

Adeesh's slap spun me around and knocked me to my knees. I wiped blood from my split lip and got back to my feet quick before she decided to follow up with that sword she was pointing my way.

Her brother caught her arm and tipped his head toward the white tunic draped over an enormous pebble. The smile that came over her face was mighty unpleasant, but she put her sword away.

"Imagine a beast thrice your height with claws as long as your arm," the pixie man said, solemn as a priest. "Now imagine that it can leap many times its own length, climb as fast as a bird can fly, reason its way through elaborate wards and defenses, and chew through wood and metal. Imagine that nothing will deter this monster from its chosen goal."

That sounded enough like squirrels, adjusted for size, to ring true. And since squirrels will eat snakes or lizards from time to time, I suppose if a dragon was small enough, it might have cause to worry.

"A fairy dragon," I said, remembering one of Ma's stories. "The squirrel is after a clutch of eggs."

"That is so." Obin sounded surprised. Another insult, I suppose. "Squirrels will eat anything, but they are fond of dragon eggs and small two-legged beings. With or without wings," he added in as bitter a voice as I'd ever heard.

"Enough talk." Adeesh scowled at me and pointed toward the white tunic. "Attire yourself."

An old tale stirred in the back of my mind, and the horror of those fine white clothes made Old Tom's bloody end a fond memory.

Adeesh's smile came back, wider and meaner. "I see you are not quite as ignorant as you appear."

"You said you'd let me live!" I protested.

"True, but I did not say for how long."

I suppose I deserved that, seeing how I knew to ask and didn't bother. What you do is less likely to cause you grief than what you *don't* do. Ma used to say that a lot, and seems she was right. Seems she was right about a good many things. When fey warriors wear white, she said, they're expecting to fight their last battle.

I had a thousand questions, but they boiled down to two important ones. "Why?"

Obin gave me a look that let me know I was too stupid to breathe. "What is life, without flight?"

One look at the pixie woman's face let me know she'd tried all the arguments she knew on her brother. Since I didn't figure he'd like mine any better, I moved on to my next question. "Why me?"

"You offered." Adeesh picked up the white tunic and threw it at me. "This much will I grant you: if you survive until moonrise, you will return to your oafish size and life. Until then, you are sworn to me."

Giving your word to a fairy is not the most foolish thing a man can do. That honor goes to breaking your word. Since I figured I had a better chance of surviving a battle, I pulled the tunic over my head and tied my belt over it. The sack Cindra had given me still hung from it, empty. That was something, I guess. I didn't want to imagine what a tomcat's heart would look like to a man in my current state.

"At least give me a weapon," I said.

"You have one." The maimed pixie nodded toward the giant knife. "Unless, of course, you'd like to look around for a larger one?"

Adeesh gave me a hard shove, and there was nothing to do but start climbing that half-fallen tree. The bark could have been a steep mountain, all boulders and crevices and small, rough handholds. My fingers were bloody, and I was blowing like a hard-ridden horse by the time we reached a knothole big as a cave's opening. Obin had fared a bit better, but he was looking none too good. There didn't look to be much fight left in him, but I didn't see why Adeesh had to die alongside him.

Another fairy oath, I supposed.

A pair of bugs, big as barn owls, peeled away from the wall and startled a yelp out of me. Adeesh sent a disgusted look my way. "Shield your eyes, fool."

I wasn't quite quick enough, and the first flash of light damn near blinded me. The bugs—summer lantern bugs, I realized—scuttled off down the tunnel, taking turns flashing to provide a steady light.

Climbing the inside of the tree wasn't much easier than the outside. I'd never walked such steep paths, nor climbed so many stairs. At last, the path ended, and we stood on a sunlit ledge.

"Why are you smiling, fool?" Adeesh pointed to a sheer cliff that rose higher than my eyes could reach. "We've reached the elm. Now the climb begins."

Summer days are long, but this one was nearly over by the time we reached the end of the ever-climbing maze that led to the dragon's den. I'd never been half so tired in my life, but nothing, not even thoughts of the battle to come, could take the shine from that moment.

Maybe some men could find words to describe that she-dragon, words that would go beyond her jeweled scales and wings like gilded green silk. I'm no poet, so I'll just say that the dragon's eyes held things that made our coming seem right and good. If I had to die today, fighting for this dragon and her young was as good a reason as any man could name.

We bowed to the dragon and settled down to wait. The more I thought about our situation, the better I liked our chances.

"Those tunnels are pretty narrow. No squirrel could fit into them. And even if they could, that maze would confound a bloodhound."

Adeesh gave me another of her looks. "Can you not hear the tree?"

"Hear it do what?"

The pixie grabbed ahold of my wrist and slapped the palm of my hand against the wooden wall.

A storm-broken limb . . . the gnawing pain of an ever-deepening wound . . . the soft brush of feathers from the sleeping owl that blocked the opening by day . . . the warm weight of many sleeping squirrels that guarded the tunnel by night . . . the tickle of claws from a squirrel running through the nearly-finished tunnel . . .

The feelings flooding me were bigger than any man was built to hold. I snatched my hand away, so spooked and shaken it was all I could do to keep from shrieking fit to drown out little Tamsin.

"It is coming," said Adeesh. "It will come soon."

She'd no sooner stopped speaking than a fearsome racket shook the den, a sound like a dozen woodcutters attacking the tree like axe-wielding berserkers. The dragon folded her wings over her eggs, and the pixies drew their swords.

You bear fairy steel as well.

The voice sounding in my head was too beautiful to have come from anything but the dragon. She nodded and reached out one glossy claw to touch the sack tied to my belt.

I loosened the knot and slid my hand into the sack. There was nothing in it but my own five fingers.

You must call it.

I couldn't think what she meant—couldn't think at all with death roaring toward us like a wind funnel.

The wooden floor shuddered under my feet. Several thunder-clap booms rolled through the den, and most of one wall exploded into splinters.

What came through that wall stopped my heart and loosened my bowels. Black as night, it was, with teeth the size and shape of war shields, claws like the Reaper's scythes. I'd expected the squirrel to be strong and quick, but this was a monster—a monster with eyes as ancient and soulless as Tamsin's when she swore me to avenge her cat.

I remembered then what she'd told me to do, and the name she'd called the thing I was to do it with.

"Heartseeker!"

Cold steel filled my hand, and I drew a pale, thin knife from the bag.

So. I had a weapon, but damned if I knew what to do with it. I'd pledged to help the pixies protect the dragon; I'd sworn to avenge Tamsin. One vow honored was another broken.

The squirrel leaped at the dragon, almost too fast for my eyes to follow. But Obin sprang up to the edge of the nest and pushed off to meet the beast, sword leading.

They came together in a burst of blue light, like flint striking steel. Some pixie magic gave Obin more power than his size warranted, and they crashed to the floor, rolling and thrashing.

Magic or no, it didn't take long for the squirrel to rise up on its haunches, holding the struggling pixie in its dagger-tipped paws. The beast dipped its head and ripped a chunk out of Obin's arm. Down clattered the pixie's sword, clean as the day it was forged.

If that sword couldn't reach through the squirrel's pelt, there wasn't much hope for me and my knife.

The thought that came to me was from no story I ever heard told, but it came from the place Ma's stories lived in memory.

I ran at Obin and cut his throat. Heartseeker, having tasted blood, leaped and twitched in my hand. And the squirrel, finding the taste of pixie blood to its liking, leaned in for another bite. I shoved the knife up under Obin's chin just before the squirrel took his head off.

Heartseeker did the rest. The death throes of that beast as the knife dug its way down its gullet and into its heart were fearsome to see, and it was a pure marvel that the dragon and her eggs weren't crushed before it was over.

And when it was over, I turned to Adeesh, half expecting to find her sword at my throat. Instead, she was looking at me with something that might have been distant kin to respect.

"Clever," she said. "And more resourceful than I expected. I will be calling upon you again."

That thought rang through my head like funeral bells as we half ran, half-slid down the maze to the tree-cave's mouth. Adeesh gave me a hard shove, and suddenly I was falling.

I hit the ground much sooner than I'd expected, and not nearly as hard as I'd feared. When I rose to my feet, I was surprised to see the pixie standing at the knothole, not more than ten feet over my head.

A tiny scrap of white drifted down like a petal from an apple blossom—all that was left of the white tunic. I hoped to hell and back that I wouldn't be seeing another one any time soon.

The forest was no place to be come nightfall, so I set out for the farm as quick as I could move. Candlelight gleamed through the windows, and the smoke rising from the chimney carried the scent of meat and onions and herbs.

They looked up from their supper bowls when I came into the cottage. Cindra's smile slipped, but she had it back in place before Da noticed.

I fetched myself a bowl from the shelf and dropped into my chair. "No place for me at the table, I can't help but notice," I said, baring my teeth at Cindra in a smile that wasn't a smile. "If I didn't know better, I might think you didn't expect to see me again."

"You were gone long enough to raise doubts," Da said in the dry tone that meant he was jesting. "Did you find Tamsin's cat?"

So that was the tale Cindra told. "No. He's long gone." I made myself reach over to ruffle Tamsin's red curls. "But I'll head over to Cotler's farm tomorrow. Word is they have kittens."

Da grunted in approval, and Cindra rose from the table, smiling. "And in return, I've got something for you."

She went to a chest and took out a length of cloth. White cloth.

"I thought I'd make you a new tunic, a fine one for you to wear to the midsummer dance."

Our eyes met, and silent words were spoken and heard. "That's fair," I said at last. And it was, after a fashion. The dance was three days away. A man could run a long ways in three days. If I was lucky, I could outrun whatever final battle the red-haired fey had in mind for me if I stayed to challenge her son's inheritance.

I didn't wait for morning, and I don't plan on ever coming back, but for all that, I don't consider myself foresworn. I fulfilled my promise to Tamsin when I killed the pixie. And since I didn't exactly say I'd bring her a kitten, no fey can hold me to that. Adeesh can call on me whenever she likes—that's my oath. But neither of us said anything about me staying close enough to hear her call.

You'd think a fairy would listen closer to the old tales.

About the Authors

Jennifer Brozek is an award-winning editor, game designer, and author. She has been writing roleplaying games and professionally publishing fiction since 2004. With the number of edited anthologies, fiction sales, RPG books, and non-fiction books under her belt, Jennifer is often considered a Renaissance woman, but she prefers to be known as a wordslinger and optimist. Read more about her at www.jenniferbrozek.com or follow her on Twitter at @JenniferBrozek.

Lillian Cohen-Moore is an award-winning editor and devotes her writing to fiction, journalism, and game design. Influenced by the work of Jewish authors and horror movies, she draws on bubbe meises (grandmother's tales) and horror classics for inspiration. She loves exploring and photographing abandoned towns; Lillian spends every fall searching for corn mazes and haunted houses— the spookier the better. She is a member of the Society of Professional Journalists and the Online News Association.

Torah Cottrill, a voracious reader from the age of three, discovered Robert Heinlein and science fiction and never looked back. But it was the original *Women of Wonder* anthologies that most influenced her. Her short fiction spans a number of different styles (urban fantasy, science fiction, fairy tale), connected by a focus on strong female protagonists. In addition to writing, Torah has also worked as a professional editor for many years on a diverse range of publications, including the *Journal of Democracy*, the women's magazine *Redfruit*, and numerous roleplaying game rulebooks for the Star Wars and Dungeons & Dragons brands.

Nathan Crowder is a writer of the dark fantastic, karaoke superstar, and connoisseur of ironic t-shirts. His writing shows a love of blue-collar heroes and pop culture. He enjoys a good sidecar, loves his friends, and has never trusted the fae. His short fiction can be found in the anthologies *Rock 'n' Roll is Dead*, *Cthulhrotica*, and *Rigor Amortis*, and the upcoming *Coins of Chaos*. His superhero novels *Greetings from Buena Rosa*, *Chanson Noir*, and *Cobalt City Blues* created the shared-world setting of Cobalt City for Timid Pirate Publishing. Nathan can be found online at www.nathancrowder.com or on Twitter @NateCrowder.

Elaine Cunningham is a New York Times bestselling author whose publications include over 20 novels and three dozen short stories. She's best known for her work in various shared-world settings, including the Forgotten Realms, Pathfinder Tales, EverQuest, and the Star Wars extended universe. *Shadows in the Starlight*, the second book in her urban fantasy series Changeling Detective, was included on the 2008 Kirkus list of Ten Best Sci-Fi Novels. A former history and music teacher, Elaine followed her lifelong fascination with folklore and ended up in the fantasy genre, which is as close to the Faerie Realm as she ever hopes to come. She has been writing about the fey folk, be they dark fairies or high fantasy elves, for over two decades. For more information, please visit www.elainecunningham.com.

Julia Ellingboe is a writer, editor, roleplaying game designer, and aspiring itinerant storyteller. Her work often draws from various folkloric traditions, such as African American slave narratives, Japanese kaidan stories, and the Francis J. Child ballads. Under Stone Baby Games, her game design work includes both tabletop roleplaying games and live action roleplaying parlor-style scenarios. With live action roleplaying, Julia combines traditional storytelling, dramaturgy, and Nordic LARP style. Her first LARP, *The Anthropophagy Society*, features a secret society of cannibals in Western Massachusetts that inducts or rejects new members. In 2012, two of Julia's short stories appeared in Stone Skin Press's publications. Julia lives in Western Massachusetts with her husband, two daughters, and three unholy cats. To the best of her knowledge, she does not know any cannibals.

Jaym Gates is the Communications Director for SFWA, as well as a freelance editor, author, and publicist and a fan of the Middle East, military history, and mechanical dragons. She can be found at www.jaymgates.com or on Twitter at @JaymGates.

Shanna Germain likes girls in red dresses, big teeth, and promises of bread and wine. She claims the titles of writer, editor, leximaven, Schrödinger's Brat, and vorpal blonde. Her award-winning fiction has been widely published; recent books include *Geek Love: An Anthology of Full Frontal Nerdity*, *The Lure of Dangerous Women*, and *Leather Bound*. She is currently the lead editor of the Numenera roleplaying game from Monte Cook Games, LLC. Walk her wild woods of words at www.shannagermain.com.

Ed Greenwood is an amiable, bearded Canadian writer, game designer, and librarian best known as the creator of The Forgotten Realms fantasy world. He sold his first fiction at age six and has since published more than 200 books that have sold millions of copies worldwide. Ed has won dozens of writing and gaming awards, including multiple Origins Awards and ENNIES. He was elected to the Academy of Adventure Gaming Art & Design Hall of Fame in 2003. He has judged the World Fantasy Awards and the Sunburst Awards, hosted radio shows, acted onstage, explored caves, jousted, and been Santa Claus (but not all on the same day). Ed shares an old Ontario farmhouse with his wife and the head of the household (a small but imperious cat). This ramshackle mansion sags under the weight of more than 80,000 books. Ed's most recent novel is *The Wizard's Mask* from Paizo, and his upcoming books include *The Herald* from Wizards of the Coast (the last book of The Sundering Saga), and *The Iron Assassin*, a steampunk novel from Tor Books.

Dave Gross is the author of about ten novels in settings ranging from the Forgotten Realms to the Iron Kingdoms. His short fiction has appeared in anthologies including *Shotguns v. Cthulhu*, *Tales of the Far West*, and *The Lion & the Aardvark*. His latest publication is the fourth Radovan & the Count novel for Pathfinder Tales, *King of Chaos*. A former teacher, technical writer, and fry cook, Dave has edited a number of geeky magazines, including *Dragon*, *Star Wars Insider*, and *Amazing Stories*. He lives in Alberta, Canada, with his fabulous wife, their disobedient dog, and two above-average cats.

Erin Hoffman, author and video game designer, was born in San Diego and now lives in northern California, where she works as Game Design Lead at the Institute of Play's GlassLab, a Bill and Melinda Gates and MacArthur Foundation supported three-year initiative to innovate big-data-powered educational video games. She is the author of the Chaos Knight series from Pyr books, beginning with *Sword of Fire and Sea*, followed by *Lance of Earth and Sky*, and concluding with *Shield of Sea and Space* in 2013. For more information, visit www.erinhoffman.com and Twitter at @gryphoness.

Jeffrey Petersen writes in a dark, secret place in the heart of San Francisco, where the paths to fairyland are open to those who know the way. He writes novels more often than short stories and is currently seeking representation for a middle grade urban fantasy fairyland novel with no vampires, brooding men in hoods, or women in tight pants with their backs to you. You can follow him on Twitter at @jeffreypetersen, where he occasionally talks about squids.

Cat Rambo lives, writes, and teaches by the shores of an eagle-haunted lake in the Pacific Northwest. Her 200+ fiction publications include stories in *Asimov's*, *Clarkesworld Magazine*, and Tor.com. Her short story, "Five Ways to Fall in Love on Planet Porcelain," from her story collection *Near + Far* (Hydra House Books), was a 2012 Nebula nominee. Her editorship of *Fantasy Magazine* earned her a World Fantasy Award nomination in 2012. For more about her, as well as links to her fiction and information about her popular online writing classes, see www.kittywumpus.net.

Andrew Penn Romine lives in Los Angeles where he works in the visual effects and animation industry. A graduate of the 2010 Clarion West workshop, his fiction appears online at *Lightspeed Magazine*, *Crossed Genres Magazine*, and on Paizo.com as well as in the anthologies *Fungi*, *What Fates Impose*, and the forthcoming *Coins of Chaos*. He's also blogged at Functional Nerds (as the Booze Nerd) and is a regular contributor at Inkpunks.com. You can also follow his day-to-day adventures on Twitter at @inkgorilla.

Amber E. Scott began her career as a freelancer for *Dragon* magazine in 2004. She soon expanded her author credits to include contributions to Wizards of the Coast, White Wolf, and Sword & Sorcery. Now she happily and frequently adds to her favorite game system, Pathfinder. Her most recent work includes

The Worldwound Incursion and *Chronicle of the Righteous* by Paizo Publishing. Amber posts writing news, thoughts on the roleplaying industry, and pictures of her cats on her professional Facebook page, "Amber E. Scott."

Erik Scott de Bie is a speculative fiction writer and game designer, probably best known for his work in the Forgotten Realms setting, including his signature Shadowbane series. He is the author of the forthcoming *Shadow of the Winter King*, first in the epic World of Ruin fantasy series from Dragon Moon Press (Spring 2014). Erik lives in Seattle where he is married with pets. Find him at www.erikscottdebie.com, facebook.com/erik.s.debie, and twitter.com/erikscottdebie.

James L. Sutter is the Senior Editor and Fiction Editor for Paizo Publishing, as well as a co-creator of the Pathfinder Roleplaying Game. He's the author of the novels *Death's Heretic* and *The Redemption Engine*, the former of which was ranked #3 on Barnes & Noble's Best Fantasy Releases of 2011 and was a finalist for both an Origins Award and the Compton Crook Award for Best First Novel. In addition to numerous game books, most notably *Distant Worlds* and *City of Strangers*, James has written short stories for such publications as *Escape Pod*, *Apex Magazine*, *Beneath Ceaseless Skies*, *Geek Love*, and the #1 Amazon bestseller *Machine of Death*. His anthology *Before They Were Giants* pairs the first published short stories of speculative fiction luminaries with new interviews and advice from the authors themselves. For more information, visit www.jameslsutter.com or find him on Twitter at @jameslsutter.

Christie Yant is a science fiction and fantasy writer and the Assistant Editor for *Lightspeed Magazine*. Her fiction has appeared in magazines such as *Beneath Ceaseless Skies*, *Shimmer*, and *Daily Science Fiction*, and in anthologies including *The Way of the Wizard*, *Year's Best Science Fiction & Fantasy 2011*, and *Armored*. She lives on the central coast of California with two writers, an editor, and assorted four-legged nuisances. Follow her on Twitter at @christieyant.

Minerva Zimmerman has touched 5,000 year old fingerprints, fallen on her head, chipped frozen squid off the floor, and been mistaken by druids for the avatar of a fiery goddess. She thinks bears should not wear pants and spiders make great minions. She grew up thinking that scary things are there to protect you and pretty, helpless-looking things are a trap. She's been unable to shake this theory as an adult. She has published a number of stories and her novella *Copper* was recently published in Crossed Genres' *Winter Well* anthology. She can be found at www.minervazimmerman.com.